THE
REUNION
POLLY PHILLIPS

**SIMON &
SCHUSTER**

London · New York · Sydney · Toronto · New Delhi

First published in Great Britain by Simon & Schuster UK Ltd, 2022

1 3 5 7 9 10 8 6 4 2

Simon & Schuster UK Ltd
1st Floor
222 Gray's Inn Road
London WC1X 8HB

Simon & Schuster Australia, Sydney
Simon & Schuster India, New Delhi

www.simonandschuster.co.uk
www.simonandschuster.com.au
www.simonandschuster.co.in

A CIP catalogue record for this book
is available from the British Library

Paperback ISBN: 978-1-4711-9541-9
eBook ISBN: 978-1-4711-9542-6
Audio ISBN: 978-1-3985-1359-4

Typeset in Sabon by M Rules

Printed and bound by CPI Group (UK) Ltd, Croydon, CR0 4YY

To my mum and dad – one of you adored Cambridge and the other was a voracious reader. While neither of you are here any longer, I couldn't have done it without you.

My eyes feel like they're about to burst out of their sockets. I can't breathe. Fingers that were curled harmlessly around the stem of a wine glass at dinner earlier are now crushing my windpipe and I'm just standing here. Taking it. I used to read scare stories in magazines like *Just Seventeen*, of girls being preyed upon as they got off the last train or walked home from school. I'd imagine that in their place I would floor my attacker with a well-aimed kick and leg it. Instead, I'm doing nothing.

I'm freezing. My brain's starting to fizz from the lack of oxygen. These old buildings retain no heat and this room probably hasn't been opened in years. I no longer know how long I've been in here. I should be fighting back but my arms hang limply by my side. No kick, well aimed or otherwise. I haven't even screamed. In all the scenarios I ran through as an anxious teen, I never imagined knowing my attacker.

The force of his grip has knocked the strap of my evening dress off my shoulder. I can feel the satin, cool against the skin on my arm. My body might be powering down but my brain is still pumping, latching on to every detail. Hands big enough to span my entire neck. Breath on my face, sour from hours of toasting. And the look in those eyes, like they're finally getting what they wanted.

My head's lolling like some macabre parody of the kind

1

of drunkenness that occurs at these big-ticket reunions. I should have seen this coming. From the moment that stiff-backed, gold-embossed invitation dropped on to our doormat, this chain of events was inevitable. I was going to be a victim again.

I start clawing at the forearms, but my hands slide off the fabric. I can't get a hold. I open my mouth to scream but his thumbs are embedded too deeply in my voice box for me to do anything but gurgle. I try to unpeel his hands from around my neck, gouging my nails into them, scraping and pinching. All I need is one flinch and I might be able to break the hold. His grip tightens.

The fizzing in my head is getting louder, like the static of an untuned television. Black clouds edge my vision. Just as I feel my focus slipping, I hear a thumping, then the scrape and creak of the heavy oak door. Hope sparks. Someone must have seen us together and realised something was wrong. I wait for the sound of footsteps pelting across the medieval flagstones. All I can hear is my own ragged breath. This room is tiny, an annex off the college's main banqueting hall, stuffed with oil portraits of important people. Even by candlelight, there's no way we can't be seen. And that door's too heavy to swing open on its own. My eyelids flicker like lights going out. My last realisation before consciousness slides away is that, whoever is at the door, they're not going to rescue me.

After what I've done tonight, I can't blame them.

One

10 hours to go

My ten-year-old daughter is lying face down on the floor, refusing to look at me. I've tried cajoling, bribery, even bare-faced threats, but nothing will shift her. If I'm honest, I'm tempted to join her. How easy it would be to slip off my shoes, sink on to the soft-pile carpet next to her and forget about the reunion entirely. But for once in my life, I'm not going to lie down and submit. I look at the Cartier watch on my wrist. Nick should be home by now; he's always better with the kids in these situations than I am. He's got the whole 'firm but fair' thing nailed, whereas I tend to be a pushover who then explodes with resentment when they don't listen. Because he spends less time at home, he's also very much the fun parent, whereas I'm the one who moans about

3

tidying their rooms and finishing their homework. It's one of the curses of being a stay-at-home mum, the other being that people think I'm good at domesticity, rather than just doing it by default. I wish I was one of those mums who sewed and ironed, could produce perfectly iced cupcakes and really revelled in the role. But I'm not.

'Do you want to talk about it?' I pat ineffectually at Artie, but she shrugs me off.

'No.'

My heart contracts. I wish Artie would confide in me. I desperately want us to be close, but I'm so worried she'll absorb all the mistakes I've made that I'm more distant than I mean to be. It's easier with Xander; I never worry I'm infecting him with my insecurity.

'Are you sure?' I try again. I wish there was something I could do to help her. I wasn't always like this. Before I went to university, I was a problem-solver, a go-getter. Now the only problems I solve tend to be laundry related. Not quite the illustrious law career I dreamed of. I clench my fists. That's why I need to go back. To reclaim the person I was – and the person I would have been. If it wasn't for them.

'Emily, are you ready to go?' My husband's voice drifts up the stairs.

I survey the child prostrate in front of me. She's had a lot to deal with over the last few months. I wonder if I'm doing the right thing in leaving her, even though I know Nick would never consider staying behind. Why is it men who put themselves first are considered dynamic and driven, whereas when mothers do it we're made to feel selfish?

'You're not having second thoughts about it, are you?' Nick bounds into the master bedroom, his face already lit up by the prospect of the weekend ahead. His smile slips when he sees Artie spreadeagled at my feet.

'What's going on, my love?' He drops into a crouch and strokes Artie's hair away from her face. When she doesn't respond, he raises an eyebrow at me.

'Doesn't want us to go,' I mouth. I can't allow myself to be sucked into staying home. I remind myself that no matter how much I think I don't, I do want to go to this reunion. I need to do this. It's been fifteen years. The shame I've worn like a cloak since I left Cambridge doesn't feel so red raw any more, though the nagging guilt hasn't faded. Neither has the sense of injustice. It's time I evened the score.

'Nonna's going to be here any minute.' Nick scratches at his shirt sleeve, trying to glance at the Rolex beneath it without Artie noticing. I know he's keen to beat the traffic. He asked me to be ready to leave as soon as he got back from the gym.

'Is there something you want to talk to Daddy about?' He chucks her under the chin, tickling her to make her smile. 'Is it Tamara and the girls at school again?'

Artie nods. I feel a wash of remorse. If I weren't so distracted by my plans for this reunion, I'd have realised straight away it was the cold-shouldering Artie's been experiencing from her friends that's upsetting her. It's triggering for me. Normally I'm all about letting the children fight their own battles (not to mention I'm terrible at confrontation) but Tamara's such a piece of work and the way she's treating Artie is so reminiscent of the way Lyla was with me at university that I could quite happily take Tamara and the rest of her cronies and drop them all from the nearest tall building. I step forwards to scoop Artie into a hug, but Nick holds up his hand to indicate he's got it.

'You know you can tell me anything, Art. I'm always on your side.'

I watch her shuffle her head towards Nick. Some of her long dark hair splays across the carpet. If I'd had a dad like him, it might have made me better equipped to deal with things. But if anything, it was my older sister Helen who parented me. My dad was too busy 'earning a crust' as he put it, then spending what he made down the pub. He left when I was eight and, if I'm honest, I scarcely noticed the difference. With Mum working two jobs to keep all the plates spinning, it was Helen who fought my corner. I press my tongue to the roof of my mouth to keep my expression neutral. Now's not the time for me to give in to self-pity.

'You know I had some trouble with my friends when I was younger, too,' Nick says. 'I expect they're just jealous of you. It happens to everyone.'

'Did it happen to Mummy?' Artie's voice is muffled by the hair in her mouth.

I tense. The million-dollar question. Of course, Nick doesn't know how to respond. He thinks I was on my own, just the victim of one glass too many, the night it all happened. He has no idea what my 'friends' did. He pauses.

'Mummy was different,' he says carefully. 'When we were at university, Mummy was the girl that all the boys wanted to go out with, and the girls wanted to be. She wouldn't have even considered dating someone like Daddy.'

'Why not?' Artie sits up and stares at me, earlier upset wiped out by natural curiosity.

'Because sometimes we don't know what's good for us.' Nick shrugs good-naturedly. 'Besides, Daddy was far too busy cracking the books so he could get a good job and live in a nice house. It's important always to work hard and do your homework, isn't it?' He winks at me. 'Here endeth the lesson.'

I manage the smile he's expecting. He's got it all wrong. It wasn't that I wouldn't have considered some-one like Nick, it's that I didn't even see him. I was too busy being dazzled by Henry, and Will and Lyla alongside him.

'She also happens to be eavesdropping on us right now when she should be getting ready,' Nick chides. 'Don't you think Mummy needs to finish packing? We want her to look and feel her best for tonight.'

'I can help.' Artie leaps to her feet, worries forgotten. Oh, to be ten again. 'I can choose what you should wear for the dinner.'

'No, that's fine.' I start backing towards the walk-in wardrobe. Artie's tastes run spanglier than mine. 'I'm already packed.'

Actually, I've been packed for days. I've checked my suitcase so many times it's like I've developed some sort of nervous tic. If I'm going to do what I'm planning, there's stuff I can't forget. A combination of fear and anticipation is driving me on, like when you're applying for a job you want so badly you're too scared to go to the interview. Or when you like a guy too much actually to talk to him. Funnily enough, I felt like that around Henry before we started dating. Will I was instantly at ease with, ironically, given what happened, but Henry made me stumble over my words and get flustered right up until he asked me out. Then I saw how sweet and caring he could be. Or at least I thought I did.

'Well let's give Mummy a minute, anyway.' Nick puts his hands on Artie's shoulders to shepherd her out of the room. 'You can go and see what your brother's up to.'

'Xander's on his switch. Again.' Artie rolls her eyes. 'He's been on it all morning.'

'Didn't school set you some work to do?' Nick frowns. 'Given that it's technically a school day.'

'It's an inset day, Dad.' Artie's eyes tilt skywards again. 'Hardly the same.'

'Ridiculous. An inset day when you've only—'

'Why don't you go and get some of the baking things out, then?' I file yet another memory away and keep my voice even to head off Nick's speech about how they've only just gone back to school after the summer holidays and the teachers are already getting a day off. I don't disagree. I could have used a morning to steady my nerves instead of refereeing between two ten-year-olds. 'I

8

know Nonna was planning to make a cake with you this afternoon.'

'That sounds like Nonna.' Nick shoos Artie away.

I keep the smile pasted on my face. Nick's mum is barely even Italian so insisting we all call her 'Nonna' is overkill, though I know better than to raise this with Nick. He's very protective of her, even more so since his dad died. They say it's a cliché to resent your mother-in-law but anyone who thinks that hasn't met mine. Besides, the acrimony goes both ways. She doesn't think I'm good enough for Nick. She's probably right.

I wish it were Helen babysitting. Last time she took them into the newsroom she used to work in so they could watch all the journalists pounding the phones and writing up stories. Xander talked about it for weeks. Even my friend Tiff, who laughingly refers to the twins as 'the vermin', would be better than Nick's mother. All Luci does is bake or watch TV. I force myself to remember I wouldn't be able to go to this reunion if she hadn't jumped in. It's ironic that regaining my sense of self-worth depends on a woman who thinks I have very little value.

'It better be chocolate.' Artie's already at the bedroom door, hollering up the stairs to the next floor where their bedrooms and the playroom are. 'Xander, we're making a cake when Nonna gets here. And it's gonna be chocolate.'

The whole house rattles as she thunders down the stairs, Xander hot on her heels.

'Well done, team.' Nick smiles at me.

I smile back, then start fidgeting. Although part of me doesn't want to go to this reunion, I'm also dying to get going. I want to see what's become of them, the three architects of my downfall. Will they wear their crimes on their faces, be shifty around me and unable to meet my eye? I bet they won't. When it comes to keeping up, I've compulsively read anything I could find, but I'm not on Facebook so, other than the odd picture in the college magazine or the press, I haven't seen them for fifteen years. From those snapshots and the trappings of wealth like expensive watches and nice cars, I can tell they're all making millions. I can also see Lyla's had her teeth capped, Will's experimented with Botox around his eyes and Henry still plucks his chest hair. But not in a single shot do any of them look remorseful. Then again, each of the three could afford an attic full of Dorian Grays; I'm sure what they did to me won't even have touched them. Especially given what they've gone on to do. I know a few things about them that haven't made the press. I run my hands through my hair, reminding myself they can't touch me now. I'm strong. 'What time is Luci getting here?'

'As soon as bridge finishes.' Nick checks his watch again. 'Good God, is that the time?' His eyes bulge. 'We really need to get moving.'

I run my hands down the front of my White Company cashmere jumper, smoothing away any pilling and wondering whether the ribbon of tension that's been underscoring everything I do is rubbing off on him. 'I'm ready when you are.'

Nick strides over to the walk-in and starts rifling through the drawers on his side of it. 'Did you manage to—'

'Yes, I packed for you.'

'Did you put in my coll—'

'I put in your college colours – socks, bow tie, the lot. You name it: you've got college stripes on it.'

'You know me too well.' Nick crosses back over and folds me into his arms. 'I know you're nervous about going back after all this time, but you'll do great. Did you pack that satin dress you bought?'

'I did.'

'You're going to smash it, then.'

I rest my face against him. The top of my head fits perfectly under his chin but even though he's only a shade taller than me, he's broad and strong. He tightens his arms around me, shutting the rest of the world out. I could stay in this moment for ever. I only wish he knew me as well as he thinks he does. He has no idea why I'm really so nervous.

'We can skip it,' Nick says. 'If you really want . . .'

He leaves the sentence hanging and I feel a stab of guilt. Nick doesn't know how much psychological trauma I still feel about what happened. We had a single conversation about that night, right when we first started dating, but I played it down. Like everyone else, he knows the surface details, that I was on the quad that morning, but he doesn't know how I got there. As things got more serious – our relationship was uncharacteristically whirlwind for both of us – I kept it to myself because I didn't want his opinion of me to change. Then it simply got too late to tell him. Even if, as every women's magazine shouts from its cover, secrets aren't good for a marriage. I nestle closer to him, taking comfort in his gym-honed biceps. I'll make it up to him when it's all over. The doorbell chimes. I try to hold on to him for one second longer, but he detaches himself gently.

'That'll be Mum.' He kisses me on the top of the head and starts leading me towards the door, leaving me no choice but to follow. 'Let's hit the road.'

Two

Now

16.00

8 hours to go

I can't bring myself to cross the threshold. Nick's already three strides ahead, scaling the steps to the porters' lodge on the left and yanking the door open to announce his arrival. He's one of our Cambridge college's most active alumni – he took the day off work for this and he comes back all the time. I never join him. Cambridge feels like a club I'm not a member of, even though I put in my three years here. Even now, I'm dawdling, picking moss off the head of one of the stone lions that squat on either side of the wrought-iron gates and eyeing up the Pizza Express a few doors down. You'd think being sandwiched between a popular chain restaurant and a chemist would make this place less intimidating but the sandstone buildings and cobbled walkways behind the gates make my gut twist. Despite how hard I've worked not to feel like a victim since I left, the sight of it makes me feel instantly smaller.

I'd forgotten how self-important everyone looks here. Mobile phones might have changed – getting smaller, then bigger (my current model is about the size of a small paperback) – but the clutch of students scurrying across the grounds still hold them up and scour the screens like they're researching the cure for cancer. They're probably all on Snapchat or TikTok but they've perfected the harried, rushed look that means you would never dare to ask. I can't believe I ever looked like that.

I should have been bricking it when I stepped on to the polished cobbles as a freshly minted first year eighteen years ago. Neither of my parents had finished their A levels and more kids in my year at school were going to prison than university. But I'd been dreaming of these historic ivy-covered buildings and the 'quad' of perennially green grass stretched between them since Helen had been accepted five years before. It felt like stepping through the pages of a novel or on to a film set when Mum and I drove her past the ornate steeples of King's College Chapel and the university's other domes and spires in our battered old Vauxhall Corsa. I remember watching Helen in the front seat, her dark spiky head bent over her detailed 'to-do' list, no fear on her face. She looked so focused that I vowed one day that I'd come too.

I memorised everything Helen said about college life, from the strange vernacular she took on – 'sets' for the bedrooms they were balloted into, 'bedders' for the cleaners who helped keep them tidy, 'bops' for parties and 'slops' for the canteen food. By the time I marched down the stony central avenue myself five years later, Cambridge was the only future I wanted. I had sun-kissed blonde hair, long legs encased in tiny denim shorts and a rucksack Helen had crammed full of Yorkshire tea bags, bottles of Sainsbury's Pinot Grigio and a crate of duty-free Marlboro Lights she had brought me back from a press trip to Eastern Europe. The perfect social currency. I ditched it all as soon as I got to my room and went straight to the library. I'd got into the habit of putting my work first at school. I don't think I went to a single party during the whole of my A levels – why change now?

I loved everything about Cambridge, from the smell of polished wood and old books in the library to cycling down to the river on Saturday mornings to watch the rowers, their long oars turning over the water in unison. Unlike many of my fellow students, I went to every lecture on my course. I couldn't get over being taught by the people who'd written the textbooks I'd crammed from to get in here. I would have been a total bluestocking if I hadn't started dating Henry.

I actually met him in the library. Such a Cambridge cliché. I'd noticed him around, of course – he and Will were about a foot taller than everyone else in college and louder and braver too – but I never thought he'd look at me. I didn't need him to; I was perfectly happy flying under the radar. Until he exploded on to the scene and transformed my bookish existence. He told me he needed the same book as me (I didn't find out until later that he was studying Classics, not Law) and that if I let him have it, he'd buy me dinner. Helen had said I should say yes to every new experience, so I agreed. His broad shoulders and Abercrombie & Fitch good looks might have had something to do with it, too. He took me to this tiny restaurant set deep into the vaults near Trinity College, with candles in bottles and wax spatters up the walls – a far cry from the 'surf and turf' and two-for-one alcopops at Wetherspoons that passed for splashing out where I was from. I remember his golden hair glowing in the candle-light and the way he had this knack of asking the right questions and really seeming to listen to the answers. I fell for him on the spot. As his girlfriend, my life opened up. I still worked hard but the entire university was stuffed full of people he'd been to school with who owed him a favour or wanted his approval. It brought me out of my shell. I'd always treated everyone as an equal (another life hack from Helen) but now when I walked across the quad, people actually noticed. I felt like a poster child for having it all. I was invited to every party, every 'bop'. Until . . .

My grip tightens around the stone lion. I look down at my hands. They're shaking, and there's moss under my fingernails. I remind myself I'm an adult now; nobody can force me into anything any more. And, as Helen would say, do or die, babe. It's been eighteen years since we started college, fifteen since I left. If I'm not going to settle the score now, then when?

I carefully scrape the nails clean of grime – no point ruining a good manicure – and force myself to step off the street and into the grounds. Objectively, it is beautiful here; the red-brick porters' lodge, square as a children's drawing, offset by the carpet of brushed gravel leading back to the blocks of sandstone behind it. I can see why so many undergrads are wowed on arrival; I was. Now, all I see are ugly memories.

My Samsonite suitcase bangs every step of the porters' lodge on the way in. I'd rather have gone straight to the hotel, but Nick wants to see if anyone's around for a drink before dinner. He doesn't understand that I'd cross the street to avoid half the people who will be here tonight. How can he when I've sheltered him from the truth?

I think I'm holding up quite well. It helps that the grounds are relatively deserted. Apart from the handful of students with their phones out on the way in, there's only a squad of Asian tourists with cameras on the far side of the quad. They're taking pictures of the Great Hall's medieval archway and its Doric columns. It was in contention as a set for the Harry Potter films back in the day, so it sometimes draws a crowd. But the academic year doesn't start for another month so there are no students stretched out under the willows by the library and the bike racks opposite the college bar are empty. Only those who've come back early for sports or have some other special dispensation are allowed in college. Henry rowed in the college eight and was captain of the rugby team. Some holidays, he didn't leave at all. I corral my thoughts back to the present. Thinking about any of them won't make me feel better.

Nick is talking to the college porter, a round-faced guy with crooked teeth and a wispy beard that looks as though it can't quite commit to settling on his chin. The badge on his black waistcoat tells us his name is Chris. The late autumn sun is blazing outside. He must be boiling in his three-piece suit. I watch as Nick grills him. The porters are not only the gatekeepers of the college but also the biggest source of gossip. I knew them all by name when we were here (one of them even used to leave chocolates in my pigeonhole), but those guys must have retired a long time ago. Chris seems so young. As my thirties recede, I find myself thinking that more and more – at the doctor's, in restaurants, meeting my children's teachers. The reality is that I'm getting older.

Chris aside, the porters' lodge is like stepping into a time warp. It looks exactly the same – a narrow rectangular room with the long counter Chris is standing behind at the front and the entire back wall divided into pigeonholes for student mail. I half expect to see my maiden name pasted on to one of them. Some of the notices on the twin magenta noticeboards on either side of the door look as though they've been up since we studied here. I wonder if I peer underneath the faded pages whether I'll see the flier for the charity calendar some of us put together when I was in my second year. It might have been dog-eared but it was still up when I was doing my finals – eleven of the most popular girls looking sultry and wistful in various beauty spots around the college. Lyla was January and December – the girl set to be January got glandular fever and Lyla was cock-a-hoop about taking out two spots – but my photograph was the front cover. I binned my copy when I left.

The claret-coloured leather on the counter Chris is leaning across has been redone but the row of beige-encased CCTV screens is the same. It only covers the front and back entrances to college. My breath catches at the back of my throat as I think of one of the many blind spots the cameras don't cover. I can almost feel the cold of the pillar seeping into my bones; the gravel scraping against my face. I run my hands through my hair, straightening my already perfect ponytail. You're safe now, I intone silently as I let my breath out slowly, yoga style. But I've always been rubbish at yoga; I can't switch my brain off. I force the shutters closed on the image. I need to stay focused.

As if he can sense my tension, Nick reaches for my hand, running his fingers up the curve on the inside of my wrist and playing with the chunky silver Tiffany cuff Helen gave me a couple of months after graduation. He jokes it's like a shackle but I like the solidity of it. Some days I need something to weigh me down and remind me that I did choose the life I've got. And how much good there is in it.

'So are we all registered?' I struggle to keep my voice light. I thought enough time had passed that being back wouldn't affect me. But standing here in the college grounds themselves, Gothic buildings looming on every corner, my skin feels itchy, like I've been rolling in sand.

'We are and I must stop banging on. Sorry about that, pal.' Nick reaches out and pumps the porter's hand. 'Couldn't resist the chance to take a walk down memory lane. I imagine you'll have a lot of people bending your ear back today.'

'You're not the first.' Chris is clearly from the West Country, though he's making an effort to iron the rounded vowels out of his voice. It reminds me of how hard I had to work to smooth my own flat accent into something plummier – for all the good it did me. I want to tell him not to bother. 'A lot of people want to wish Will Jenkin well.'

I fight back a shudder. Will is sponsoring a champagne reception before the fifteen-year reunion dinner tonight. He invented some kind of portable flatscreen and made a fortune in tech. Now he's lobbing some of it at the college. Nick says rumour has it he's planning to get into politics and be Cambridge's answer to Boris Johnson and this is how he's kicking off his campaign. Not if I can help it.

'It's nice how many of us want to come out and support one of their own. I know he'll be pleased, whether or not he decides to run.' Nick's tone sets my teeth on edge.

'Did you know him?' Chris sounds impressed.

'On and off.' Nick chooses his words carefully. 'More since we left, if I'm honest.'

I shudder again. Yes, *I* knew him. But the porter's too preoccupied with Nick to ask.

'Were you a member of those Odysseans like him, then? They say there was a few of them here at this college.'

'Not my scene, really.' Nick drums his fingers on the desk. I look out of the window until I can master my expression. The Odysseans' drinking society was out of control long before the university forced them to disband. Made up of the richest, best-connected male students across Cambridge, they spent their time scaling college walls and climbing buildings late at night, going on benders, smashing up restaurants and paying them off. Each of them had a revolting drunken party trick, which ranged from the lanky one who could snort condoms up his nose and through his mouth to the fat one who downed drinks out of a top hat. Yet, because most of them hailed from legacy families with parents known for making extravagant donations and they threw a magnificent garden party at the end of every year, any misdeeds were swept under the carpet. One year they had caviar shots and the Brit band of the day performing. I remember I wore a skintight yellow dress in honour of the hit song 'Yellow' and Henry pulled me on stage at the end. A few people griped that the Odies were throwing their money around, but it didn't stop them wanting to come. It's one of my abiding memories – watching members of the college faculty swaying to an acapella version of 'Trouble' while half a dozen Odies vomited champagne and caviar into the bushes a few feet away. College calibrated into a single moment.

'Of course, that was all disbanded long before my time,' Chris probes. He obviously thinks Nick's being cagey. 'But they say the Bullingdon Club had nothing on you guys.'

Nick's Adam's apple bobs as he looks for the words to answer Chris's question. 'We moved in different circles, but I always enjoy seeing him at these things. Clearly, I'm not the only one who feels that way.'

'Of course, it's nothing to do with all the free booze,' I say, the memory of Henry buying me that yellow dress souring my tone.

'I hardly think our cohort has to worry about

getting their money's worth on champers,' Nick says, but Chris chuckles.

'It's certainly one of the more popular reunions. The bedrooms on every staircase are sold out.'

I feel a renewed sense of relief that Nick suggested staying in a five-star hotel a few minutes away. When he comes up for other alumni events, he usually stays in college. He says it's all double beds and en-suites now, whereas in our day you were lucky to get a sink and a mattress with springs.

'And there he is: the man himself. Will Jenkin.' Nick pulls open the door to the porters' lodge and my heart free-falls through to my stomach. Think of the devil and he shall appear, as my mum used to say, though she was usually talking about my dad. The sentiment just as readily applies to Will Jenkin 'no S, there's only one of me, sweetheart, haha'. I force myself to take another deep inhale, holding the breath in my diaphragm. When my pulse has stopped racing, I turn slowly, the way they do in horror movies when they're told, 'It's behind you.'

It's not him. At least not in the flesh. My internal organs rearrange themselves. One of the kitchen staff is planting a life-size model of Will in the middle of the path, holding up a tray of champagne with details of where in the college the reception is being held (in the Great Hall, just like the dinner, rendering the entire sign totally superfluous). Will's teeth twinkle and his dimples flash.

If anybody else tried to pull this off, it would be beyond tacky, but the graphics on the figure are so retro and the whole thing is so irreverent that it works. It's got the hallmarks of Will's tech company all over it. He's been described as the next Elon Musk. He was integral in organising the government's last three elections and there's talk of a knighthood for all the work he's done with technology in children's schools. As a grammar school-educated child himself, he never misses the opportunity to tell everyone he's 'paying it forward'. The college can't get enough of him. My eyes catch on his tanned hands, strong, tapered fingers tucked on either side of the tray. I could tell them a very different story.

'Do you mind if we go back to the room now?' I touch Nick's arm. 'We don't have that long until dinner.'

'And some people take longer to get ready than others.' Nick rolls his eyes affectionately, but I can tell he's distracted. He's looking at the sign and running his hand through his short curls, trying to work out how it was done. He works in oil and gas now, directing operations and flying to summits in exotic locations. But at times like this, the long-haired engineer that he's papered over with a golf habit and an encyclopaedic knowledge of wine appears. My heart softens. It's when he's vulnerable like this that I feel most affection for him.

We start walking back, tracking across the gravel path to a stone one that rounds the side of the Old Court to the tiny car park behind the library. I half expect to see Will's old MGB parked up. You weren't allowed cars when we were at university because of congestion in the city centre. But people like Will and Henry got away with it. The Odies used to hightail it through town and out along the river up to Grantchester, college scarves flapping in the wind as they revved the engine. Rumour has it they nearly ran Stephen Hawking down once. I remember there was a cafe a few miles away that served its own cider that the four of us used to go to, Lyla in the front next to Will because she didn't want to get her clothes wrinkled, Henry and I squashed into the bench seat along the back, heads low until we hit the back roads. If I wanted to, I could still conjure up the smell of petrol and old tyres and feel the weight of Henry pressed against me, the sound of our laughter over the engine.

Today the car park is almost empty. Our Range Rover dominates the space, alloy wheels gleaming in the September sun. I let the leaves crunch under my feet. Autumn's always been my favourite time of year – the smell of bonfires in the air, the way the trees shed their leaves, ready for renewal.

Nick flips on the radio as I buckle myself in. It's a slow news day; they're still talking about an unsolved hit-and-run from six weeks ago. I breathe in, reminding myself why I'm here, what I've come to do. The leather seats have that new car smell; I took it to the car wash to rid it of the stench of spilled snacks and stray PE kit earlier this week. I felt stupid; nobody was going to be judging me on the smell of my car. But I did it anyway. We pass Will's cutout again on the way back down the drive. This time, I stare right at it, taking in the overconfident grin, dimples and eyes the colour of midnight. His whole face lit up in glorious technicolour. I square my shoulders. I half expect to see Henry and Lyla propping him up on either side – faces I thought I knew as well as my own but didn't really know at all. I steel my nerves. Earlier, I let Nick give Artie the majority of the pep talk about how when people do mean things to you, you have to forgive them because they might not have meant to hurt you. But when he'd ducked into the kitchen to get Luci a coffee, I told her she needs to stand up for herself and not let them get away with it. It's the advice Helen gave me fifteen years ago. I didn't listen then. But I'm listening now.

Three

'I'm not coming back for the summer holidays.' We're in the Old Court and the wind is whipping off the ancient buildings so I have to holler to make myself heard. Lyla squealing while the boys pelt her with grass in the background isn't helping.

'What? I can't hear you. The connection's bad.' Helen's voice sounds tinny.

'I'm going to Europe.' Even though the wind twists my hair around my face so I end up talking through a mouthful of it, I can't keep the smile off my face. This is going to be the first holiday Henry and I go on together, even if we do have Will and Lyla in tow. We were planning to do a week somewhere last summer, but Henry's family took him to South America. He asked if I wanted to go with him, but I had to make up an excuse. There was no way I could afford it.

This trip will be pretty much the first time I've been

abroad (aside from one cheap package holiday to Rhodes before my dad left), though of course I haven't shared that with the other three. Unlike them, I couldn't afford to take a gap year and see the world. I'll save my travelling for after college, when I've got law school tucked under my belt.

'You're what?' Despite the bad connection, the concern in Helen's voice comes through clear as a bell.

'Henry's parents have got a place in Tuscany.' I bite my lip. I was so caught up in the excitement of the plan, I didn't really stop to think about Helen's reaction. Or the fact that I'm abandoning our plans to spend the summer together. 'We're going to Interrail our way there.'

Now it's my turn to shriek as Henry abandons Lyla and scoops me up and throws me over his shoulder in a fireman's lift. 'Put me down, you idiot. I'm going to drop the phone.'

I can see a couple of girls further towards the library looking over at me enviously. Henry's hair is even blonder in the sun and he's tanned already, even though we haven't been away yet. When they see me notice them, they look away.

'You better not drop that phone,' Lyla warns, picking tufts of grass out of her tight vest top. 'Or you'll be buying me a new one.'

I grip the phone tighter. This model is the very latest Nokia; it's even got a camera that takes decent pictures on it. There's no way I've got the budget to replace it.

'What's going on over there, babe?' Helen's voice is still in my ear. 'I can't really hear you. It sounds mental. I would have thought you'd be at King's Cross by now.'

'Yeah, about that . . .' I look down at the ground. I was looking forward to spending the summer at Helen's new place in Canary Wharf. She's been up to visit a couple of times, but this would have been the first time we'd have spent any length of time together since Mum died. And I know she'd made plans for us. I feel guilty about letting her down.

'Look, why don't you just give me a call when you arrive, and we'll do lunch? The newsroom's pretty crazy today but I can sneak out for a sandwich. This line's bad. Two seconds ago, it sounded like you said you were going to Europe.'

'I am.' I raise my voice so I'm practically shouting again. I beat my fists against Henry's back to make him put me down. When he does, they all frown as though I'm the one disturbing the peace. I stick my tongue out at them and turn away.

'Now, I'm confused. Give me a sec. I'll close my office door.' I hear the squeak of Helen getting out of her chair and the clink of a glass door shutting. 'Okay, shoot. You're doing what?'

'I'm going to Europe with some friends from uni. We're going to Interrail.' Something stops me adding that we're going to stay at Henry's parents' house. If she didn't hear it the first time, I don't need to tell her about it now. Helen's a bit funny about inherited wealth; she thinks it's part of the patriarchy.

'Who's we?'

'Me and Henry. And Lyla and Will are going to come along as well.'

'Quite the double date.'

'It's not like that.' Am I imagining the disapproval in Helen's voice because I feel guilty? 'Lyla and Will aren't a couple ...'

'She wishes,' Will calls from where he's now balancing on a low wall. The porters should be telling him to get off it, but I can see them laughing at him through the windows of the porters' lodge. Lyla makes vomiting faces and then immediately pulls her face back into line as a group of rowers walking past wave at her from across the quad. Henry starts running his hand up and down my bare arm. 'Everything okay?' he asks, sotto voce. I lean against him and mouth, 'It will be.'

'We got last-minute tickets to leave today. Is that okay?' I telegraph his concern to Helen. I know she's not my parent; I don't need her permission. But it is just the two of us now and I don't want to upset her. 'I'm sorry I'm not coming to see you.'

'Don't be daft,' Helen scoffs. 'You don't have to worry about me. I've got loads on. Have you got the cash to cover it? I don't want you to run through your student loan. Do you need me to sub you?'

Typical Helen. Even when I'm blowing her off, she's offering to cover my costs. I tell myself I'll make it up to her by going to visit her as soon as I get back.

'Don't worry, I'm fine. We got a really good deal,' I say quickly. I don't want her to know that Henry's covering my tickets with the money his parents gave him for getting a first in his summer exams. Or that we're staying rent-free at his parents' place. To be honest, I wasn't that comfortable with it myself. Being shouted drinks in the bar and cinema tickets is one thing; having a holiday is quite another. But without Henry paying for me, there was no way I could go. And he was really sweet about it.

'And it's just the four of you?'

'Yeah. What's wrong with that?'

'Nothing.' She hesitates. 'It's just ... quite an intense grouping.'

'How do you mean?' I take a step away from Henry and the others. I have a feeling I'm not going to like what Helen says and I don't want them overhearing. They already tease me about how much I report back to her. Will gave me a copy of the book *My Sister's Keeper* for Christmas and he does a Nazi salute and calls 'Hel Hitler' every time she comes up to visit. Luckily, she thinks he's funny.

'You just want to be a bit careful.'

'Careful how?'

'Look, I know you're infatuated with this guy, babe, but you've got to remember that makes you vulnerable. They're a fast crowd, they don't have the same concerns that we do. I don't want to see you get hurt.'

'I'm not going to get hurt.' I scowl like a toddler getting a telling off. Henry and I have been dating for almost two years. As far as I know, Helen's never had even a sniff of a serious relationship. And she's hated men ever since Dad left. She doesn't get it.

'Fine.' For someone who swears they don't want kids, Helen's got the martyred maternal sigh down to a tee. 'I'm only saying it because I care.'

'I know.' I look back across the grass at where the other

three are standing. Will is tapping his foot exaggeratedly and pointing at his wrist as if there's not a second to waste. Lyla's playing with her hair, pulling wavy sections of it over her shoulder and tugging them until they're straight. Henry's throwing cashew nuts in the air. The salt on them makes them sparkle in the sunlight as he catches them in his mouth. He doesn't miss a single one. Without this phone conversation, I'd be standing over there in the sunshine with them. I feel suddenly resentful of Helen and then ashamed for feeling that way. 'Look, I'll be fine.'

'I'm sure you will be.' Helen sounds a bit more placatory now she's offloaded all her concerns on to me. 'But it's my job to worry about you.'

'There's nothing to worry about. Anyway, you're always telling me I need to be more decisive.'

She ignores the dig. 'How about I lob a bit of money into your account anyway, just to see you through? Make sure you've got enough to bring me back a present.'

'You don't have to.' Already I'm breathing a sigh of relief. Money from Helen means I won't be quite so dependent on the others.

'I want to.'

'I promise I'll pay you back when I'm a hot-shot lawyer.'

'You better. So, whereabouts are you going?'

'Loads of places,' I fudge. Again, I don't want to admit that we're going to Henry's place. Or that I haven't a clue where we're stopping on the way. This plan only sprung up a couple of nights ago, after Henry and Will had got back from a particularly epic Odysseans bender. All I had to do was say yes and Henry was making calls and booking tickets. I didn't even realise the other two were coming until Lyla mentioned it at slops yesterday. I thought it was a romantic getaway. But the four of us makes it an adventure. One last hurrah before our final year. I can already tell that Will's exuberance is going to get us into scrapes that Henry's wallet and his charm will have to get us out of. And that Lyla's going to flirt with every man in sight, single or otherwise. We'll be making memories. 'Look, I should probably get going.'

'Sure. Don't let me keep you. Just remember you can call me any time. Use a payphone and reverse the charges if you're worried about your phone bill.'

I look at the bright pink handset in my hand guiltily. My phone doesn't have any credit – that's why I'm using Lyla's. I'll have to top it up on the way to the station.

'I'll top your phone up for you if you like,' Helen volunteers. I can hear the smile in her voice. Sometimes it's scary how well she knows me.

'Thanks, Hels.' I look back at the group. Will's doing handstands, his rugby shirt rucked up over his tanned torso, while Henry and Lyla applaud. One of the first-year Odysseans has brought over a bottle of Moët for them and they're drinking straight from it. The crowd of students sitting outside the porters' lodge can't take their eyes off them. I don't know whether it's the champagne or the aura around them. They all look so sure life's going to go their way. If I wasn't a part of their group, I'd want to be. 'Anyway, I've got to . . .'

'I know, I know. You've got to go. Just remember what I said and be careful, babe. Take care of yourself.'

'I will.' I hang up with a frown.

I know she only worries because she cares but some of what she said has dented my good mood a bit. She came out of Cambridge with a first; her university experience was very different to mine. If I hadn't met Henry, I might have followed her path. But with them in my life, it's so much more. I'm still maintaining the good grades and the bright future I've promised myself but I'm wringing joy out of every moment. Just because they don't have to worry about money doesn't mean I can't trust them. Will's got an overdraft, too. He's not that different to me. I jam Lyla's phone into the pocket of my shorts and rejoin the group, grabbing the Moët from Henry. I take a big swig, relaxing as the bubbles hit the back of my throat.

'All sorted?' Lyla smiles at me sympathetically. She called home about half an hour ago and although her mum's concerns were different from Helen's – where would she sleep, did she have enough luggage, was she travelling first class – she copped an earful too.

'Sorted.'

Will flips himself into standing position.

'I think I liked you better before, when I couldn't see your face,' I tease.

He gives me the finger.

'This is going to be so fun.' Lyla links arms with me. 'Think of all the shopping potential.'

'You better put your dad's Amex on standby,' I joke. 'Italy doesn't know what's going to hit it.'

'It's not just the fashion,' she says dreamily. 'Think

of the bars and the restaurants. The food ... I heard Florence's got like thirty Michelin-star restaurants. Is that near where your place is, Henry?'

He nods while necking champagne and ends up having to spit a mouthful on to the floor. 'This is going flat,' he says. 'We should get another before we go.'

'And we can stay home and cook too,' I add hastily, thinking of my overdraft. I'd planned to do some temping while I stayed at Helen's but that's obviously not going to happen now. 'I bet the ingredients will be amazing.'

'I'm not going on holiday to cook,' Lyla sneers.

'Who cares?' Will interrupts. 'We're going to Europe!'

'Yeah!' Henry gets to his feet and smacks his hands against his chinos. He puts on a fake 'frat boy' American accent. 'We're going to Europe, baby.'

He and Will high-five and then he slings an arm around me, tucking me into his chest. His hand's the size of my entire bicep. I detach from Lyla and snuggle closer into him, into the nook between his bicep and his pec that he calls my 'safe space'. I breathe in the familiar scent of Allure aftershave. Sometimes being this close to him feels like a drug. I'm sure we'll get plenty of time to ourselves; Henry's pictures make the villa look huge. Tennis court, swimming pool; we may as well be staying in a five-star hotel. I make myself look out at Will and Lyla, giving them each a wide grin to include them.

'The big question is ...' I let the words linger. 'Will we have time to get smashed before we go?'

I take the champagne bottle back from Henry and put it to my lips like I'm raising a salute. There's more than half left. I don't stop swallowing until I've finished the entire thing.

'Now we can get another,' I say, the sounds of their laughter ringing in my ears. This trip's going to be perfect. Helen doesn't know what she's talking about.

Four

Now

17.00

7 hours to go

Nick slides his arms around my waist suggestively as soon as we get into the room. I know I should reciprocate but my brain's already spinning like a tumble dryer, picking at the details of tonight. I can't afford to get anything wrong.

'Freedom!' he croons in my ear, twisting away from me to do a Robbie Williams-style shimmy as he deposits both our suitcases in the hall of the suite. 'One whole night without any mounds of ironing, umpteen help-with-homework requests or having to referee over who gets the remote.'

He's so demob happy that it would feel churlish to point out that by the time he gets back from the office the homework has been supervised, the battles refereed and the ironing done. Helen calls me Mrs Stepford but it's easy to be dismissive of household chores when you don't have a family. She's been on at me to restart my career and now the kids are getting older, I can finally start thinking about it. I'm not moving quickly enough for her, though; she blames Nick. She thinks it suits him to have me at home. But she's my big sister; it's her job to think my husband's not good enough for me. Nick is as hands-on a parent as his job (and the extensive travel it involves) allows. Given that same job, which pays the mortgage on our townhouse in Dulwich Village, the private school fees and kits us out with two holidays a year, is now under the threat of redundancy and his investment portfolio (whatever that is) is affording us the same standard of living, I should be grateful.

It would also puncture his libido, which might not be a bad thing, given how bloated I feel. I felt so nauseous in the car that I scoffed two M&S roast chicken sandwiches and a packet of crisps from the services on the M11 on the way up. These days, sex feels a bit like the way people talk about the gym. You know you should be doing it more often and that you always feel better for it afterwards but there are other things you'd rather be doing. Tiff says I should be scheduling it in like a workout, if I feel like that. 'Role play you're doing it with a hot gym instructor if that's what it takes to get you off,' she shrieked halfway through a bottle of Pinot Grigio when I raised the topic. I'd blushed and changed the subject. I'd like to be the type of empowered *Sex and the City*-style woman who takes ownership of her sex life and shares all the gory details with her girlfriends, but I've been burned by that before. Besides, Tiff's single. No kids. She thinks getting in the mood is as simple as playing the right song. She doesn't get that there are always a hundred other things I should be doing instead rattling around in my head. Especially lately.

'Come on, Em, we're away.' He lifts up my hair and starts kissing the back of my neck.

'Do you think Artie and Xander will be okay?' I wriggle away. 'With everything going on ...'

'Mum's more than capable. She brought yours truly up, didn't she?' He mock preens. 'And we're going to be gone for a single night. Speaking of which, let's make the most of it.'

'I know, I just worry about Artie. I can't believe Tamara could turn on her like that.'

He strokes a hand along my cheek then trails his fingers down my neck. 'It's because she's so pretty. Like her mama.'

'But they were such good friends. I don't understand how she could become such a cow.'

Although maybe I do. At one point I thought I trusted Lyla with my life, but she was pretty quick to flush our friendship down the drain when it suited her.

'She's probably always secretly resented her for being such a star. It's a pretty unequal friendship.'

Was that what happened with Lyla? I think of all the secrets we shared, the good times we had, all of them now stained by my loathing of her. She was always richer and more confident than me. Was our friendship unequal from the beginning? Or is it just easier for me to think like that?

'Artie will be fine,' says Nick dismissively. 'Do her good not to have us mollycoddling her for a night.'

'You mean me.' I pull my mind back from my past problems to the present. Nick's much better at switching off from the twins than I am. He's prodigiously proud of them but he doesn't let their dramas affect him the way I do because he has a separate identity. With all the time I spend volunteering in the classroom and heading up the PTA, the fundraising panel and the 'green team' sustainability committee, I feel like I'm just as much a part of the school as they are.

'I mean you could use a break. Those two are a handful, and then there's your ... school commitments. You need a rest.'

'You're right.' Nick always says school commitments because he says 'volunteer' doesn't begin to describe everything I actually do for my two-day-a-week voluntary role at the school, particularly when I'm better qualified than some of the teachers. It's sweet, even if it's not true. 'I'll give Luci a call later anyway to check in.'

'If you must.' Nick bends his head to my neck. 'Now, where were we?'

'Just let me unpack us and get things a bit sorted.' I detach myself. 'I'll be there in a minute.'

One excuse too many. He makes a frustrated sound at the back of his throat and goes over to the bed. He lifts the TV remote from its cradle on the bedside table and throws himself on to the huge four-poster. It's all pared-back dark wood and white cotton. I can almost feel the high thread count from here. It's a bed built for sex and as I bend down and unzip the first suitcase, it feels like Nick and the bed are both staring reproachfully at me.

'Maybe later, okay?' When my stomach's less knotty.

I make a mental note to initiate something when we get back from the dinner tonight. I've seen enough marriages fall by the wayside to let too long go by without sex. Besides, if everything goes to plan tonight, this will be a victory shag. Nick won't know what's hit him.

I leave him to the flickering screen, hoping the blare of the sports commentary will soothe him, and start opening doors at random like some sort of gameshow contestant, looking for the grand prize of some hanging space. The first door is the bathroom, which opens to reveal a slick black and white chequered floor and walls covered with stylish white tiles designed to look like bricks. There's a shower in the corner big enough to have a house party in and a free-standing claw-footed bathtub in the middle. It's a far cry from our bathroom at home with its scram of Artie's brightly coloured lotions and potions spilling over the sides of the bath and at least one sodden towel perpetually on the floor. I turn the taps on. If I fill the room with enough steam it should smooth any creases out of the two dresses I brought with me, and I can have a bath at the same time. It's sad how much I count these domestic shortcuts as wins. I nip outside to locate the rest of the cupboards and finish unpacking quickly then head back in, trailing the dresses behind me.

This is the kind of bath Lyla probably has in her house, I think, as I sink into the steaming water. Even at college, she scored one of the few rooms with an en suite, which she decked out with plush towels, her own mirror and so many scented candles it looked like a show home, not a student bathroom. Not that I should complain; the lighting was better in there than my room so it's where I always got ready for nights out. Lyla was one of the first people to sign up to this; her name was right at the top of the list. She's probably using it as a networking opportunity; she never could resist bragging rights.

She lives in an eight million-pound house in Hampstead, a few roads back from the Heath. Even if she hadn't boasted about it in the college mag, she regularly appears in women's magazines and Sunday supplements, promoting her string of award-winning fertility clinics, which she had the audacity to call The Artemis Fertility Clinic. What a coincidence. Not. In the process of relentlessly promoting the latest opening, she was careless enough to give away her address. I looked at it on Street View. Her house is double fronted, set back off the road with a huge paved driveway. There's often a Mini Cooper or a Range Rover parked outside it, although I know she's currently single. Not that I've driven past that often. I'd be mortified if she could see how much time I've invested in her. She probably hasn't given me a thought since that night – other than to appropriate the name of my daughter. Nick says the name of her clinic is a coincidence, as though Artemis is like Olivia, Amelia or some other contender for this country's most popular name. But I know the truth: Lyla has never been able to keep her hands off my things.

God, I hate her in the way that you can only hate

someone you used to love. Someone who's betrayed you. I take off my jewellery, casting my engagement ring, wedding band and the Tiffany cuff on to the edge of the sink more roughly than I intended. My hands and wrists look naked and exposed without them. I slide into the bath quickly and stick my head under the water, letting the heat close in to soothe me. I never get the chance to have a bath at home. There's always something to be done. Chairing committees, playing chauffeur for the twins' rapidly expanding after-school clubs schedule, keeping on top of the housework and running Nick's social calendar might not be rocket science but it is time-consuming. I never thought I'd end up as a 1950s-style housewife. I was going to change the world. I'd love to fuel my energies into something more worthwhile than cushion plumping and cabinet reorganising but at the moment I'm trapped. Nick and I agreed I'd stay at home while the kids were little and now they're older his career is too big to accommodate mine. We talk it over a couple of times a year but always end up agreeing that it's not fair for me to have too much on my plate.

I've started having more and more *The Good Wife* fantasies with me retraining as Alicia Florrick, the kick-ass later-in-life lawyer from the show (minus the incarcerated, cheating husband). I know Luci would trip over herself to help and we could always hire a nanny or au pair down the track. Jess down the road had a French au pair a couple of years ago while she did a masters and one of her kids took GCSE French early as a result. That's the kind of argument that would sway Nick. In my vision of a Gallic goddess who'd help Artemis and Xander get fluent, I gloss over the fact that Jess's au-pair ended up shagging her husband.

I push my head deeper under the water and let my long blonde hair fan out around me. Although her hair's much darker than mine, Artie used to love doing this when she was younger, blowing bubbles to the surface and pretending she was a mermaid, while Xander splashed around on the other side of the tub. She used to be so sure of herself. Nick thought being named after Artemis, Greek goddess of hunting, was a lot to live up to, but I wanted to endow my kids with a strength and power that I didn't have. It's the only thing I've insisted on over the years. Schools, houses, holidays; I'm happy to defer all that to him. But there's a lot in a name. She might have become a die-hard feminist who thinks men are superfluous to requirements, but Helen still got to be the face that launched a thousand ships. The only famous Emilys are depressive authors or poets, all of whom died young.

I feel a twist of pain. Tamara going out of her way to make Artie feel excluded, through nasty notes and sleepovers she isn't invited to, is so petty but I see Artie shrinking into herself, the way I did. I have to do something. I want her to grow up strong and capable like Helen, who was running a national news desk and a team of twelve by the time she was twenty-five, not someone who lives her life framed around other people the way I do. As if to prove my point, Nick is tapping on the door before I've even had time to finish shaving my legs. I glance at my watch – more time has passed than I thought.

'Give me a second.' I skim the razor over my calves (one advantage of being married – you never have to bother shaving above the knee) and rinse off the excess foam. Then I pluck one of the thick, saffron-coloured towels from the heated towel rail next to the bath. Tucking it around my stomach, which is protruding more than I'd like, I pad over to the door. 'Sorry, I've been ages. Did you want to get in here?'

'Actually, I wondered if you wanted a glass of champers. Special occasion and all.' Nick's proffering a bar menu and smiling, good humour restored. His team must have won.

'From the minibar?' I look at him dubiously. 'Won't that cost a fortune?'

'Who cares? We're on holiday.' Nick raps me on the nose with the menu. 'Anyway, we can afford it. So, what'll you have? Glass of bubbles?'

'There's bubbles in the minibar? I'm impressed.' I'm normally careful around alcohol but tonight I could use the Dutch courage. 'Sounds good.'

'I'll be right back.' Nick disappears around the corner. I hear the smooch of the fridge opening and then he reappears with two glasses and a bottle of champagne, which he pretends to shake in the air like a rally driver. I can't help laughing.

'Stop it, you idiot, or it'll be totally flat.'

'So we'll open another.' He pops the cork and fills both glasses halfway, waiting until the bubbles dissipate and then filling them to the top. He nudges his glass against mine and then takes a swig.

'It's good to see you smiling. Tonight's going to be fun, I

promise,' he says. 'I know you hate these things but there's nothing to be nervous about. You've got me.'

'I know,' I lean into him. 'And I feel very lucky.'

I am lucky. Tiff calls it my Cinderella story. If Nick hadn't found me after we left Cambridge, who knows where I would be? Still flipping pizzas in a neighbourhood Italian? We were so young that he proposed with a Diet Coke ring pull instead of a ring. I could never imagine him doing that now; he's always gifting me fancy jewellery and designer labels. But I still smile every time I drink Diet Coke.

'Preloading.' Nick rolls the champagne around his mouth. 'Is that what you cool kids used to do?'

He's smiling but there is a tightness to the way he says it. You wouldn't know it from his vintage watch, Tom Ford tux and the various other trappings of success, but Nick wasn't 'cool' at university. He didn't hang out with the in-crowd of assorted rugby players and Odysseans like I did. Which is ironic when you look at the trajectory our lives have taken since, his rise being meteoric, me clinging on to his coat-tails.

'I don't think there was anything cool about me at uni, really,' I say, brushing off the discrepancy in our college experiences. 'I listened to S Club 7 and I got my style inspiration from Britney Spears. And it's not like I have much to show for it.'

I don't add that I was weak, letting my own existence melt into my boyfriend's. I went to Cambridge fully expecting to be a trailblazer like Helen; to come out of it with an impressive degree and a plethora of career opportunities. But Cambridge was like this beautiful present that I wasted. I came out with nothing but fear and shame. I expect Nick to stop talking about it now. For a couple who both went to Cambridge, we mention it surprisingly rarely. But I suppose being on our way to the reunion makes it inevitable.

'Maybe not, but you didn't see yourself the way I did.' He sounds wistful. 'Clattering up and down the stairs in those red shoes of yours. You remember the ones?'

I know exactly which ones he means – cherry red and covered in glitter. I used to feel like Dorothy from *The Wizard of Oz* every time I put them on. I was wearing them at the last boat club party. After that, I never wore them again. 'I remember,' I say. Now I'm the one parcelling out my words as if I'm reluctant to part with them.

'Do you know I used to lie in bed at night and listen out for the sound of those heels?'

'Liz must have loved that.'

While Nick likes to tell everyone he fell for me the moment he saw me across the lawn at the freshers' barbecue but I was too cool to notice him until we left, he also dated someone else throughout university. The end of his relationship didn't have such brutal consequences as mine did.

'She wasn't your biggest fan.' Nick gives me a boyish 'what can you do?' shrug. He laughs confidently. 'I'm sure she's over me by now, though. You don't have to worry about her tonight.'

I don't say that seeing Liz tonight doesn't worry me. Nor do I mention that I only knew who she was because she lived on the same staircase as Henry. That and her uncontrollably frizzy hair that didn't sit flat no matter what she did to it. Henry used to joke she and Nick looked like Brian May from Queen and his wife Anita Dobson. With his curls cropped short and dusted silver and his muscly torso, Nick is one of those rare George Clooney types who have got better looking with age.

But when it comes to university reunions, everybody's egos could do with a little boosting. It's kinder to let him think that his ex-partner gives me a little frisson of discomfort, rather than confessing the idea of seeing mine with his cronies produces a dull but insistent ache at the base of my skull.

'She knew nothing about you,' says Nick, misinterpreting my expression. 'Do you know how much I wish I'd had the guts to come up and approach you at that barbecue? Bowled you over with my chat about thermodynamics and my bad dad jokes? I should have told you that one day I'd be the father of your children and you'd have been putty in my hands.'

'I'm sure I'd have melted like jelly.' I slip out of his grasp and start fixing my hair in the mirror. I try to assess my appearance objectively; my hair looks thick and shiny, my skin plumped. I've felt too tense and queasy about this reunion to run as much as usual lately, which means there's an unexpected fullness to my chest. I look good. Do I look good enough?

Nick reads my thoughts. 'You look gorgeous. I'd better make sure I don't let the side down.'

'As if you could. I'd better start getting dressed. I still

don't know what to wear but I'm leaning towards the Stella McCartney.' Not least because of its more forgiving shape, I think, but don't say.

'Wear the satin one. It looks great.'

I take my pot of Chanel foundation out of an over-stuffed makeup bag and start stroking the cream on to my face, imagining how different my life would have been if Nick had approached me at that barbecue. I hadn't met Henry by then; my encounter with him came two weeks into the first term. I hear Nick whistling as he straightens his cuffs. How much pain and humiliation I could have spared myself. If I'd never agreed to that dinner or just let Henry have the stupid library book, who knows where I'd have ended up? That whole night wouldn't have happened and I wouldn't have been walking around for the past fifteen years feeling vulnerable and ashamed. And I probably wouldn't be working myself into stomach ulcer territory about coming back here.

I finish smoothing my cheeks and reach for the lipstick I know Nick likes. Lady Danger. How apt. I swipe it across my lips in two blood-red slashes and move on to my eye-liner. I think of the last time I saw Henry, the shock and disgust etched on to his golden features.

I close my eyes as if I can block the image out. He never came to see me afterwards. None of them did. Not Will, nor Lyla. Not once. No apologies, no final reckonings. In the mirror, the pencil stutters. I force myself to iron out the brackets between my eyebrows. I haven't come to dwell on the night they brought everything crashing down around me, or the low, dark days that followed. I've served my time, living as the outline of a person, blaming myself for what happened. I look myself square in the face. The skin between my eyebrows unfurrows. I don't need to worry. Things are different now. I've changed; tonight gives me the perfect chance to prove it.

Five

Then

I can't believe how hot it is here. Or how perfect. The last two summers in the UK have been total washouts; it's like the weather gets nice in April and then runs out of steam by the time we break up for the summer holidays and can actually make use of it. But here in Tuscany, the sky is like a stripe of clear, royal blue and it's so hot that I don't think a single one of us has been fully clothed since we got here. Which, given that Henry has a physique straight out of *Men's Health*, makes for quite a pleasant view. Even Will's looking good; broad shoulders tapering down to tight abs and skin the colour of caramel. I wonder if Lyla will notice. It would be nice for those two to get together and complete the square. She brushes me off every time I suggest it, but I'm sure she must have considered it. There's something innately lovable about Will.

'Do you want me to top you up? Your shoulders are

looking a bit red.' Henry holds out the bottle of Nivea I've been religiously applying. I'm not like the other three; one glimpse of sunlight and they're golden. I burn.

'Yes please.' I flip my hair over my shoulder and lower the straps. 'Make sure you do it properly; you missed a whole chunk at the back of my neck yesterday.'

'Perhaps it was all part of my evil ploy to get you to come inside and out of the sun with me?' Henry raises his eyebrows and slides his hand into the top of my bikini.

'Get a room, you guys,' Lyla groans from the lounger next to me.

'That's exactly what I'm suggesting,' Henry laughs, holding out his hand to me. 'What do you reckon? Are you up for a "siesta"?'

'Seriously, it's gross.' Lyla sits up and pushes her sunglasses on to the top of her head so she can glare at us. I feel bad. Henry and I have been all over each other this holiday. It must be the freedom of not having our time carved into by lectures or the Odysseans. I've been so swept up in the joy of moving forward with our relationship that I haven't really stopped to think how it must be for Lyla and Will. Will doesn't seem to care – he's currently doing lengths of the pool underwater – but Lyla's been a bit restless the last couple of days. She claims she doesn't want to be in a relationship but that doesn't mean she needs mine rubbed in her face.

'Sorry,' I say, slipping out of Henry's grasp. 'I'll try and keep a lid on it. Do you want me to come in for a dip?'

'Don't worry about it. I'll go in on my own. I don't need babysitting.' She stands up and adjusts the minuscule metallic gold bikini she's wearing. I'm forever pulling my tired Topshop two-piece out of my bum – I think the fabric must have shrunk in the washing machine – but Lyla does the opposite, making sure the briefs ride high up on her hips and expose more of her perfect posterior. Once she's satisfied, she flounces off to the pool and executes a perfect dive into the deep end, barely even making a splash, and starts floating on her back.

'I guess we should cool it a bit,' I say to Henry, watching Lyla floating on her back.

'What if I can't control myself around you?' Henry springs on to the lounger next to me and wraps his arms around me.

I laugh. 'You'll have to try. I'm hardly that irresistible.'

'You have no idea what you do to me.'

'I might have some idea.' I nod at the tent-shape in his trunks.

'What can I say? I've got chills, they're multiplying,' he starts to sing off-key. 'And I'm losing control.'

'Very nice, John Travolta. Isn't that the bit when they're singing about the car?'

We watched *Grease* last night. The villa has an odd selection of DVDs that Henry claims belong to his sister. So far, we've been through *Clueless*, *Dirty Dancing*, *Grease* and *Three Men and a Little Lady*. The perfect selection for a tweenager or a gay man.

'Tough crowd.' Henry shrugs. 'Anyway, there's something I wanted to talk to you about while those two are busy.'

'Sounds serious.' I try to sound playful, but my pulse

speeds up a bit. It's not like him to want to discuss something serious.

'I've decided I'm going to apply for law school.' He says it like he's presenting a prize. I'm almost expecting him to do jazz hands.

'Law school?'

'What can I say? You've been banging on about it so much you've finally converted me.'

I pause for a moment to take it in. I always thought Henry would go into the City like his dad. It's like all my Christmases have come at once.

'That's amazing,' I beam. Although I'm excited about going to law school, worrying about the impact it might have on my relationship with Henry has dampened my enthusiasm a bit. Now I don't have to worry.

'It is a bit, isn't it?' He preens. 'As a classicist, I'll have to do a conversion course and get you to help me with the application and all that crap and I haven't done any vacation work schemes but I'm sure it won't be a problem. Nottingham, here we come.'

'Nottingham?' I frown.

'It's the best, baby. And we deserve the best.'

He's got a point. Nottingham has one of the best-regarded law schools in the country. I'd just always planned to go to law school in London. Helen's said I can live with her and I figured it would be closer to Henry, whatever he decided to do. I suppose I don't have to think about that now.

'We can get a place together and be all grown up.' He leans over and kisses me.

I can feel the euphoria bubbling up inside. I can't believe I can have law school and keep Henry. I lose myself in the feeling of his skin against mine until what feels like a bucket of cold water is tipped over my head. I jump to my feet, freezing water running down my nose and face on to my shoulders and chest. Will is standing there with the bucket and laughing.

'You two looked like you needed cooling down.'

'You are such a dick.' Henry shakes water out of his hair like a dog.

'You suck, Will.' I wring my hair out.

'Oh, come on, Emmy, you look like a mermaid. A furious mermaid, but still a mermaid. I was only messing around.'

I stick my tongue out at him. Actually, in the heat the water feels refreshing, but forget mermaid, I probably look like a drowned rat. Inside my bikini top, my nipples are standing to attention and I've got water on my eyelashes. I cross my hands over my chest. 'You'll get yours.'

'I look forward to it.'

'Anyone feel like an afternoon beverage?' Lyla pulls herself out of the pool slowly, pouring her body over the edge in slow motion, like a *Baywatch* model.

'I've got some of the miniatures from the plane in my room.' Will nods back at the villa. 'Vodka, gin, what's your poison?'

'I meant wine. We could have a couple here and then go into town for dinner? We still haven't tried that place we talked about.'

I try to look blank, even though I know exactly which place she's talking about. We've walked past it two or three times and she says she wants to go in every time we do. Apparently, it's had a write-up in *Vogue*. It's also hideously expensive. I've tried to budget for this trip as best I can but Helen's money is long gone. Even though we've stayed in the villa quite a lot, eating cheese and cooked meats, each time we go out, I have to hold my breath when every bill comes.

'Come on, you know the one.' She comes over and bumps her hip against mine. 'It'll be fun. You can borrow that red Valentino dress I bought in Florence.'

'You haven't even worn it yet,' I say distractedly. I'm still trying to work out if what I've got left on my overdraft will cover dinner.

'So?' She links arms with me. 'I've got loads of things to wear and it looked much better on you than me. Have it if you want.'

I hadn't even meant to try it on. I was only looking at it because I was bored. The boys were long gone – into a smoky bar with green awning that we passed on the way to the main shopping strip. I'd much rather have been with them but Lyla insisted she needed a second opinion on her purchases. And someone to help her carry her bags, as it turned out. Valentino was the fourth shop we went into. She was in the changing room for such a long time that I started flipping through the *saldi* racks. Before I knew what was happening, the sales assistant had set me up in a changing room with a stack of clothes to rival what Lyla was trying on. I didn't buy anything but when Lyla saw me in the red one, she decided to buy it.

'Er . . .' I don't know what to say. She might be my best friend, but I can't accept a designer dress when they've been subbing me all holiday.

'Ugh, it's too hot to get dressed up and go out.' Will saves me. 'Save your designer shit for graduation week. Why don't we just throw on some things, go into town and grab some pizza and some booze to bring back here?'

Will's the only one who gets that money doesn't grow on trees. I shoot him a grateful look and he winks at me.

'I'm easy,' Henry yawns. 'I don't care whether we're in or out as long as I've got a beer in my hand.'

'Fine,' Lyla says. 'You should keep the dress, though, Em. Next year's going to be awesome. There'll be plenty of places to wear it.'

'Starting with the Odyssean garden party,' Henry says. 'Now you're looking at El Presidente, I think I'm going to make short dresses mandatory. For the ladies, of course.'

I flick water over him jokily. 'You'll be lucky if we come.'

'The kinds of parties I'm planning on throwing, everyone will want to come. I'm thinking champagne, I'm thinking caviar. At least one a term. Anyone who's anyone will be there. And baby, we're not just anyone. College is going to be ours for the taking. This is the year we rule.'

He says it as though he doesn't already walk across the campus like a war hero.

'You better believe it.' Will throws his arms in the air

like he's winning a race. 'It's going to be unforgettable. I can't bloody wait.'

With mine and Henry's future stretched out like a band of gold in front of me, neither can I.

Six

18.00

6 hours to go

Nick insists on taking a selfie when we've finished getting ready. Photography's his thing – our house is wallpapered with hundreds of beautiful black and white shots of the twins. Normally I hate having my photo taken but tonight I get into it, twisting my head and pouting while he applies filter after filter on his phone, sweeping it the length of my body so he can get my Victoria Beckham satin evening dress in all its glory. I couldn't decide between it and the velvet Stella McCartney I brought, but Nick really wanted me to wear it, so I did. Underneath I'm Spanxed to within an inch of my life, but from the outside I'm svelte. It's amazing what good tailoring can do. Lyla had dresses like this at college and she was always happy to lend them out after she'd worn them but back then I was Topshop or Warehouse the whole way.

Nick's faffing with his bow tie so I tell him I'll meet him in the lobby. I've had two glasses of champagne and I'm second-guessing my own every move. Hanging around in the suite is making me nervous. I'll feel calmer in the lobby. I stuff a room key card into my bulging evening bag and step out into the hallway, and straight into a statuesque blonde in a shimmery evening gown that suggests she's going to exactly the same place as I am.

'I'm sorry.' My nerves start to thrum with anticipation. 'I should have been looking where I was going.'

'It is also my fault,' she says in a faintly accented voice. I watch her take in my evening dress. She's wondering whether we've met. We haven't. But I know exactly who she is. She's taller than she looks in photographs, with boyish hips and long legs, one of which flashes through the slit in her dress. When she opens her mouth, I see even white pearls. Good legs and teeth. Like a racehorse. And, of course, about a decade younger than me. Henry married disappointingly predictably.

I'm so busy rating every part of me compared to every part of her that I hardly notice Nick coming out of the room behind me. I do notice when he crosses the corridor and pecks each of her cheeks.

'Freja. So great to see you again. Have you met my wife, Emily?'

I feel wrong-footed. Of course, he would know her; that's what comes of attending every alumni event. But

I want to tug him back, to bring him on to my side. I recover myself.

I smile graciously. 'In a manner of speaking. We bumped into each other. Quite literally.'

'Freja is Henry Hawksmoor's wife,' Nick continues. He once told me the key to forging conversations is to introduce each new person with two facts about themselves to ignite discussion. I wait for the second. 'She works in oil and gas, too, so we often get thrown together at these things while everyone else bangs on about law.'

He doesn't realise I already know everything about Freja. I might feign disinterest in the college but I scour the quarterly alumni magazines in secret when Nick's gone to bed. I know where she works (Shell), where she met Henry (Copenhagen, where she's originally from) and how many kids she has (none). I take pleasure in this last fact, although I know I shouldn't.

Freja smiles. 'Though I am also a tax lawyer, so I straddle both camps.'

'How nice,' I say, as though I haven't noticed Nick's gaze flick to her exposed leg on the word 'straddle'. No Spanx required there; the advantage of being the other side of thirty. I pluck the material of my own dress, feeling enormous.

'It's a pleasure to meet you properly,' I say.

'It's good to meet you too,' she says. 'I've heard many things about you.'

My smile freezes. To anyone else this would be a conversational banality. To me, it's taut with the knowledge that once I was the college laughing stock.

'Nick talks of you often,' she clarifies.

'All good, I hope.' I shuffle the tension off my face, hoping she hasn't seen it. I'm being paranoid. What happened that night might have defined me, but everybody else will have moved on long ago. It's me that's stuck.

'Very. He tells me you are a teacher. That must be rewarding.'

'He's being too kind.' I nudge Nick with my hip. 'I'm just a classroom helper.' I shouldn't say 'just'. I know what I do is valuable, shoring up old concepts while the teacher pushes on with new, and making the classrooms look like inviting places to learn. But in the company of tonight's assorted lawyers, bankers and other captains of industry, volunteering at the school your kids go to doesn't quite pass muster.

'You're hiding your light under a bushel.' Nick nudges me back. 'She coordinates the entire year group and works across all three of the Year Six classes at the best prep school in London.'

I blush. Nick's so relentlessly proud of all my achievements; his enthusiasm almost diminishes them. He'll be talking about my running next, as if I'm some kind of international athlete rather than an occasional park runner. Freja's eyes have taken on the glaze that people who don't have children reserve for when those that do start talking about them. I vow that next time we come to any kind of reunion I'll have more to talk about than my children.

'So you guys are staying at this hotel as well?' Of course

she is. Idiot. People don't tend to roam the corridors of hotels they're not staying in.

'A whole group of us are.' She glances behind her as if mentioning them will summon them. I feel a rush of adrenaline. It's the fight-or-flight reflex; the twins studied it at school last term. Wherever she is, *he* can't be far behind.

'Lots of familiar faces,' I say, adding another bland topic to the pile. I think of the garden parties I swanned around at when I was a student, the small talk I could slip into like a second skin. I used to be better at this.

'But perhaps not for you? Nick explains you are often unable to come to these events.'

I trot out my practised excuse. 'Childcare issues.'

'When you have twins it can be hard to get a sitter,' Nick confirms loyally.

Freja nods sympathetically, even though she doesn't have kids. The sound of Nick's mobile stops her from having to find a suitable response.

He squints at his screen. 'I need to take this. It's all going belly up in the Gulf of Mexico. I'll only be a sec.' He presses the phone between his cheek and his shoulder and takes a few steps down the corridor.

Freja, who looks more interested in the Gulf of Mexico than my small talk, reorients her attention back to me. I fear she's already pegged me as some dowdy housewife but she's trying to be nice. 'So how did you two meet?'

'Nick and I?' For a second I don't understand the question. Then it dawns on me. She doesn't know I went here. Any fantasy that Henry might have referenced our three-year relationship ebbs away. I shouldn't be surprised. He demonstrated how little I mattered back then. What could possibly have changed? It's almost amusing that I've spent so long worrying everyone would remember what happened to me; it hadn't occurred to me that some of them wouldn't know who I am. I look back down the corridor at where Nick's plucking at his sideburns and spitting out instructions. I draw strength from the fact that he's in his element. I'm not on my own here. 'We were in the same year.'

'At Cambridge?'

I can practically see the cogs in her head turning. She's wondering how I ended up volunteering at a primary school if I have a degree from Cambridge. I almost will her to ask me. I'd love to tell her how her husband and his friends' actions shrank my career choices down to nothing. But she doesn't.

'That's right.' I pretend I haven't followed her train of thought. 'Although we didn't get together until much later. We both dated other people at college.'

I picture Henry, wet hair hanging in his face, fresh off the rugby field after a win, picking me up from the sidelines and carrying me back to his room. How he used to lie on the narrow single bed under his sloped ceiling, a cigarette hanging out of his mouth like Leonardo DiCaprio. I wonder if the betrayal shows on my face. I want to tell her I dated him, to make her see I'm not some dullard with nothing to commend me. But the comment slides past.

'How nice to come back at last.' When she smiles her face lights up. She seems genuine. I wonder how someone like her ended up with Henry. 'So, you will know everyone here?'

'All too well.'

My comment hangs in the air. It's my turn to stoke the exchange but I'm finding it hard to let the images go. Lyla was my best friend; Henry was my first love. And Will? I thought he had my back. That's why it all hurt so much. I look at her again, wondering if she knows as much about him as I do; whether she'd be with him if she did.

'What did I miss?' Nick's hung up the phone.

'Nothing really.' I take a step down the corridor to where I can see the metal of the lifts glinting in the foyer. Normally I'd worry about being rude but I'm sure I'm doing Freja a favour not forcing an already stilted conversation. Her being so nice is making me feel uncomfortable, anyway. 'Should we get going?'

A door slamming further down the corridor cuts off Nick's answer. I hear Henry's chuckle before I see him. I freeze, my earlier adrenaline bleeding away. I wait for the sound of Will's mockney 'boy done good' laugh to underscore it but a tinkly laugh rings out instead. Then they round the corner and I'm confronted by the sight of Henry striding down the hall with Lyla hanging off his arm.

Looking at them together makes me feel light-headed, the way you see spots if you stare straight at the sun. It's been fifteen years but it could all have happened yesterday. The years have given the lines of his face gravitas, mussed him up a bit. He no longer looks baby-faced; he looks devastating. Especially with Lyla next to him. I've read enough self-help books to try to subscribe to the theory that everything happens for a reason, but it seems a particularly cruel twist of fate to deliver my first sighting of him and involve Lyla. I think of all the times the four of us linked arms and strode across campus. Will, Henry, Lyla and me. My eyes snap back to Freja but she seems supremely comfortable with Lyla's proximity to her husband. Does she know any of this history? Maybe she's so confident in his affection that she thinks she doesn't have to worry about a woman like Lyla. She thinks Henry will never let her down, that she can rely on him. I made that mistake once. I won't make it again.

Nick steps forward.

'Aren't you a sight for sore eyes?' he tells Lyla, and she shakes her long dark hair over her shoulders like she's on a photoshoot. She's wearing huge pink earrings like chandeliers and a fuchsia halter neck that wouldn't be out of place on a beach. She makes me feel stiff and formal, like I'm trying too hard. I remind myself that Freja is as smartly dressed as I am. Lyla used to underdress at university, too. She used to say she couldn't be arsed to make the effort, but the reality was she thought she was too pretty to have to adhere to a dress code like the rest of us, as if the rules didn't apply to her. She laughs up at Nick and my hatred tightens a notch. First Freja, then Lyla. I had no idea he knew everybody so well. He never talks about any of the college functions he comes to. I've always thought it's out of consideration for me. Now I'm wondering if there's something more to it.

You're jumping at shadows, I tell myself. You should be grateful he's given you a moment to recover yourself. To get off that back foot you perpetually find yourself on as one of life's underachievers. Having to describe myself as a classroom volunteer to Freja hasn't helped. As if to live the metaphor, I step forward.

'Henry. Lyla.' I give them both a wide smile, trying to channel Helen. Fake it till you make it, as she would have said if she found herself in this situation. 'Long time no see. Don't you two look a picture?'

Lyla fluffs her hair again and ignores the dig but the skin under Henry's left eye pulses the way it used to when he was tired or stressed. I wonder whether Freja will notice. They've been married six years, twice as long as I dated him. But there's something about the cosseted university experience, how much time we spent cocooned in each other, that makes me think there are some parts of him I know better, some habits only I will pick up on. The way he has to run the tap when he goes to the bathroom, that he hates nuts but loves cashews, the special pair of threadbare Gap boxer shorts he wore for exams – they're all homage to the beginning of a life together. I wonder on a scale of one to pathetic how tragic it is that I remember all these details. I can forget my house keys on any given day and have to use the spare, but I can still remember that Henry Hawksmoor only sleeps on his left side. Of course, those are the innocent details I know about him; lately, I've filled in some darker facts.

'It's good to see you after all these years,' I lie. 'Neither of you has changed a bit.'

Actually, Lyla looks significantly harder, her taut forehead suggesting she's had any essence of personality

Botoxed out of it. Her cheeks are fuller; her lips a little too cushiony to be natural. It is Henry who looks identical to my memory of him – the same patrician cheekbones, same thatch of blonde hair. That same effortless charisma. I can't look at him too long.

'Nice to see you, Emily.' Henry flashes a smile but he looks vague, as though we're old business acquaintances; colleagues who once did a deal together. 'It's been a long time.'

I wonder what he sees when he looks at me. Does he see the laughing girl whose belly button he tried to drink champagne out of one summer afternoon by the river? Or remember the time I capsized a punt with the four of us in it under the Bridge of Sighs, how we all tumbled head-first into the foetid mix of bird poo and algae floating on the surface? I think of the Cambridge bubble we existed in together, cloistered in buildings seeped with history, convinced we were going to change the world. Or is it that night he sees, me equal parts vengeful and pathetic? I can't tell. Perhaps it's neither and he scarcely remembers me at all. I don't want to know.

'You haven't changed either!' Lyla darts forward to embrace me. 'Still that tiny waist. You look gorgeous!'

She carries on raining down exclamations of how amazing I look. I refuse to be moved by the barrage of flattery. Once her opinion was the one I deferred to. She helped me choose shoes, haircuts, points of view. Not any more. I volley the compliments back as we make our way towards the bank of lifts. They're art deco, like the rest of the hotel, and the gold plate is so shiny it makes me blink.

Lyla immediately checks out her reflection, while I keep buttering her up. The chain of clinics, the media presence; I lay it on thick. Like most women defined by the way they look, she's always had a weakness for being told how clever she is. She's so arrogant that she has no idea I don't mean a word. But I need her to think I'm not a threat.

'Gorgeous and a leading light in the IVF world. I can't open a magazine or Sunday supplement without seeing your face. If I wanted any more children, I'd know where to come. Thankfully twins are more than enough.' Nick is twitching in my peripheral vision. Ideally, he'd have liked more children but it's easy to be wistful when you haven't had two of them cut out of you. I steer the conversation back to safer, blander waters. 'Anyway, you look great.'

'Thanks.' She says it smugly, as if she's claiming a birthright. 'So do you. We've come a long way from crowding around that tacky mirror, haven't we?'

That she has the audacity to evoke a shared memory makes me want to poke her in the eye, dislodge the lashes I can see from this distance are extensions. I nod instead.

'I haven't seen you at any of these.' She wags a finger laden with diamond rings at me. 'You make your poor husband come to them all alone!'

I look at Nick and Henry, wrists together, now comparing watch brands and laughing heartily. 'He seems to be doing okay.'

Lyla holds my arms and swings them, like we're fresh-faced students, mincing through college together. I think of all the times our arms have risen and fallen together.

For a moment, we're back there, before my spectacular fall from grace. 'But it's been for ever. Surely not graduation?'

The bubble bursts.

'Actually, I didn't make graduation.' I snatch my hands away, my words snapping out harsher than I intended.

Lyla's smile falters.

I dig my nails into my palm and try to raise a smile to defuse the situation. 'So, it's been a pretty long time.'

Then Nick's at my shoulder, cupping his hand under my elbow, the way you might cradle a baby. I let myself melt into his strong grip, telling myself not to let Lyla get to me. 'I think we should make a move? Don't want to miss anything.'

'Here he is.' Henry's voice cuts over Nick's. The door down the corridor bangs shut and a tall, dark man runs down the hallway. I fix my gaze on the floor. Moment of truth. I give myself a mental pep talk. 'You don't have to be a victim any more.' This is what I came for. When I eventually tear my eyes away from the blue and gold swirls on the carpet, I start in surprise. I was convinced they were waiting for Will. This guy, with his designer stubble and a jaw so chiselled he might have been cut out from a magazine, is Lyla's date. Of course, she wouldn't be dating anyone below supermodel level. He'll be a hedge funder or a surgeon or something; Lyla always aimed high. He nods at Henry and Freja and hands Lyla a tiny Chanel clutch without bothering to acknowledge Nick or me. 'You left this.'

Hedge funder, I mentally amend. You'd expect a surgeon at least to be polite.

'You're an angel.' Lyla turns away from me and gives him a showy kiss. He's so tall she has to reach upwards. As she does, she flicks her left heel up, like she's so enraptured she's floating on air. She used to do it at uni. Like all of her signature moves, it's borrowed. She stole it from *Sex and the City*. I wish my memory wasn't jammed with her idiosyncrasies. I suppose in a twisted way that's what tonight is all about. Wiping the disc clean and moving on.

'Shall we?' We've been together so long Nick can read my mind. He knows I hate PDAs. He presses a button as huge as a shiny gold gobstopper. I try not to imagine stuffing it into Lyla's glossy mouth. When the first lift arrives, I throw myself into it even though it's too snug to fit everyone. I know it's rude but I figure if we get in first, the rest will stick together. I'm right. I breathe a sigh of relief as the others demur and the doors close.

'That was a bit . . . hasty,' Nick says, as I start jabbing the button to the ground floor.

'They're not my favourite people to hang out with.'

'Fair enough.'

'I don't get why *you* would want to, either.' I pick at the emotional scab. He's so reasonable. I don't know why I'm trying to goad him into a fight when he's the one person here on my side. Not for the first time, I wish he knew what they'd done to me.

'I'm not too fussed either way.' He's so chilled out my stress just rolls off him.

I stop jabbing the button and step back into him. 'Promise?'

'Promise. Now, are you okay? You looked upset back there. What did Lyla say to you?'

I look at his eyebrows, folded together in concern. The timing's terrible but for one moment I want to tell him everything. From the very beginning. To the end I'm planning tonight. It's too late now. I'll tell him when it's over.

'It's a lot coming back,' I fumble. 'I haven't seen most of these people since I . . . left. I didn't expect graduation to come up.'

'I think it was just a one-off. A turn of phrase.' He doesn't understand that his second comment contradicts his first. 'I promise half the people here won't remember that you never graduated.'

Hearing the words out loud is like a swift blow to the head. I've packed up the fact I flunked out into a little box alongside the other painful things I never want to think about. I've become adept at never referencing it. If I tell people I went to Cambridge, they assume I graduated. Why wouldn't they? My grades were good enough. But I never sat my last exam. And without it, all the other work I'd done, and the exams I did sit, meant nothing. A Cambridge degree is split into two parts of a 'Tripos' over the three years. You can ace Part 1 but if you don't sit the exams for Part 2, you fail. So it all comes down to your finals. They presume that getting in in the first place means you're good at dealing with pressure. It turns out I wasn't. At least not the kind of pressure I found myself under after that night. Leaving without a degree meant my options narrowed into nothing, like water down a plughole. That's when

71

Nick found me. I know all this. Hearing him say it so bluntly stings.

'There's bugger-all difference between you having a degree or not, anyway,' Nick says as the button I've just stopped worrying lights up. 'We've got the kids, the house, the car, the life. All that's only possible because of you. I've got two interviews lined up next week and the board wants me to stay on. We want for nothing. I'd say we were doing okay, degree or no degree, wouldn't you?'

I don't point out that it's him that has the degree and the high-flying career, which pays for all the accoutrements he's mentioned. Other than a small inheritance, I've contributed nothing to our standard of living. But Nick's always impressed on me that he couldn't do his job without me at home, taking care of all things menial. He genuinely believes that, even if I have my doubts.

The question's rhetorical, anyway, so he doesn't leave room for an answer. He squeezes my hand and checks his reflection, lit up in gold, by the door. When it slides open, he steps straight into the lobby. I look at him standing, mop-headed and grinning under an enormous art deco chandelier that looks like an upside-down wedding cake. He doesn't get the spike of shame and self-loathing I feel being back here. His eyes are sparkling like he's come home. He might think differently if he knew the full story. But I made a calculated decision not to tell him what really happened. I didn't want it to sully what we had.

I pat my evening bag, fingering the contents through the beaded material. The things I paid to find out. The photographs that prove them. It's the best money I've ever spent. Once they've seen those, the rest of the college will look at Henry, Will and Lyla the way I do. And after I've proved what they're like now, I'll tell Nick what they were like then. Not all of it but the bits that matter. I step into the light and reach for his hands. It might have taken me almost two decades but tonight they'll finally pay for what they did.

Seven

Then

In the mirror, my hand is shaking. I put the eyeliner down and take a deep breath. Tonight, of all nights, is not the time to give myself panda eyes. Outside on the quad, someone is whistling and I can hear the three medics who live down the hall whooping. It's the start of Cambridge's May Week end-of-exams celebrations so everyone is completely crazy. There's a mass of garden parties and balls on the horizon and even the porters are acting like heightened versions of themselves, clicking their heels together and saluting each time I go in to check my pigeonhole for mail. One of them's even been leaving little 'good luck' notes in them. I'm the only one in college not walking on air. My hands are trembling so much it takes five separate attempts to get my eyeliner straight. It's not nerves; the cheap Cava I'm necking straight from the bottle takes care of those. It's anticipation. There's so much riding on the boat club party tonight. I can't afford to get anything wrong.

I shouldn't really be going. Most people might have finished their exams but I've got one final left. It's the bridge
between me and law school. Without it I can't graduate.
At Cambridge it all comes down to these exams. It's ridiculous, really; I could blow every exam before my finals
and come out with a first if I ace these. I doubt that I'm in
any danger of a first the way my revision's tailed off this
week, no matter how well I did in Part 1 of the Tripos. I'm
not Helen. A nice safe 2:1 is all I'm aiming for. As long
as I don't get a Desmond, as 2:2s are derisively referred
to around here. A 2:1 will be enough to get me into law
school, secure me a training contract and set me up for the
rest of my life. I've got all the places I want to see marked
out with pins on a map on the wall. I want to have all the
opportunities denied to my mum. It's what she would have
wanted. I can't lose focus now. Or give in to the pressure.
I think of the sixth-form student I was, the one who got
up two hours before school every day for a year to prep
for my Cambridge interview. That's who I need to channel
now. The one who knew what she wanted.

But I can't not go to the party. It's a week to the day
since Henry broke up with me and I don't know what to
do with myself. This could be the one chance I have to
win him back.

I shudder, remembering.

'I think we should take a break.' He was wearing his
college rugby strip and leaning against one of the library's
columns. The sun bouncing off the marble and the tips of
his blonde hair made him look like some sort of Adonis.

'I'm game if you are.' At first, I thought he was talking

about a break from revision. 'What do you feel like? Bar? Cinema? Late afternoon picnic in Grantchester? I've got strawberries back in my room if you fancy? Your wish is my command.'

I cringe, thinking about how I slapped my hands against my jeans and jumped up. A group of first-year girls passed, eyes on us, trying to pretend they weren't looking at us. I'd helped the girl at the back of the group with her bike combination lock outside the bar a few weeks before. I told her I lost my room key in my first term and had to try to stop myself bursting into tears in the porters' lodge. She said 'thank you' like I'd given her a present. It feels funny to think that I was that clueless once. I didn't tell her that Henry had hustled me out of the porters' lodge before they could charge me for another key, hitched up some trailing wisteria and climbed through my window to let me in. Forget the cheap wine and fags Helen furnished me with on arrival; he's been the only social currency I've needed. Cambridge can say whatever it likes about trying to be inclusive but there's still a core of about three or four public schools that rule the roost. As an old Etonian and a rugby player, Henry's top of the tree. Because it's so small here, it gives people the chance to become larger-than-life characters. At another university, even dating Henry, I might have got lost in a crowd. Here we stand out. I turned back to Henry, ready to make a comment about how far we'd come. But he was pulling a clump of weeds out of a patch growing at the base of the column and looked at them spread out in his hands without saying anything. That's when it clicked: Houston; we have a problem.

'Henry?' I hated the question in my voice.

'Emmy.' He couldn't meet my eyes. He kept looking at the grass, rubbing it between his fingers like it was a rosary. 'I just think maybe we met a bit young.' He sounded like a newsreader, reciting someone else's script. At this point, a second year he played rugby with wandered over to say hello.

'Fuck off,' Henry bellowed as the guy held out his hand to shake.

'Oh, right.' The guy took one look at my blotchy face and veered off. I should have been embarrassed but I barely even registered the interruption except to note that Henry looks even fitter when he's cross. It brings the colour into his cheeks.

'Sorry about that. Look, you're a great girl but having a bit more freedom before we graduate might be a good thing for both of us,' he carried on, as if there had been no interruption. 'It doesn't have to be for ever.' The last platitude offered up like a consolation prize. Or a back-up option.

What about law school, I wanted to scream. My whole future was riding on him. I chose Nottingham over London because that's where *he* wanted to go. When he started talking about getting a flat together, with a pizza oven for him and a window seat for me, Nottingham instantly became the better option. To him, they might have been ideas but, to me, they were promises.

'Is it something I've done?' I fumbled against the column to sit down like an old person needing support, barely managing to keep the wobble out of my voice.

'God no, you're perfect.' He actually sounded like he meant it, which somehow made it worse. 'But I think I need a bit more time with the boys.'

I nodded briskly like we were concluding a business deal, even though I felt like my chest was cracking open. He tried to hug me but I moved away.

'Emmy . . .'

'I'll be off then. Exams and all that.' I will not break, I thought. With two weeks of college to go, I will not crumble. I managed to keep the smile hitched on my face but as I got up to leave, my legs were shaking.

Henry called after me but I didn't turn around. My dignity was the only thing I had left.

It was a different story when I got back to my room. I blocked him on MSN messenger and ripped down the picture of us at last year's college ball next to the map above my desk. I lit cigarette after cigarette, sparking each on the butt of its predecessor. Now all of a sudden Henry wants more time with the boys? I let him bring his best mate on our romantic holiday. I haven't been able to talk to him on Friday nights for the best part of three years. Friday nights are Odysseans night. If you're lucky enough for them to choose your college to hang out in that weekend, you have to watch them get drunk and start singing along to Robbie Williams's 'Angels', swaying in a semicircle until one of them inevitably drops their trousers and they all get kicked out of the bar.

I'm sure other girls think it's a bonus going out with the president of the Odysseans. I get invited to every bop and garden party going and I can jump the queue at any club in town. But when he's been out with the Odysseans, Henry spends most of Saturday too hungover to do anything. Occasionally, he goes AWOL for the entire weekend. Even Will pretends not to know where he is, although it's perfectly obvious he's passed out at someone else's college or on an epic bender. I never complain. He comes back to my room on Sunday night to scribble out his weekly essay while I make curry or run out for pizza. It never occurs to him that things won't be fine. And they always are. The library's named after him, for God's sake. He's got the world at his feet. It's made him careless of other people's feelings.

After I'd finished smoking the entire packet, I called Helen who, to her credit, didn't say I told you so. She tried telling me I should be focusing on my finals but she could tell from my tears and angry crying that that wasn't going to happen so she said I should go out with a girlfriend and get smashed instead. I texted Lyla and suggested we head to one of the other colleges for the evening to let our hair down. It was a Sunday night in the middle of exams, but she agreed. I held it together as I was doing my hair and makeup and choosing what to wear. But when I got to her room, I couldn't do it. Her smile was too bright. I made up some excuse about exam stress and feeling a migraine coming on and scuttled back to my room to brood alone. I felt guilty for keeping it from her. What kind of person doesn't tell their best friend they've broken up with the love of their life? But admitting it to her was like admitting it to myself.

**Hey stranger, you about? Fancy a
sharpener? I could come over**

It's the third message along these lines that I've sent to her
this evening. She hasn't replied, even though she's surgi-
cally attached to her mobile. She's got the N90 and she
spends her life taking arty photos on it and showing them
off because nobody else's phone can take pictures as good.

I don't want to be desperate. Just because we usually go
to these things together doesn't mean that I can't walk in
on my own. She probably wants to make an entrance. She
finished her exams two days ago; I know she was going
to the hairdresser today. She's got this froth of black curls
that fall perfectly down her back but she doesn't like styl-
ing it herself, so she goes to the hairdresser twice a week. I
could go to her room and see if I can catch her on the way,
but I've messaged her enough. I don't want to be like a dog
begging for scraps. Sometimes, when we're getting ready
in her bathroom, our faces lit up by the mirror with bulbs
around the frame, I wonder what she sees in me. She's
got the designer clothes and handbags, the perfect hair
and a body that makes men lose their place in sentences
and I've got … Henry. Going on my own will be good
for me; it's not as if I'm going to have Lyla as a sidekick
at law school. She read economics and management; she's
headed straight into the City when we graduate.

I take another swig of my Cava, trying not to wince
at its sharpness. All summer long we drank crisp Pinot
Grigios and heavy Italian reds. Henry bought them by the
caseload, barely even bothering to look at the price. It's

different when I'm on my own. This Cava was £3. The more I drink of it, the less my taste buds protest. I'm being stupid. I should have bitten the bullet and told Lyla about the break-up; she might have been able to help. I'll find her tonight and fill her in, I decide. Before I find Henry. She might have some advice; unlike Helen, men are her specialist subject. She's had a different boyfriend each term; I've only ever dated Henry.

I take up the eyeliner again, bracing my right hand with my left to keep it steady. The rest of my face is flawless – my skin is creamy and my cheeks are flushed. I've managed to conceal the plum-coloured crescents under my eyes. The last thing Henry needs to know is that I've spent the week in sleepless agony. I think of the last time I got insomnia after my mum died, and how sweet he was, going to Boots and loading up with every over-the-counter medication he could get me, and buying a ton of DVDs and magazines to distract me until I was ready to leave my room. That's the Henry I want back.

I sweep the brush from the corner of my eye outwards for the sixth time and this time it catches. A perfect cat's eye. It must be a good omen – aren't cats supposed to be lucky? I repeat the movement on the other side and load on some mascara. Then I stand back from the mirror to see the full effect. I'm wearing a push-up bra, white faux satin bustier top that I got on eBay and a pair of denim shorts that I know Henry likes. Because I haven't been eating properly this week, the waistband is loose so I secure them in place with a couple of safety pins. Even then they hang low, exposing at least an inch of my waist. If I were in sales, you might say I've got all my wares on show. I hope they're enough.

I smash more Cava down my throat and crank the music up high. The Pussycat Dolls belt out of my laptop speaker, harmonising about being hot and wanted and filling me with confidence. I can practically feel my bloodstream humming as the alcohol hits it. I'm bouncing as I slip my feet into my favourite glittery crimson platforms. Why wouldn't Henry want me back?

I heave the sash window up and look out on to the quad. Diagonally across the grass, I see a stream of people heading towards the Great Hall where the party is. The bright colours and tight clothes are at odds with the majesty of the buildings behind them. I can almost imagine the gargoyles perched on the roof gutters judging them for their dodgy fashion sense and drunken shrieking. I can hear the noise from here. Even though the formal college balls don't start until next week, everyone who's finished their exams wants to let their hair down. I grab my fake Prada handbag (a Helen gift – she did a news story on fake handbags last year) and head for the door. I need to make an entrance, but I don't want to be so late that Henry's forgotten to look for me. Before I flip my door open, I readjust my Wonderbra. I've always been a believer in faking it until you make it. Nobody watching my hips wiggle as I strut down the central path would imagine that my insides are churning.

I've deliberately avoided contacting Henry this week, though my fingers have been itching to text him. I haven't gone to slops, the river or the college library. Will's knocked on my door a couple of times, but I've pretended not to be in. I know it was him because he left a tube of Smarties (my favourite chocolate) and a miniature bottle of vodka like you get on aeroplanes and I know he collects them. I've tried to focus my attentions on my final paper, though it feels like most of the information has gone in one ear and out the other. I haven't even told people we've broken up. As far as I can tell, Henry hasn't either. Apart from Will. That has to be a good sign. But what if it's not enough?

Getting him back isn't as simple as clicking my fingers and looking hot. Henry's used to having things served up to him on a plate. I know the way his mind works. I've seen him bristle when Will and I share a joke in the corner of the Eagle. And we always end up arguing if someone else offers to buy me a drink at Cindies or Life or one of the other clubs in town. He doesn't want somebody else playing with his toys. If I want to get him back, I'm going to have to make him jealous. Normally I'd feel bad about leading someone on, but I've seen the guys from the Odysseans all over girls one night, blanking them in the college bar the next. They rank their conquests depending on bra size and once had a bet to see which of them could shag the 'poorest' girl in college. When Henry found out, he went mad. Said it brought the whole club into disrepute. They deserve everything they get. Any one of them should do. Not Will, though. We're mates. We look out for each other.

It's not as if I'm going to do anything, except flirt a little. I've been off limits and on a pedestal for three years, the prom queen to Henry's king. All I need to get Henry worked up is for one of them to believe for one night that I might be in reach. Then I simply have to withdraw gracefully and wait for him to warn whoever it is off and reclaim me. I've seen him start fights for less. Then there's two more weeks of college before we graduate and head off to law school and into the rest of our lives, safely back together. What could possibly go wrong?

Eight

Now

18.30

5½ hours to go

From this position by the edge of the quad the buildings seem smaller than I remember. On the surface, nothing has changed. The sandstone bricks are buffed to within an inch of their lives; the ivy climbing them neatly cut back. The sea of grass that stretches from one side to the other, filling the middle, is impeccably shorn and brilliant emerald, despite the dry summer we've just had. But they don't seem as stately as they did when I marched down the gravel drive eighteen years ago. I remember finding out two prime ministers had had my room before me and being scared to sit down at the desk in case I damaged it. I propped my laptop on my knees and wrote my essays that way until at least the beginning of the Christmas holidays.

'Let's go and get lashed.' Nick tugs me towards the Great Hall. He's champing at the bit. Having the champagne at the hotel has encouraged him. Even though I don't drink much normally, we finished the bottle.

'Slow down,' I laugh. 'We've got plenty of time.'

'The reception started at six,' Nick reminds me. 'It's not on to come in too late.'

'So we'll sneak in and make sure nobody sees us.' I stare at the buildings and remind myself how far I've come. I feel stronger than I did when we arrived a couple of hours ago. I'm strong enough to be here. When I crawled out of this place, I didn't think I could make anything of myself. I didn't care where I ended up. Here I am, a wife and mother. Life might not have turned out how I'd planned it to but it hasn't been bad. I wonder whether now's the time to mention law school to Nick, but he's tugging at my arm like an impatient toddler.

'You don't know how these things work. There are usually speeches.'

'I thought those were after dinner?' I frown. I'm relying on those speeches.

'I'm not a hundred per cent sure of the running order. Speaking of which . . .'

I let him pull me along, trailing my hand along the bricks as we walk down the flank of the building, towards the large square hall jutting out on the end. I've walked this route so many times, I wonder if the individual gravel stones kicking against my heels have kicked against them before. Or are they the ones that I felt against my face that night? I feel my chest getting tight and force myself to look anywhere but at the gravel. I'm being stupid again. These sorts of things get recycled. We're all replaceable.

I find myself slowing down as we get closer to the hall, as though my body is resisting being pulled into its orbit. I notice two trundle tables positioned outside the entrance, covered in thick magenta cloth, a crystal hurricane lamp perched on each one. The table on the left is piled high with champagne glasses, next to a tower of Moët bottles. How tacky. Typical Will. I think of the endless rounds he used to buy at the cafe in the meadow, competing with Henry, even though he probably couldn't afford them. He can't do anything by halves. I take one and force myself to sip it, reminding myself I need a clear head if I'm going to do what I set out to. Nick's taken a glass and gone over to the other table, where he is laughing to himself.

'What's so funny?'

'Talk about a blast from the past.'

He picks up something that looks like a driving licence from the table and holds it out. When I step closer, I see it's a name badge, complete with passport photograph in the corner.

'I don't get it.'

'They're our matriculation photos, the ones they took in our first week.' Nick chuckles, dangling the badge under my nose. An image of Nick at eighteen in his first week at college, the frame entirely covered by wild, curly hair, stares back at me. He looks like an Ewok. Thankfully neither of the twins has inherited his unmanageable locks.

'I think I've improved with age.' He fixes his badge to

the front of his tuxedo and turns back to the table. 'Do you want me to help you find yours?'

I recoil. I have no interest in seeing my own photograph. I was a different person back then. It's like what people say about grief. You can never be the person you were after you experience a loss. The blonde peering out from underneath her fringe in that photo may as well be a stranger. I look down at the table. There are about half a dozen badges left. Most people must have already taken theirs and gone inside. I wonder how many will be here; how many of them feel as nervous as I do.

'There you are.' He points at one of the badges at the corner of the table. I'm surprised he can tell. Despite the light the hurricane lamps are emitting, it's hard to see the individual faces unless you hold them up. He picks it up and holds it out, stroking the edge of the badge. 'Aren't you going to put it on?'

'I'm not making a hole in this satin. It cost a fortune.'

'Let me do it. I'll make sure it doesn't make a mark.' Nick gestures at his own breast pocket, where his badge is hanging.

'I don't want to risk it. I'm fine like this.' I feel myself getting tenser. It's being this close to the hall, and the anteroom off it, that's doing it. I know I'm back for a reason, that I promised Helen, that tonight's finally my chance to get my own back on Henry, Will and Lyla. But a tiny part of me, the part that clearly doesn't share Helen's DNA, just wants to leg it.

'Then how will people know who you are?'

'They'll see us together and know that way.' I sidestep

around the fact that we were never a couple at university. 'Or they won't. To be honest, I'm fine with being anonymous.'

'I really think you should—'

'I don't want to wear it, okay?'

He looks surprised. Normally I bow down to his suggestions. Emily Toller is a people-pleaser. I take the badge out of his hand and put it back on the table, resisting the temptation to hurl it into the darkness.

Nick backtracks. 'It's completely up to you.'

A gust of wind scuffs off the trees and whistles past us, making me shiver.

'You're cold,' Nick tells me. 'Come on, let's get inside.'

He bounds up the steps two at a time. The huge oak door is open; I can see the rooms off the corridor glowing behind. The sight of the brickwork lit up like that and what's behind it makes my skin start to crawl. I stand there, feeling a wave of claustrophobia, then Nick says, 'After you,' and I take a deep breath and follow him in.

I was able to hurry past the anteroom, clutching Nick's hand and not looking, but the hall looks completely different to how it did last time I was here, which stops me feeling quite so ill at ease. No strobe lighting for a start. Tonight, it's entirely lit by candles, tall white columns set in holders flickering from the walls and on all the tables. This college was founded by one of the Plantagenet kings and though various buildings, like the library and the bar, have been added on by generous alumni, the main hall has maintained its medieval feel. The windows at either end are stained glass and usually there's a huge Holbein painting of the founder on the far wall opposite the entrance. It was commissioned by Henry VIII to celebrate his favourite ancestor and it's often roped off because it's so valuable. Tonight, the patch of wall where the frame normally hangs is covered by a dark magenta curtain. The alumni magazine mentioned the painting is at the Courtauld Gallery being restored, but the effect is eerie, as though even one of England's blood-thirstiest kings can't stomach tonight's reunion – Cambridge's equivalent of the nation crumbling if the ravens desert the Tower of London. I tell myself off for projecting and carry on looking around. The top table is laid for eight, on the raised platform at the right of the hall, diagonal to where we came in. It runs parallel to the edge of the dais and only one side of it is laid, wedding style, so the diners can observe and be observed by the other guests. Normally the master of the college sits there with his guests. Tonight, that's where Will, as host, will sit. My eyes fix on the screen situated halfway up the wall behind it, next to the founder's curtain. Even I, who still think of an iPad as cutting-edge technology, can't help being impressed. The screen is so paper-thin it can be unrolled and stuck to the wall like a poster. When the event is over, it will be peeled off, rolled up and stored somewhere safe. It's worth a fortune. Those screens are how Will made all his money; their portability has revo- lutionised conferences. All his graphics and apps pale in comparison. I know this because the financial pages of every newspaper tell me so. I think of the contents of my handbag and how easy they will be to beam up on to it. Ironic that his greatest achievement is going to be part of his downfall, too.

I look at the sleek plasma sitting on the wall. It's supposed to enhance the Great Hall's appeal for conference hires. This college isn't rich like some of the better-known Cambridge colleges. It has to pay its way. It's certainly going to be doing that tonight. I take my phone out of my bag and log in to the college's free WiFi in case I need it later, then I look around the rest of the room.

'Why don't we check where we're sitting?' Nick nods at the table plan on an easel next to the door.

I shrink into him. Because the event is already under way, we've missed the bit at the beginning where people flounder around and look for people. Even though I was dreading mingling, at least it would have given me a distraction, something else to think about. Without that, my mind is starting to wander. I start to remember what happened here.

'I expect we'll be on one of those.' Nick points to the two slightly less ornate wooden tables facing the top table, each laid for a three-course meal, or 'formal hall' as we used to call it. 'Will's saving the top table for his nearest and dearest. Look, they've really gone all out.'

There are crested college plates, thick linen napkins and huge silver candelabras spearing the centre of each table, the metal flashing in the candlelight. A menu at each place tells us exactly what we'll be eating. I force myself to focus on all the details to pull my mind out of the past.

The left-hand side of the hall has been cleared, except

for half a dozen tall circular tables. Each is topped with a champagne bucket overflowing with bottles. Around them, knots of people are collected. Men in tuxes and dinner jackets, women in evening gowns that range from black across a spectrum of metallics. Other than Lyla, nobody's wearing bold colours and only the odd person is brave enough to get their knees out. I can tell by the way some of the men are standing and the cut of some of the dresses who has come back with something to prove. Some people are smiling and laughing, having immediately reconnected with old tribes. Others look shell-shocked to have found themselves back here. For those who were in the in-crowd at Cambridge, college was *the* place to be; memories were made, lifelong friendships formed. But there were people who didn't fit in, didn't form connections and were probably anxious to get the hell away from this place as soon as they graduated. And not come back. I hold the dubious honour of having started in the former and ended in the latter.

Focusing on the details works and I start to relax. It's not as if this building was responsible for what happened to me. I need to be braver and tougher than this if I'm going to get through tonight. More like Helen. Nick raises his hand to wave at a few people and some smile and nod. Nobody looks at me twice and I wonder what I was expecting – for people to point and laugh or swerve out of my way? It was a long time ago. And I'm the only one who's had to carry the hard nugget of guilt and shame around with me that I asked for what happened. Everyone else must have forgotten.

I can see Henry, Freja, Lyla and her date – I heard him say his name was Jon – among a clutch of people near the window. They are with Ollie and Hugo, the other two Odysseans from our year, and their wives. They all have the shiny moneyed look that privilege gifts you. I have to remind myself that, thanks to Nick, I have it too. Still no Will.

'Shall we go and grab a drink?' I make an effort to press on. 'Look, they've got a proper bar over there. Let's go and get some cocktails or something. I don't really fancy more champagne.'

Nick perks up when he sees the slab of marble serving as a bar and the guy behind it, rattling a cocktail shaker. Despite its compact size, there's a backboard full of optics and spirits bottles. It's much grander than anything I've seen in the pictures from previous reunions and a far cry from the crates of beer and alcopops that we got at college. It must be another Will import.

'What do you want?' Nick has already ordered his beer and both he and the barman are looking at me expectantly. The barman's got one of those pretentious twiddle moustaches that make him look as if he's from the 1920s. He throws his cocktail shaker up and I watch the silver cylinder plummet through the air.

'Er, a vodka, lime and soda, please. With cordial, if you've got it.'

The barman looks disappointed. But Nick's enthused.

'Do you remember when this was what everyone used to drink to sober up? Of course it was doubles back then, wasn't it? A DVLS.'

I swallow. DVLS was a Henry and Will stalwart. It was a classic Friday night finisher for them; an attempt to neutralise the effects of a bellyful of beer and a night of revelry. If he was feeling generous, Henry would shout the entire bar a round, hold his drink aloft and raise toasts. Nothing buys goodwill like a free drink at the end of the night. I'm surprised it's on Nick's radar. But he's looking at me eagerly as if it's a memory we share. I've read about this, people putting themselves at the centre of something they weren't even present at. Memory can be a mercurial thing. I should know. Parts of that night are still hazy to me. That's why I'm here.

'Excuse me,' Nick calls over to the barman, who's cranking the cordial into a cut-glass tumbler. 'Can you make that a double?' He downs his pint. 'And I'll have one, too.'

I accept the drink even though it's stronger than I wanted. I can always pour it into one of the ornamental trees if I need to. Nick and I nudge glasses and I take a sip. The sugary cordial gives me the kick I need. I'm finding it draining, being here. I'm not good at big functions at the best of times. I take a bigger gulp and my shoulders start to loosen.

'Not too bad so far?' Nick is smiling at me. I look at the drink, then realise he's talking about the reunion.

'Not so far.' I look around. Everybody's caught up in their own conversations, phones out, no doubt swapping numbers or snaps of their children and talking about house prices. Helen said that's what her reunion was like. She said it was so boring she wished she hadn't bothered going. Whatever happens tonight, it won't be boring. She and I have seen to that.

I notice Lyla look over and shift uncomfortably. How many of these black-tie events have I attended with her, standing side by side and passing comment about how pretentious some of the guys were. I remember she slept with someone so pleased with himself he signed her bedsheets when he left. They were Frette, and she was furious, so I made sure to accidentally knock against him next time he was in the bar so that he tipped his own drink down his tux. It was a snakebite and black and his face turned purple to match it. We thought it was hilarious.

While I'm all for playing the long game, an idea, so deliciously subversive I can't believe I didn't think of it before, strikes and I turn my back on the room and start rummaging through my handbag. I never normally carry much cash but Nick and I were caught out by a cash bar once at a wedding a couple of years ago so I got some money out at the service station on the way up. Five twenty-pound notes. Is that enough? I look around at the waitresses. In term time, these would often be students looking to earn a bit of extra cash. I donned a white shirt and an ill-fitting waistcoat myself to serve smashed alumni and captains of industry. But we're in the university holidays so these guys are seasoned professionals. There are one or two who look younger. I wonder if they're from one of the local sixth-form colleges. My eyes skip over the middle-aged one bustling between the tables, polishing already sparkling candelabras and straightening menu cards, her shirt Persil white and her regulation heels buffed, and fix on one with badly cut hair and a lot of eyeliner. The scowl on her face gives me hope. I track her with my eyes, working out how to catch her on her own, when conversations across the hall suddenly still. One after the other, heads turn to the doorway like a Mexican wave. I tear my eyes away from the waitress. Standing in the entrance, raising his hand and ducking his head as if he's already on the steps of Downing Street, is Will. My stomach drops away and my courage deserts me.

Nine

Then

From the outside, the Great Hall sparkles like Christmas. It's the middle of summer but the boat club has slung fairy lights across the columns at the entrance and threaded them through the box hedges on the window ledges. Even the gargoyles are wearing coloured tinsel collars. The early evening sun bounces off the buildings and the lawn is laid out between them like a blanket. People are already strewn across it, necking champagne straight from the bottle and staggering as if they've just finished a war. In twenty years, these people will probably be running the country. It's frightening. There's a girl in a short silver dress chucking her guts up in the bushes by the entrance to the master's private garden and a chunky guy in an expensive-looking top hat braying into his mobile, trying to persuade whoever is on the other end to come to the party.

'Come and bop it up,' he shouts. 'No, I've just arrived, you chump. I haven't been in but it's carnage in there.'

He's an Odie from the year below us; his name is Crispin. Or maybe Tristan. Often, when he gets really drunk, he necks pints out of that hat. I can't imagine what the inside smells like. I make a face at the idea and accidentally catch his eye.

'Emily.' He hangs up the phone immediately and sweeps into such a deep bow he nearly trips himself up. 'A vision, as always. Can I get you a drink?'

'I'm fine, thanks.' Lyla never turns down the opportunity to make one of the Odies get her a drink – she says it gives them a sense of purpose and they've all got money to burn – but I try to be a bit more genuine. I flash him a smile and hurry on. Flirting with one of Henry's friends is pointless if he's not around to see it. I need to find him.

I walk past him, up towards the steps into the Great Hall. There's a trio of girls in black dresses on the middle step, huddled over a cigarette. I recognise the one in the middle – she lives next door to Lyla – and raise my hand in greeting. She doesn't acknowledge it. At first, I think she hasn't seen me. Then she cups her hand to the ear of the girl on her left like she's giving it mouth to mouth and starts whispering. That girl side-eyes me and they all burst into hysterical giggles.

It's times like this I can't wait to leave this place. I've spent three years making my As into Es so I sound like the queen and trying to be something I'm not. Up until a week ago, any one of them would have jumped up at my greeting, offered me a cigarette and made room for me in the conversation. Now they're laughing in my face. It feels like Cinderella in reverse. Without Henry, my coach turns into a pumpkin.

'Excuse me.' I slide past.

The news can't have seeped out. These girls are just being bitches because they can be. I've never gone in for that side-eyeing and one-upmanship; even going out with Henry, I focused on my studies and never acted like I was better than anyone. I give them a wide smile, even though they're acting like idiots. I'm not going to start now.

I clip up the remaining two steps and step inside the building, telling myself I'm imagining things. I can hear Beyoncé's 'Crazy in Love' pumping out of the speakers. I stand just inside the entrance, next to the anteroom that nobody ever uses, and move my lips in silent prayer. 'You can do this,' I say. 'You're strong. You're desirable. He'd be lucky to have you.' I hear Helen's voice in my head. 'And if he doesn't, it's his loss, babe.' It's easy for her to say. She's never cared what anyone thinks of her. I wish I could be like that. But I do care. Desperately. I give myself one more second to call up my courage then I straighten my shoulders, puff out my chest and sashay down the corridor and into the hall.

It takes my eyes a second to adjust. The long tables have been pushed to one side and every available surface is covered in a sticky mess of bottles and plastic glasses. The boat club has put up their usual strobe lighting and the whole room is flashing. People throw back their heads and pour drinks down their throats in a series of frantic snapshots, like they're being papped at some sort of Bacchanalian feast, all watched over by the imposing portrait of the college's founder.

I look around briefly, trying to see Lyla, but I can't

see her signature dark curls anywhere. Maybe she's still getting ready. It can take her a while to achieve the 'I just threw this together' look. I keep scanning the room for her but who am I kidding? My whole body is thrumming with the need to find Henry. I'll catch up with Lyla later.

I see a row of men in the magenta and gold-striped blazers of the Odysseans snorting tequila shots off the bar and patting each other on the backs. With their Roman profiles and identikit flopping hairstyles, they all look the same. Henry isn't with them. Neither is Will. They're usually inseparable: the ultimate bromance. I wonder if they're already on the dancefloor, throwing shapes and bumping shoulders. There's a DJ – some second year with his own set of decks – up near the dais where the master normally dines. I make my way in that direction, my eyes zeroing in on the cube of bodies dancing through his smoke machine. And my heart stops.

Henry is standing in the centre. He's got a cigarette in one hand – rules like no smoking inside don't apply to Henry. The other is wrapped firmly around a girl's waist. She's coiled herself so tightly around him that she's got to be crushing his ribcage. Even with her face half covered I'd recognise that hair anywhere. But in case there was any room for doubt, he chooses that moment to drop the cigarette on the floor and run his hand through her hair, pushing it out of her face. Lyla tilts her chin up and he bends down and kisses her.

It feels as though a thousand panes of glass have shattered in my chest. My pillows still smell of his Allure aftershave. It's only been a week. I thought Lyla and I were friends. I thought Henry loved me, but it turns out he barely cares at all. At least not enough to avoid sticking his tongue so far down my best friend's throat he can probably taste the supper she didn't eat. I think of the life I'd planned and my body feels like a building coming down, the very structure crashing to the floor. Now I know why the girls outside were laughing at me and why she hasn't been returning my calls.

I reel as if I've been struck. I don't know which betrayal hurts more. I want to run and hide but how can I pass that coven outside? Even now, people are probably looking at me and revelling in my humiliation. That's how it is here. Like being at the top of the mountain where the air is thin and there's not enough for everyone. We pull each other down. I hold myself steady, forcing my face into a rictus grin in case anyone's watching. I think of how hard I fought to get to Cambridge, all the extra work I did at school, the crappy supermarket job I take in the holidays to pay my way. This cannot be how it ends. But when I look around the hall, I can't see a single friendly face. There's one thing for it. I'm going to get steaming drunk.

I start minesweeping tables, picking up empty bottles and rattling them. I need a drink. Any drink. I feel eyes upon me but nobody approaches. It's like there's an invisible forcefield around me. I shake a can of Fosters, but there's only the dregs left. The bottle of Peroni next to it is empty too. While there's a cluster of magenta and gold blazers there, I can't go up to the bar. My fingers close around a Bacardi Breezer, which seems promisingly heavy. I haven't got any money, anyway. I spent the last of my student loan on an expensive graduation present for Henry. Cufflinks that I haven't seen him wear since I gave them to him. What a joke.

'Do you need me to get you a drink?' A voice at my shoulder. I snatch my hand away. Some long-haired guy that I vaguely recognise from around college. I look at him blankly. His voice is so kind it makes me want to cry but I don't know who he is. I screw my face up with the effort of trying to recognise him.

'Just leave her. She's enough of a mess as it is.' The frizzy red-haired girl hovering by his side tugs at his arm and they shuffle off before I can answer. I recognise her. She lives on the floor below Henry. Now I know who the guy is. Before I can even acknowledge him with a thanks, she's dragged him away, tutting at my rudeness and giving me daggers over her shoulder.

I pick up the Bacardi Breezer and peer at the label. Watermelon. Not my favourite. I take a glug. It reacts badly with the vat of wine I've already consumed, tasting overly saccharine, like it's starting to go off. I take another gulp. Beggars can't be choosers. That's when the idea hits me. It's watermelon flavoured. And coloured. I start walking. I know what I have to do.

Henry and Lyla are now smooching openly in the middle of the hall. There's a circle of well-wishers around them, as though this is a wedding. Or prom. Well, she's about to lose her crown. A couple of people nudge each other as I start pushing my way through, not caring who I bump into. I hug the bottle close and reach out and tap Henry on the shoulder. Adding insult to injury, I have to do it twice before I get his attention. I feel the bottle sweating in my hand as he pulls away from Lyla and turns around. I don't acknowledge her. Henry's eyes widen like he's shocked, but he's obviously getting a kick out of this. Otherwise he wouldn't be flaunting it. He opens his mouth to speak but I don't give him a chance. I pull back my arm, like I'm pitching a ball, shake the bottle and then let rip, spraying the contents all over them. I'm spattered with sticky dark orangey pink liquid like lava in the process but it's nothing compared to how drenched Henry and Lyla are. They look as though they've been tangoed. I drop the bottle like a bad pop act dropping the mike and then I spin on my heel and turn and walk out of the hall with my head held high.

I know the music is still playing but all I can hear is white noise. I half expect Henry or Lyla to come after me. They looked furious, like two angry orange jelly babies. But nobody comes. I make it to the stone corridor that leads outside, closing the door to the hall behind me. I take a few steps towards the exit but the reality of what I've done hits me and I feel like I might collapse. I flatten myself against the wall. Through the window, the guy with the top hat is still on the phone. I can see the backs of the girls on the steps, the red cherry of their cigarette tip glowing as they pass it between them. The world's shifted on its axis but hardly any real time has passed. Euphoria mixes with horror. What was I thinking?

The skin between my fingers is coated with Bacardi Breezer. It's sticky. There will be globs of it in their hair, on their skin, in their faces. Like gunshot residue. I need to get out of here. Lyla will want to go back to her room and get changed. It's horrible to know her so well that I can anticipate each of her next moves. She'll laugh this off like she's not fussed about the way she looks, while secretly seething. Then she'll suggest going back to her room to change and of course she'll open it up for Henry to go back with her. I could kick myself. Way to win someone back by driving them into the arms of your enemy and making them hate you. At least she won't be able to get the smell of Bacardi out of her hair. Right now, that seems little comfort.

The volume of the music from inside the hall increases. I look over to the door to see the handle rattling. Someone's coming. I peer around, like a cornered rat. I can't face anyone. There's not enough time to get outside. My only option is the tiny anteroom I passed on the way in. It's so small that half the college doesn't know that it exists. I only know it's there because Will and Henry keep the booze for their rugby team in it. It's pretty creepy. This building was used as a hunting lodge before our founder decided to convert it to a college and that room's where they used to dry out the game. They say that in some lights, you can see bloodstains on the walls, even though they've been whitewashed a thousand times since. Right now, I don't have any other options. On the plus side, it's a storeroom. There might be wine inside.

I hurry over to the oak door. I take a quick look over my shoulder to check nobody can see me then I turn the lock and slide inside, pulling the door to behind me. It's pitch black and I stumble on the uneven floor. I put my hand out to find the light switch and it brushes something that could pass for fur. I give a shriek and stagger backwards. I fumble along the wall, checking every whorl in the plaster to see if it's a light switch and trying not to think of the blood. Eventually I find one and flip on the overhead light to see it's just a stack of the old college gowns we have to wear on formal occasions. As the light from a broken-looking electric chandelier brightens, I can pick out the oil paintings on the wall, each of a lesser alumnus the college isn't that proud of. This room is like an upper-class junkyard. I spot a pile of branded umbrellas in the corner, spokes sticking out at odd angles, and a bank of broken oak tables piled up against the far wall. A creak from the corner makes me flinch. I'm not alone in here. Leaning against the wall, cigarette in one hand, bottle of port in the other, is Will. Standing in silence, smirking at me.

Ten

My gaze swings wildly around, checking for exits. In a room full of almost two hundred people, I feel cornered. I didn't expect him to have this effect on me, but looking at him in the doorway, the light gilding his face, the whole idea of being here seems flawed. The plans Helen and I have made seem juvenile, outlandish even. I'll go back home and I'll go to the police, the way I should have done in the first place. I stand up and push the bar stool away, hoping nobody will notice my legs are wobbling. I need to get out of here.

'Nick? Why don't we slope off and give tonight a miss?'

'What?' Nick takes another swig of his drink.

'We've come, we've shown our faces. Why don't we

head back to the hotel and make the most of the room?' I try to raise my eyebrows seductively. Nick looks as if I've just cancelled Christmas. 'We won't miss much. Formal hall food is always crap, anyway. It always has been.'

Will's circulating now, working the tables nearest the door and greeting everyone by name. I see people opening up to him, their faces lit up as he says something to make them smile. He's a born baby-kisser; the consummate politician. I think of the scrapes he got the Odies out of. Henry threw money at situations; Will used charm. He always knows what to say.

I don't want to see him. Coming here was supposed to make me feel stronger but I feel weaker instead. Memories I don't want to think about are already flooding my brain. The four of us lounging by the pool, the time we climbed on to the roof of the student bar and watched the sun come up. The good ones are almost more painful than the bad. And undercutting it all: guilt. Because I know on some level my actions kicked everything off. If I'd never thrown that drink ... I stroke Nick's sleeve, trying to keep the pleading tone out of my voice. 'We could get room service, kick back, watch a movie, relax. Since you got back from Houston, I've barely seen you.'

Nick sets his jaw the way he does whenever I bring up Houston. 'Emily, at the risk of sounding like a dick, I think you're overreacting a bit. I know you're nervous but nobody even remembers that far back. Anyway, who among us hasn't got batfaced and done something they're not proud of? I know I have.' He sighs and runs his fingers through his hair, tugging at his curls. 'Why don't we stay for a bit longer and see if we can have a nice evening. I guarantee people aren't thinking what you think they're thinking. Stick with me and it'll be fine. I see a couple of people from my lab group that we could catch up with.' He points to a trio of bespectacled men nursing half-full champagne flutes and looking out of place. I know he's consciously picked the least intimidating people in the hall. 'Shall we go over?'

Will's drawing closer. Any minute now and he'll be upon us. My breath feels trapped in my chest and I can feel acid from my stomach edging up my throat. I've never had a panic attack but I imagine this is what they feel like. I can't be here. This man destroyed me. Henry and Lyla betrayed me, but what Will did was worse. In a funny way, he was the one I trusted the most.

'I'm going to go outside and get some air.' I detach my hand from Nick's arm. 'I'll give your mum a call to check on the kids.'

'You're not going for a cheeky fag, are you?'

He eyes my evening bag. A few months ago, he found the emergency packet I keep in one of the kitchen cup-boards. I haven't smoked properly for years but I keep it for those days when the kids are being too much. Nothing raises two fingers to parenthood like the illicit pleasure of standing at the edge of the patio and lighting up while your children are upstairs in bed.

I've got about a minute before Will reaches us.

'I've given up.'

'Well, if you are going to speak to Mum,' Nick begins. I feel my leg start to pulse. Now is not the time for a shopping list of parental concerns. 'Remind Xander that he needs to leave his footie kit out if he wants me to do his boots before—'

'I will.' I'm already starting to move.

'And don't forget to—'

I nod and duck away, like a fish slipping through a net. Behind me, I hear Will's banter. 'Nick Toller! And where's your missus off to? I haven't seen her for about a decade.'

I pick up my pace. Will's voice has been described as the audio equivalent of a six-pack and a killer smile. A journalist from the *Sunday Times* went nuts for it. To me it's nails on a blackboard.

I hurry towards the fire exit at the back of the room, hoping it isn't alarmed. I can't go out of the main entrance because it means passing the anteroom. I managed it on the way in because I was with Nick. I don't want to go past it on my own. My heart is beating at about sixty miles an hour. I hate the idea of Nick and Will in conversation. I keep my eyes down, counting the flagstones on the floor to calm me and almost bang straight into a petite woman with glossy chestnut curls and a Roland Mouret Galaxy dress walking in the opposite direction. She's towing the man next to her along as if he's a dog on a lead. He is so tall and broad that he looks like a gorilla in a suit.

I see her shoes with their blood-red soles like the ones Nick bought me for Christmas – and manage to swerve just in time.

'I'm sorry,' I say automatically.

'Don't worry about it, Emily.' There's something disparaging about the way she says my name. She looks familiar but I can't place her. Nick's idea that I could be anonymous is ridiculous. I may as well be wearing a scarlet letter.

I don't bother to stop and look at her badge. I want to get out of here. I say sorry again and step round her. After they've bustled off, I realise why she looks familiar. That was Liz, Nick's college girlfriend. The hair might look less like she's been electrocuted but the watchful eyes and air of busyness were the same. I don't turn back. I punch a number into my phone and keep walking. There's only one person I want to speak to and it's not Luci.

Straight to voicemail. I listen to my sister's voice, telling me to leave a message after the beep and that she'll get back to me. I press my teeth into the soft flesh of my cheek and try to think what she would say if she answered. I picture her at our scrubbed-pine kitchen table instead of Luci, hands curled around a cup of tea while the kids lounge on the sofa next door, and want to be there so badly it hurts.

At least I've bought myself some time. If I can't speak to Helen, I can always try Tiff instead. I just want to speak to someone who gets me. I pick up my pace and start striding away from the college, back towards the meadows behind this strip of buildings, where the grass is longer. My feet are killing me. This is why I never wear heels, no matter how many pairs Nick treats me to. 'That and the fact that you're married to a midget,' as Helen would say, uncharitably. She and Nick often butt heads. He thinks she's a man hater; she thinks I let him make all the decisions. They're probably both right.

I key in the number.

Tiff answers straight away. 'S'up?'

I launch in without preamble. 'Ugh, I don't know if I can do this.'

She knows exactly what I'm talking about. 'Bullshit. Of course you can.'

It might seem disloyal that I've been open with Tiff in a way that I haven't been with Nick. But Tiff and I have always had that kind of relationship. We used to work together. Aside from that job, our lives have never intersected, which makes us each other's perfect secret keepers. And because our lives don't overlap, there's never been any rivalry. We trust each other. When she was cheating on her boyfriend, I was the person she told. Not her sister, not her childhood best friend. Me. And I never once judged. That's the other thing we offer each other. No judgement. When I told her what I was planning tonight, her eyes widened. But that was the only reaction she gave.

'Seriously, I mean it. I don't know if I can do it. I can't even be in a room with them.'

'And *I* mean it. You can do anything you want.'

'It's this place. Being back here. It makes me feel like less than I am.'

'If it were easy, everybody would be doing it.'

'Any more platitudes you want to share?'

'Not all heroes wear capes? This too shall pass? Don't hate the player, hate the game,' she rattles off. 'And don't get all pissy with me. I'm on your side.'

'I know you are.' I bite my lip. 'I guess I didn't think it would be this hard.'

'Yes, you did. That's why you left it fifteen years.'

'Seeing them all again . . .' I trail off. 'They've all done so much. And I . . . haven't.'

'You've got a lovely husband, two gorgeous kids. A life some people could only dream of.'

'I know.' I flush guiltily. 'I know I'm lucky. But when I come back here, it doesn't seem enough.'

'Okay, let me lay it out for you.' There's a muffled sound. 'Give me two seconds.'

'What are you doing?' I feel instantly guilty. 'I'm sorry, have I interrupted something? Are you on a hot date?'

'Why is it you married people always imagine I'm on a hot date? A hot date with my stove.' Tiff laughs her rich throaty laugh and I feel instantly grounded. I can picture her standing over the stove top, wooden spoon in hand, multiple pots gurgling. 'I just needed to take something off the heat. Anyway, where was I? Oh yes, your free therapy. Of course, you're going to feel inadequate going back there. It's Cambridge, darlink. But you're in control of this.'

'But what if—'

'What if nothing! Do you know when I first met you I thought you were this quiet little mouse? I used to dread shifts with you. It took about six months to discover you had a personality and that was only because that drunk guy with the spaghetti spilled his wine all over you. I had no idea you'd even been to university, let alone Cambridge. So tonight is not about what you have or haven't done. It's about you as a person. Go in there and kick some butt.'

'Kick some butt? You know you're not actually American just because you watch *Scandal*, right?'

'Doesn't mean I'm not right.' I can picture Tiff shaking her head, her dreadlocks clicking. 'So, are you going to do it?'

'Yes,' I say doubtfully.

She puts on a stern voice. 'I said, are you going to do it?'

'Oh my God, you sound like one of those dreadful children's entertainers who makes them all say hello about a thousand times until he's worked them up into being all shouty. But at least you've made me laugh.'

'Happy to help. Seriously, though, you got this.'

'What if I crack under pressure?'

'As far as I see it, there is no pressure. You've done the hard bit, right? You showed up. I thought all you had to do now was play the stuff on your phone?'

'That's the pressure,' I say. 'What if I mess it up?'

'You won't.'

'But what if I do?' I scratch at the skin just underneath my Tiffany cuff.

'You've got to believe in yourself,' Tiff clicks her tongue. 'I don't know why you give yourself such a hard time about everything. If you knew the mistakes I made on a daily basis – yesterday I sent a reply-all email about grabbing a coffee to the entire company. I just rolled with it. We're all human. Even you.'

Inspiration strikes.

'Tiff, you're a genius.'

'It has been said.'

'I mean it.' I stop scratching and start pacing instead. 'I know exactly what to do. Gotta go.'

'Call me any time, you nutter,' I can hear Tiff saying, but I'm already taking the phone away from my ear. 'Don't worry about waking me up.'

'I will,' I shout just before I hang up.

I'm so pumped up that I tap in my passcode wrong the first time but second time lucky I open up my Gmail app. It takes only a few minutes to set up an anonymous account. Once I've done that, I take the file out and drag it into an email, addressed to the entire reunion class list. I press the schedule send option and select midnight. Nick and I should be safely tucked up in bed by then. I don't want to be around when this bomb goes off. I tell myself I can delete it at any point in the next five hours; it's only an insurance policy. One that can go straight to the police in the morning. Before then, I will have played that presentation on Will's stupid flatscreen. But just in case I don't, this way justice will be done.

I snap my handbag shut and start towards the Great Hall. The buildings glowing against the inky sky light the way and I feel righteous, like I'm on a mission. It seems ridiculous that the sight of Will was enough to drive me out. I clip my way across the gravel, mount the steps to the hall and breeze past the anteroom with my head held high just in time to see my waitress collide with Lyla, tipping a trayful of red wine glasses all over her fuchsia dress. I have to physically stop myself from clapping my hands. I'd only asked her to spill a glass; she's taken the idea and run with it. Lyla has that effect on people. It's the best £100 I've ever spent. I must raid Nick's wallet later and see whether there's any more cash I can give the stroppy waitress. She looks completely unfazed when Lyla starts shouting at her, gesticulating at the stain and waving her hands. I watch the stain eating into the dress, spreading across the material like a blood stain. There's something so perfect about Lyla having a drink tipped over her tonight. It's as though life has gone full circle. Perhaps I'm not that different from the girl I was back then, the girl who was brave enough to take down someone who wronged her. Because, tonight, after a fifteen-year hiatus, I get to be her again.

Eleven

Then

'Jesus, you made me jump out of my skin. What are you doing here in the dark?' I ask. 'You look like you've been dragged through a hedge backwards.'

'One woman's trash is another woman's treasure.' Will gives me a pantomime wink and I can't help smiling. His hair is sticking up in all directions and his tie is askew. He looks like he's been climbing trees. I wouldn't put it past him. I swear he's got ADHD; he can never sit still. Now I can see that it's him, the room seems less creepy. The dim light flickering overhead makes the room seem almost cosy. I wonder how desperate you have to be to think that a glorified dungeon is like a refuge.

'Cool shoes.' Will nods at them. 'If you click your heels do they send you home?'

'I wish. Seriously, what are you doing in here?' I start rummaging through boxes for the wine I hope might be in here. I find stacks of tea, sachets of coffee and empty glasses. But no wine. 'It's a bit weird lurking here in the dark. Like a bat. Though I suppose you'd have to be upside down to be a bat.'

'Better a bat than a ball. A human wrecking ball, that is.' Will raises the bottle of port in an ironic salute. 'Hell hath no fury, right?'

The last wave of the adrenalin leaves my body like a balloon deflating. Of course, he knows. He probably knew what Henry was going to do before I did. I open my mouth to say something clever and burst into tears instead.

'Shit. Sorry, Emmy, I was only messing with you.' Him calling me Emmy makes me cry harder. When Henry found out that's what I used to be called as a child, he latched on to it. It's what they all call me. I feel tears leaking out of my eyes and running out of my nose.

Will crosses the room, throws the bolt on the door and then comes over and circles a clumsy arm around me. 'Come on, mate. Hawksmoor isn't worth your tears. And neither is she. He should know better.'

'I'm such an idiot. I made a total fool of myself.'

'From where I was standing, she's the one who looked like a dick, not you. Mind you, I don't know what all the fuss is about. I've always had a soft spot for a Breezer myself.'

I don't know how to laugh and cry at the same time so I hiccough instead.

'You're worth ten of her. Probably more. I mean, not monetarily, obviously, she's got buckets of cash. But in every other way.'

I smile through the tears. Even though it's pathetic, hearing that Will's on my side makes me feel better.

'I'm sorry. I'm being so lame.' I didn't even cry when my mum died; Helen said we were stronger than that. I'm not going to shed tears for this. 'I'll be all right in a minute.'

'You're too good for him, Emmy.'

'Yeah, well, whatever. Clearly not.' I find a scrap of tissue in the pocket of my shorts and rub my eyes. I'm probably smearing my makeup across my face but I don't care any more. I look at the door. I wish I really could click my heels and go home. Much as I appreciate Will's loyalty, I want to be back in my room, curled under my duvet with the rest of the world shut out. 'I should get going.'

'Don't let those dicks chase you away. Stay and have a drink.' Will rattles the bottle at me. I can hear the liquid sloshing around at the bottom.

'I'm all right. I don't like port anyway.'

'She doesn't like port.' Will shakes his head in mock horror. 'How can you come to Cambridge and not drink port? It's at the end of every fancy dinner we've ever had. It's the only thing in this place that's free, for Christ's sake.'

'I had a bad experience one Christmas. Seeing it again the morning after was enough to put me off for life. Even sniffing it now is enough to make me want to vom. Sorry, you probably didn't need the visual.'

'Tasty.' Will smirks. 'And I'll let you in on a little secret. We're not so different, you and me – I can't stand the stuff, either. If the lads back home caught me standing up and toasting the university with it in a gown, they'd rip the shit out of me. Guess that's why I never go back.'

I look at him curiously. Although Will never hides where he came from, he doesn't talk about it much. In all the time I've spent with him, he's never referenced feeling out of place when he's at home.

'Other than at formals, I only drink this crap after rugby matches. Which is why –' he goes back to the corner and starts rummaging around in a canvas holdall I didn't spot earlier '– I can offer you white wine, red wine, vodka, bubbles, beer.' He pulls out bottles at random and holds them up. 'You name it, I've got it.'

'What did you do? Rob an off-licence?'

'Close but no cigar. Cleaned out the rugby clubhouse. Won't be needing it when I graduate. No more rugby for me.'

'You're not going to play again?' Will plays rugby at university level. It's what got him into the Odysseans. He got a blue for playing against Oxford. I'm surprised he's ready to give it all up.

'Tell you the truth, 'snot really me.' Will scratches his nose. 'I've got big plans.'

'Doing what?'

'Tech.' Will's face lights up. He sees my expression and rolls his eyes. 'I know, I know. I'm too cool for tech but it's the future, sweetheart. That's where the dosh is.'

'I hate to tell you, but the Internet's already happened. You missed the tech bubble.'

'You wait.' Will points his finger at me. 'You'll be sorry. Tech's going to change your life. You've got no idea. Anyway, enough of that shit. What are we going to get you lashed on?'

119

'I'm all right.' I shake my head and look at the door again. Now the high's gone, the reality of what I've done – and how publicly I've done it – has sunk in and I feel totally exhausted. 'I think I'm going to go.'

'Go on, you wouldn't make a man drink on his tod, would you?'

I consider the pleading expression he's pulling; the puppy-dog eyes the university's female rugby fans go for. Right now, he's about the only friend I've got.

'Won't you get in trouble?' I say mockingly. 'For being in here with me after what I did?' There's a strict honour code among Odysseans. There are rumours that way back in the annals, one of them went to prison for another. 'I doubt Henry'll take too kindly to you being in here, mopping me up. And Lyla will give you shit as well.'

I've sometimes wondered about the nature of Will and Lyla's relationship. The four of us spend so much time together, it would have been logical, symmetrical even, if they paired up. But when I mentioned it to Lyla this summer, she wrinkled her nose. 'Not my type, darling...' I thought she was biding her time, scared to connect with Will in case it was something real. I didn't realise she'd had her eyes on a different prize all along.

'I couldn't give a shit what either of that gruesome twosome thinks.' Will grins. 'As long as you have a drink with me.' He sees me wavering. 'Go on, what's your poison?'

'Gimme some white wine, then. A bucket or a vat, anything. I don't care, just hurry up. I want to numb the pain; I'll drink it out of the bottle,' I say when he starts rummaging through a cardboard box for a glass. Anything to drown the image of Lyla plotting her move. I think of the times I've confided in her, all the things I told her about Henry. The things we did together, what he likes and doesn't like. I practically gave her a 'how to' guide on getting together with him. I didn't realise she was taking notes. I groan and hold out my hand for the bottle. 'I need something to block this out.'

'Naturally.' Will unscrews the cap and takes a gulp. His fingers scuff against mine as he passes the bottle over. 'This too shall pass. Now get your laughing gear around that.'

'How profound.' I take a big pull from the bottle and hand it back. 'I can't wait to get the hell out of here. Graduate and leave this dump behind.'

'And that's our happy thought for the day.'

'Sorry.'

'It hasn't been all bad, has it?'

'Mostly.' I'm in one of those moods that my mum used to call the 'wallpaper blues'; when I'd spiral into such despair that I'd look around the room and criticise everything, even the wallpaper. Usually only Helen can bring me out of them.

'You're breaking my heart. Come on, why don't you let your uncle Will cheer you up?'

'You sound like a paedophile.'

'How kind. Gimme your shoe.'

'What?'

'Your heel, your kicks, your ones and twos,' he rattles off. 'Whatever you want to call 'em. Give me your shoe.'

He leans over and shucks a shoe from my foot.

'What is this? I don't think you're quite Prince Charming material.'

Will ignores me and balances the shoe between his knees.

'Ew, you're not going to do what I think you're going to are you?' Henry's told me about Will's party piece – the trick Henry makes each Odyssean perform at their initiation – but I've never actually seen it. I cover my nose and mouth with my hands as he fills the shoe to the brim with wine, puts it up to his lips and knocks the whole thing back.

'That is the most disgusting thing I've ever seen in my life.'

'Got a smile out of you though, didn't I?'

My lips twitch. 'Why is it the cleverer you guys are, the stupider you act?'

'Maybe I like making pretty girls smile.'

I grab the bottle and take another swig so he can't see me blushing. 'Cheesy line. It's beneath you.'

'All right, hellraiser.' Will snatches the bottle back and puts it to his own lips. 'You don't have to down it all in one.'

'At least I'm not doing it out of a shoe.' I knock my shoulder against his. My shame is slackening. Maybe I'm overreacting. All it takes is someone else doing something more scandalous than me tonight and me throwing the drink will be old news. Until then, why shouldn't I stay here drinking with Will? At least he gives a shit about me. We both know Henry isn't mourning me. While I want to tell myself she lured him away from me, I know him too well. He likes the thrill of the chase. And he's probably already back in Lyla's room.

'What's yours is mine and all that.' Will hands me the bottle.

'You wish.' I try and nudge shoulders again but this time I lose balance and my back slams the wall. My limbs are sloppier than they should be. The additional alcohol must be taking effect. 'Oops.'

Will grabs me by the upper arms to straighten me up. 'Easy, tiger.'

'Sorry, I feel a bit floppy. Are you sure it was wine you gave me and not rocket fuel?'

A shadow crosses his face. 'I've always rated you, Emmy,' he says instead. 'Thought Henry was batting above his weight.'

'Thanks.' I try to shuffle up to give him more space, but he doesn't let go of my arm.

'You could do much better. This thing with Lyla'll burn itself out. I said it in Italy. She's not a patch on you. Then you can have him back. If you still want him.'

'In Italy?' An uncomfortable truth is looming towards me. 'You don't mean . . .'

'Hawksmoor really isn't all that, you know,' Will barrels on. 'He wouldn't even be here if his dad hadn't bought the college a library.'

'I thought he was your best mate.' My brain is still picking at what he said, worrying at when and where Henry and Lyla got together, who started it and how long it's been going on.

'It just pisses me off how easily everything falls into his lap. I don't like to see him not appreciating it.'

I look down. On the stone floor, our shadows have melted into one. His hand is on my arm, though I no longer need holding up. I slide along the wall. The idea of Henry and Lyla behind my back when we were all away makes me feel sick.

'I think I'm going to head. I'm knackered.'

'Don't go.' Will pushes himself back off the wall with one leg and turns to face me. 'Stay a bit. I'll get you another drink.'

'I shouldn't.' I yawn as I feel another huge wave of tiredness wash over me. I know myself well enough to know when I've had enough. More than enough. I'm starting to feel really weird. 'I think I need to go to bed. Thanks for the drink. And the pep talk.'

I peel myself off the wall and start for the door. All my limbs are heavier than they should be. It feels like walking through mud. And then Will's there, blocking the way.

'You know I like you, Emmy.'

He takes a step towards me. Realisation dawns. I should move or let him down gently, but his dimples are dancing in his cheeks and his teeth are gleaming. I've never looked at him like this before but for some weird reason – probably desperation – I think about what it would be like to kiss him. I move my head slightly and he lunges at me. His teeth scrape against my lip as our mouths connect. My head is swimming. His other hand is in my hair, tugging at it to bring me closer. I close my eyes and let myself slide into the kiss as he manoeuvres me against the wall. His lips are soft and warm. At the back of my mind, I know this is probably a terrible idea, but my impulse control is shot. It feels nice to be wanted. I can't deny there's a spark of attraction. Maybe this makes sense. For a moment I cling to him, wanting to hold on to the feeling.

His kisses get more demanding. His hands are inside my top, slipping under the waistband of my shorts. My body responds, pushing itself against him. Every part of me feels like it's on fire. He's turning me on in a way that Henry never did. With that, the image of Henry and Lyla together on the dance floor, their limbs intertwined, slams into my mind. It's like an off-switch; reality comes crashing back. I can taste the blood in my mouth from where our teeth bashed together. My neck's at the wrong angle and my spine hurts from where it's being pressed into the wall. Will keeps kissing me.

I twist my head to the side to break away, but he follows the movement. I press my hand against his chest to try to push him back. 'Will,' I say against his mouth. 'Stop.'

My voice sounds faint, even to my own ears. Maybe I'm not being firm enough. I wish I could rewind a few minutes, back to when the kiss felt good. Or back past that, to when he was being a friend. I turn my head away again and push him with both hands, leaning in to force him back.

'I mean it,' I say. 'You've got to stop.'

But he doesn't.

Twelve

Now

19.30

4½ hours to go

Lyla is doused in red wine. She looks furious but she's trying to hide it. She's finished berating the sulky waitress who, to her credit, looked like butter wouldn't melt (she should funnel the £100 I gave her into acting classes), and now she's holding a large white napkin to her dress and dabbing it. Another waitress – the sensible-looking woman with short grey hair – has come over to her with soda water and together they work on the dress like it matters. I turn away; I can't keep the smile off my face. I feel about three stone lighter, like my shoes have got springs in them and every step feels like a little bounce. The night's starting to turn. Just like I planned. Lyla flounces out of the hall, the woman with the grey hair scuttling behind her. There's not enough time for her to go back to the hotel and change. Even if they manage to get the stain out, there's comfort in knowing the smell of her expensive Chanel will be drowned out by the stench of red wine for the rest of the evening. She'll smell like a wino. Appropriate, given her recent behaviour.

I grab a flat-looking glass of champagne off one of the remaining trays in celebration and start looking for Nick. He must have gone to the bathroom. I spot several people I lived near in my first year, one of whom gives me a shy wave. A girl who had the pigeonhole beneath me taps me on the shoulder and says 'hey' as if we've just bumped into each other in the porters' lodge. I smile back and exchange a few words. She's an art therapist now, practising in Liverpool. I tell her I'm a stay-at-home mum, looking into retraining, and she doesn't bat an eyelid. No judgement. She doesn't seem to have any memory of that night. She doesn't look at me funny or anything. Maybe I can actually have a pleasant evening. Then the smart screen at the front of the hall blinks into life. I tighten my grip on my champagne. It didn't occur to me that anybody else would want to use it. A series of images of the college in various seasons fills the screen. Seeing the building shrouded in winter fog brings a December image of Henry holding me and Lyla down while Will filled the back of our parkas with snow one winter. The picture is as crisp as the snow dusting the quad on the screen. I wonder whether the amount of time I've spent raking over memories of this place exceeds the time than I actually spent here. Probably. How lame. But not any more.

I spot Nick at the bar and see he's got stuck with the Odysseans there instead. He's the only one in the group not wearing an Odyssean bow tie. He sticks out like a sore thumb, mainly because he's the only one with no more than one chin. Aside from Nick, there's a circle of empty space yawning around the men wearing those ties. At college, the Odysseans were the ones who set themselves apart. They loped through college like a pack, breaking rules or having them bent to fit round them, as if they were a different breed to the rest of the students.

'I can do anything I want. I'm on for a 2:1 from Cambridge,' I heard each of them say on more than one occasion. As if those around them weren't going to achieve exactly the same accolade. Tonight, the tables have been turned. People seem to be actively avoiding them. I notice the girl who said hey to me a few minutes ago go to the other side of the bar rather than stand shoulder to shoulder with them. While the drinking games and back-slapping make it seem like they're having a good time, they're clustered together for want of other opportunities. Perhaps this is a new age for the college and for men like them.

I'm not surprised. The Odysseans were forced to disband a few years after we left when two of them picked up a fresher girl and tried to carry her back to the set of rooms they shared. When she said she didn't want to go, they dropped her on the grass and she broke her ankle. One of them then got on top of her and tried to dry hump her. Luckily for her, it was caught on CCTV and one of the porters came running out to stop it. The two Odysseans involved were 'sent down', or expelled, from the university and the rest of the society outlawed in perpetuity. It made all the papers. Some of the reports alluded to a culture of acceptance and previous incidents around the university being hushed up. There was a story about a girl being cornered by three boys from another college and thrown into their fountain when she refused to kiss them all and another about a group of fresher guys made to drink their own urine and then jump into the River Cam. Helen told me I should come forward with what happened to me. She said she'd use the paper to make sure I got a sympathetic hearing. But I was starting to get my life together. I didn't want to bring it all up again.

As I slide past a group of people reminiscing about the bacon and egg sandwiches college used to serve for breakfast, I wonder if Will ever thinks about that night. How can he think he did nothing wrong and make conversation with my husband as if I'm an old friend he regrets losing contact with? His actions hounded me out of college. Unless he's a psychopath. I think of an article I read once about how psychopaths rise to the top of the business world because they're not troubled by human traits like empathy or regret. It's definitely possible.

A screech rips through the air: feedback from the microphone. Will is on the stage. Of course he is. I knew he wouldn't be able to resist the spotlight. He taps the top briskly with his palm and beams.

'Ladies and gents, sorry to drag you away from your drinks. I promise I won't take up too much of your time.'

There are a few grumbles from the back of the room that sound so good-natured I wonder whether he's planted them.

'All right, all right, you lot.' Will winks. 'I know many of you are enjoying a well-deserved break from the rug rats, so I'll keep this short. I've had nothing to do with the organising and planning of this event. We've got Liz Tripp and her girls to thank for that. Thank you, Trippy.'

In the audience, Liz beams and the big guy squeezes her shoulder. As far as I'm aware she's never been called Trippy in her life, but Will has a way with nicknames. It's part of his skill for establishing intimacy in about two seconds flat.

'Short of being told where to sign the cheque, that is,' he carries on confidently, 'I've done diddly squat. That's about all I'm good for these days. Don't worry, I made it a big one.'

He winks lewdly as if the size of the cheque is reflective of the size of his penis, and one of his lackeys at the front gives a small whoop. Will holds up his hands like Hitler at a Nazi rally. Look what happened to him, I think spitefully. Tonight might be your final bunker moment, Jenkin.

'Settle down. Seriously, though, this is where it all began for me and I couldn't let the night go past without paying tribute to that. When I came up to college, I'd never had a three-course meal before. At matriculation dinner, I didn't know which fork to use. I was like Julia Roberts in *Pretty Woman*, only not nearly as fit.'

I stifle a yawn. He grew up in a two-up two-down: not exactly the ghetto. But from the glazed faces around me, I see everyone else eating it up. He shifts on his feet modestly, twitching his broad shoulders as though he's uncomfortable in the spotlight. I can't believe people have forgotten he greeted us with a life-size model of himself. I bet he's basking in the attention.

'This college gave me the chance to develop into the person I wanted to be without judgement for that. It might sound trite but I found myself here and I'm willing to bet a lot of you did too.

'Would we all be standing here today, having achieved what we have, without it? Would we all be looking so goddamn ancient?'

On cue the screen behind him flashes up to our matriculation photo; a landscape of the entire year group standing together in our first week. Clad in suits and blazers, most of us look as though we could be wearing our school uniform as we blink into the camera and smile nervously. We were frighteningly young. The screen crackles and then all of a sudden our faces start ageing until our fresh-faced teenage selves look like pensioners. It's both a horror show and a feat of Will's clever graphics. Around the room, people gasp and laugh.

'We don't look that bad,' I hear someone shout.

'Your eyesight's going, mate. Blind as a bat.' Will smirks at the catcaller. He turns back to the screen. 'Glad that's working. Bit of a clusterfuck if I can't get my own technology in order. Though of course I'd die trying.'

He winks and points his phone at the screen. A moment later, a cartoon grave, complete with gravestone, appears on the picture, a superimposed skeleton death mask appears on Will's face and a lion dressed in the college's colours pushes Will into the open grave.

Another bubble of laughter. I think it's creepy but nobody else seems to share that opinion. I notice his faux mockney accent drops away when he's trying to make a point.

'Okay, okay, we don't look that bad.' Will points the phone and reverses the ageing process and the cartoon burial until we're back to the original shot. Then the screen shuffles it back to a generic image of the college's crest.

'Now, it wasn't all a walk in the park. Lectures were hard. If you actually went to them. Or at least that's what I'm told. The advantage of doing a land economy degree. Never had to bother.' More laughter. With each smug word, my desire to see Will humiliated increases. I just hope it sticks. People like him are Teflon.

'Timetables were punishing and exams exacting.' The crowd is lapping it up. 'I picked up some bad habits, some of which have stayed with me. The foot fetishists among you will be relieved to hear I can still down a pint out of a shoe.' He pauses for laughter and the crowd obliges. My skin crawls. I can't believe he can refer to these things so flippantly. Him drinking from his shoe is one of my clearest memories of that awful night. I feel that tightening in my chest again and take another gulp of champagne. Not the most sensible way to feel calmer, but certainly the quickest.

'But I regret to say, I can still burp the National Anthem. Not my finest hour.' He clears his throat. 'Don't worry,

I'm not going to do it now.' More gameshow laughter. You wouldn't know some of the finest minds in the country were among this crowd. I purse my lips disapprovingly.

'Along with bad habits come bad decisions and there's a couple of apologies I need to make.'

Now the skin on my upper arms puckers. I want Nick but I'm sure as hell not wading through a sea of Odies to get to him. Henry is moving towards the front. I dig my thumbnail into the skin around the nail on my index finger. Surely he can't be about to admit what he did? But why else would he be going up there? My heart thuds in my chest. Is Will about to acknowledge me? Is Henry going to join him in a mea culpa? Have they finally realised what they did was wrong? Is Lyla going to come back from the bathroom and walk into the room as a pariah the way I've had to?

'Firstly, to the person among you who has the bad luck to be staying in N1, the ground-floor room on N staircase. I have it on good authority that they've replaced not just the mattress but the entire bed since I lived in that room. I suspect, however, that the U-bend will never be the same. I give you my apologies for that.'

I can't believe I could be so naive. Of course he wasn't going to acknowledge me. I'm an idiot for thinking he would. It's one thing to admit you vommed in your bathroom a few too many times; it's quite another to admit to what he did that night. But how dare he stand up there and make jokes?

'Alongside those apologies come my thanks,' Will carries on. 'I had some of the best years of my life at this college and I want to thank it and all of you legends for that. Eat, drink and be merry – it's all on me. I've asked college to reimburse you all for the tickets and my company will pick up the tab for any poor sucker staying in one of the college's rooms. It's the least I can do.'

Now the applause is deafening. Who doesn't like a free meal? I make a mental note that I'll write to the college and refuse the refund. I don't want to owe Will anything.

He pauses to take a sip of water from the glass on the lectern. 'Now I know you all thought I might be making a big announcement tonight. Sorry to disappoint you. While I might be ready for the Houses of Parliament, are the Houses of Parliament ready for me? You won't see me in number ten – or Maggie's Den, as I prefer to think of it – any time soon.'

The rhyming slang's back. He must be nearly finished. Good. A staged boo erupts from the back and Will holds up his hands. 'All right, all right. Settle down. Just one more thing before I hand you over to the lovely lady who made this happen . . .'

Liz is waiting at the side of the dais, quivering like a cycling peloton at a traffic light. She can't wait to get up there. But she's not the only one on the move. Henry's nearly reached the stage. I wonder why he's bothering now it's clear that Will's not going to spill his guts. It's not until he moves Liz to one side and climbs the steps that I see he's holding a single black stiletto. He bows his head and grins as he hands it to Will. The Odysseans at the back bang on the bar. As Will takes the shoe, fifteen years fall away. I feel like I've been physically struck.

'That's right, boys and girls.' Will raises his voice from politician calm to sports stadium frenzy. The Odies are now stamping their feet against the floor. 'It wouldn't be a college reunion without a little nod to the past. *Per ardua ad alta.*' He throws out the college's motto, ducks his head and takes a small sip. When he looks up there's a foamy moustache around his mouth. He points the clicker several times and a picture of him in his prime appears, hair tousled, blue eyes twinkling. There's a loafer full of beer at his lips.

'I usually prefer my own ones and twos, but back in the day I did this to make a girl smile and now they think I'm anyone's.' He raises the shoe in the air, like a glass. I can see his eyes combing through the crowds and I shrink back. What little I remember of that night comes in shards. Him drinking from my shoes. Strong hands unclipping my bra, my back against the gravel. That fragment has sharper edges. The moment when I thought I wanted him, followed by the moments afterwards when I knew I didn't. I fight back a swell of nausea.

'While this might not be Oz, "there's no place like home". Those who want to hear a cracking rendition of the National Anthem, come and find me later. Now let me welcome the indomitable Liz Tripp to the stage. Over to you, Trippy.' He puts the stiletto up to his lips again, tips his head and downs the whole thing. The room explodes in a series of flashes as people hold up their phones and start taking pictures like he's some kind of rock star. I fade out of view, fist clenched. I stare at the screen, imagining what I've found out about them all illuminated;

the photos, the charts. Finally, I'm taking control of the narrative. I stand up taller. Tonight will be the last time I end up cowering in the corner while Will gets to stand on stage like a king, his eyes flickering in the dark, trying to find me.

Thirteen

Then

I'm not enjoying this any more. I feel guilty because Will obviously is – I can tell from the way he's stroking my cheek and cradling my chin with both hands. And the fact that he hasn't stopped, even though I've asked him to.

I feel a flutter of fear. I've seen Will all over the girls who swarm around the University Rugby Blues at the end of a night in Cindies or Life or one of the other clubs in town. 'Blu Tack' they call them. But I'm not like that. I'm the person he comes to complain to about girl trouble. I thought we were friends. I twist my mouth away again. More firmly. I don't know whether he's so wrapped up in the moment he can't read my signals or if he's choosing to deliberately ignore them. I didn't think I'd drunk that much but I'm finding it hard to think straight. Maybe I do want this on some level. I raise my knee and press it against his groin. I don't want to piss him off by making a fuss but I want things to stop.

'Will.'

'Sorry.' When he pulls away his face is flushed and his pupils are huge, like he's on drugs. He looks like a stranger. My hair's all mussed from where my head's been pressed against the wall and my lip feels swollen from where his teeth cut it. It's throbbing, banging in time with the splitting headache that's suddenly come on. I feel an overwhelming desire to go home.

'We can't do this.'

A muscle clicks in his jaw.

I carry on, stumbling over my words in my haste to get them out. 'I really like you but it's not worth it. I'm not worth it. You don't want to lose Henry over this.'

Will smirks. We both know what I really mean is that *I* don't want to lose Henry over this. The part of my brain that was screaming, 'Screw you, Henry' when Will kissed me has died away. I feel a gutful of regret. Why do I keep making such terrible decisions?

'If things were different . . .' It sounds like a consolation prize but a part of me means it. When Will kissed me, I felt something. But that doesn't make it right. 'So, er, what do you think?' His silence is making me feel nervous. Maybe it's the atmosphere in here, the way the light keeps throwing weird shadows across his face, but he looks like a stranger. An angry stranger. I keep talking to try to fill the gap. 'I could go back to my room and we could both forget that anything ever happened. I'd take it to the grave.'

I draw my hand across my mouth and mime zipping my lips up, managing to swipe myself in the eye in the process. I'm not naturally co-ordinated but my hand/eye co-ordination is way off, even for me. Will blinks but the rest of his face doesn't move. My eyes flick back to the door, noting the heavy iron bolt. He shut it when I started crying. It seemed thoughtful at the time. I welcomed the privacy. Now it makes me feel uneasy. As does the fact he's blocking the exit. He's 'the best back row Cambridge has ever seen', according to Henry. It was his prowess on the rugby pitch that got him into the Odysseans when his lack of public school accent and palatial country home should have kept him out. I don't know what a back row does, but I know enough to realise I won't be getting past him if he doesn't want me to. I tell myself I'm being stupid. This is Will we're talking about.

'What do you reckon, then? Shall we call it a night?' My voice sounds weird. Maybe it's nerves. I look at the door again.

Will shakes his head. 'Why don't you stay for another round? Then we'll call it quits.'

There's something in the way he says it that tells me it's not really a question. I tell myself I'm overreacting. Will's dated a revolving door of the hottest girls at university. He probably couldn't care less that I've knocked him back. If I insist on leaving and don't stay for a drink, I'll be the one making it weird. I put my fears to one side.

'Okay.'

'Here. See this away.' He plucks the bottle of port from the ground.

I put the bottle to my lips, wincing as it hits the sore spot. There's a sour, chemical taste, the way there is when you know you've drunk too much.

'Don't you want some?' I offer him the bottle but he shakes his head and goes on watching me.

'I don't like port, remember?'

'You won't say anything to anyone, will you?' I ignore the fact that he knows I hate port too. 'About ... you know.' I look at him pleadingly. Right now, I've got very little chance of getting Henry back. If he finds out what's happened that chance shrinks to zero.

'You mean, I won't tell Hawksmoor we were practically at it?' I've never seen him sneer like this. It's like he's had a personality transplant. His feelings can't be that hurt by me stopping our kiss, can they? 'You don't want me to give him a bell right now and see if they want to come down and join us? Get the gang back together again?'

I shudder at the idea of seeing Henry and Lyla again.

'Don't worry, I'm just fucking with you.' Will flips the words off. 'I won't say a word.'

'Thank you.' I've obviously hurt his feelings, but I don't want things to be weird. I tell myself I'm reading too much into what he's saying, that he's only messing around. That it doesn't mean anything that he's blocking the door. That's when the freight train hits. The last sip of port must have tipped me over the edge. I can barely stand up. My legs feel as though they're made of rubber. I lurch towards the wall but misjudge the distance. The heel of my hand scrapes the brickwork and I wince. I try to take a step but my ankles knock together and my legs get tangled up in each other. I'm sliding down the wall with zero control over my own body. I've never felt like this before, no matter how much I've drunk.

'Will?' I can barely get the word out without slurring it. My tongue feels thick against my gums, like it's swollen. 'I feel really weird.' My voice sounds like someone's slowed down a tape recording. I try to find his face but it's all fragmented. His mouth seems huge and his eyes are out of alignment, floating around like a surrealist painting.

'Don't worry. I've got you.' He puts out a hand to steady me and then I'm floating too. My legs splay from under me and I find myself sprawled on the floor. I can see shadows dancing on the walls around me. They look like they're made out of blood. I open my mouth to scream but no sound comes out. Will's on the floor beside me in seconds, sliding to his knees by my head.

I flail my arms and legs as I try to get up, but I can't lock my knees to stand.

'Hold still.' He pins me in place. 'If you can't stand up straight, I'll help you.'

He grabs my hand and tries to pull me up but I can't seem to move. The sight of his face turning slowly red with the effort of heaving me up from the floor now seems hilarious and I start laughing but it's more of a howl. I don't sound like me.

'I'm a coyote,' I tell him, throwing back my head and howling at the moon. My head cracks against the floor but I don't even feel it.

'If you're going to act like a sack of spuds, I'll have to carry you. So, can you stop kicking off?'

I'm laughing too hard to stop.

'Have it your way.' He slides one hand underneath me and lifts me up as though I weigh nothing. His face is so close that I can see the different shades of blue in his eyes. I think of Henry and Lyla going at it on the tiled floor of Henry's villa in Italy and suddenly it seems like the best idea to try to kiss Will again. He puts his hand over my mouth. 'Sssh . . .'

The whole room seems to turn red and the walls start wobbling. The only thing solid is his grip on my arms. My memory slips after that.

Fourteen

'Ahem.' Liz clears her throat to try to gain the attention of the room. She sounds like a headmistress trying to silence an unruly school assembly. I try to focus. Now she's up on stage, I take the chance to really look at her, noticing the figure poured into that Roland Mouret Galaxy dress, the high heels, the perfect makeup. At the end of her fluted designer sleeves, her fingers are trembling. I can hear overconfident male voices at the back, placing bets on how long her speech is going to last.

'Three minutes,' says either Ollie or Hugo. After all this time, I still can't tell them apart.

'You can get a lot done in three minutes. Especially in that dress,' jeers the other.

I feel a wave of affiliation. She's obviously heard them. I can see it in her over-bright smile and the way her arms are rigid at her sides. A few people are tutting on her behalf. The guy she was with earlier turns his head, scowling as he tries to work out where the comment came from.

'Come on, lads, show a bit of respect.' Will bounces back on to stage again. 'She's put a lot of work into tonight.'

The volume drops immediately.

'Thank you,' Liz says pertly. 'I promise I won't take up too much of your time. Just a bit of housekeeping.' She goes on to tell us the college bar, a sweaty oblong room with some bar stools and a pool table situated in a glorified shed behind the library, will be open for one drink after dinner. She reminds us that we must keep the noise in our rooms down after eleven as there are students on the premises and that we're still not allowed to walk on the grass. She alludes to how much work she's put into the reunion, without saying it directly. My eyes glaze over. Of course, Liz would be the one to organise the reunion. She was that kind of student. She played netball, she rowed, she was on every committee going. If you needed to know where to buy a book, no matter what subject, she had at least half a dozen suggestions. She was always all over the college message boards. I grimace.

I don't know why she irritates me so much. But the dislike is mutual. That was clear from the way she spoke to me earlier. I suspect she's never forgiven me for marrying Nick. She's pulled out all the stops in her appearance tonight – she's dripping in designer and her upper arms scream personal trainer. The guy she's with is already putty in her hands; it must be for someone else. I don't buy all the women's magazine mulch about women wanting to look good for themselves. And Nick's always been cagey about how things ended between them. Maybe I'm just tarring her with my own brush. Not everybody is incapable of moving on.

'It's an absolute pleasure to be back here after so many years.' She puffs her chest out like a pigeon ruffling its feathers as she reaches the crescendo. 'And what an exciting programme we've got for the weekend. Tonight's champagne reception courtesy of the honourable gentleman who has just left the stage and forced me upon you all.' She trills out a laugh as if Will pulled her on to the stage spontaneously, when even from this distance I can see she's holding laminated cue cards. 'Shortly we'll sit down to a delicious three-course meal, crafted by the college's very own award-winning chef. I'm proud to say that we're the only Cambridge college with a Michelin-starred chef. Certainly a world away from slops.'

People are slower to laugh for her than they were for Will. She obviously doesn't have half a dozen audience members primed. Despite her relentless keenness, I don't remember her having a great many friends at college. Not that I'm one to talk. She had Nick; I suppose she thought she didn't need anyone else.

I take my eyes off Liz and start scanning the room. Nick's managed to get away from the Odysseans, who are in the process of pouring the tops of their various drinks into a pint glass, presumably with the aim of forcing one of their number to drink it. A game I remember well. It was called Arrogance. How apt. I see Henry detach himself to whisper something in Freja's ear and now Nick is standing with Lyla, of all people. Out of the frying pan into the fire. A small section on the midriff of her dress is darker than the rest of it but other than that she did a good job of getting the stain out. I grit my teeth. Why can't she leave my husband alone? So much for him not leaving my side. It's about time I went and reclaimed him. I fantasise about tipping another drink over her in the process. Nick would be mortified.

I'm walking past a group of natural scientist graduates, or natscis as we used to call them, talking about skiing holidays, when Liz flicks the screen and a picture appears. It's a photo from graduation – a sea of grinning people wearing black gowns with white fur trim at the collar like particularly ecstatic-looking penguins. They look considerably more confident than in Will's photo of us in first year; three years of Cambridge entitlement must have seeped in. Even from halfway down the room, I can pick out Lyla, her black hair shining in the sunshine, Henry, standing head and shoulders above those around him. Will's front and centre, standing with the scholars, the fur trim on their graduation gowns crimson rather than white. Nick and Liz are off to the side, huddled together, their hair blowing in the wind. The sight of them together should sting, but I've got too much on my mind.

'I know, right? Weren't we all so young?' Judging that everyone has had enough time gawping at the photo to pick themselves out, Liz starts speaking again. 'Of course, I've been lucky enough to see most of you at one law event or another or some of our annual year rep bashes but it's been half a decade since we've been back here all together. The ten-year reunion. Wasn't that a blast?'

Actually, Nick told me it was poorly attended. Half the year group was knuckle-deep in changing nappies and the other half was too busy chasing career opportunities to attend.

'And haven't we come a long way, even since then? Among us are doctors, oil magnates –' of course she'd have to mention Nick '– lawyers, CEOs and possibly the next prime minister.' She puts her hands on her hips flirtatiously. 'No matter what he says . . .'

The screen flicks on to a picture of Will, standing on one of the university's prettiest bridges, bare-chested under an Odyssean blazer with a pint glass on his head and a drunken expression on his face. 'Always had an eye for the camera. And the ladies.'

This draws roars of laughter. I don't even try to feign a smile. To me, there's nothing funny about Will's inability to control himself around women.

'Of course, Will Jenkin is not the only one of us who has seen our name in lights,' she continues, her voice louder and more confident. 'Among our number we count Romily Simmonds, who was nominated for an Oscar for "Best Supporting Actress" last year. Romily's currently treading the boards on Broadway so can't be here tonight but asked me to send her very best. Here she is in the latest Tarantino.' Click. The screen changes to a movie shot of Romily in a leather catsuit. One of the Odysseans obviously makes a lecherous comment because there's a hoot of drunken laughter from the back. 'And music scholar Rob Aldwych has turned his considerable talents to composition with several of his scores featuring in Tom Hanks's latest film. If we twist your arm, perhaps you can give us a rendition of some of them on the piano when we adjourn to the bar for last orders.'

She fixes her gaze on someone towards the front, presumably Rob, though I can't tell from the back of his head. When he's nodded, she continues briskly.

'They've both come a long way.' She flicks up a picture of an impossibly young-looking Rob and Romily dressed up to the nines on their way to a ball. I'd forgotten they were ever a couple. I wonder what the woman in the mauve dress who has just let go of Rob's hand thinks of the picture and how many people leave a reunion feeling smaller and worse off than they did when they arrived. I brace myself. This time, that's not going to be me.

'Then again, as a college we've always had a flair for the dramatic, wouldn't you agree?' Liz puts on a confidential voice as if she's drawing us into a secret. 'As a cohort we've certainly gained a reputation for making a splash ... so how's this for a trip down memory lane?'

She points the clicker at the screen. At first, I don't register what I'm seeing. Then I feel the blood rush to my head. The glass I'm holding falls from my hand and shatters on to the floor, drenching my ankles in champagne.

'Taxi,' calls a male baritone.

I can see people turning, trying to work out where the sound of smashing glass has come from. I look over at Lyla, expecting to see guilt splashed over her face. Her face is expressionless. I should have known better than to think she'd even feel a smidgen of remorse. Even through the utter humiliation, I feel furious that she can act so unconcerned when she's the one who took the photograph on the screen. Then Will's on stage, handing Liz her phone back and taking the clicker off her.

'Technical hitch.' He points his own phone like a remote and a benign image of graduation hats appears. He's so quick that perhaps some people will only have seen the chapel blazing in an early morning sunrise, its columns brilliant white against a cloudless sky. But the image Liz conjured up is burned on to my retina. Even though I haven't seen that picture for over fifteen years, it's slammed me right back to the pain and humiliation of that night. I start scratching at my wrist, twisting and tugging at the Tiffany cuff. I feel like I've been violated all over again. I can't stay. I ignore Nick charging towards me and step out of the puddle of champagne. Then I shake my feet free of the glass and turn and walk out of the hall.

Fifteen

Then

The crunch of gravel wakes me. My head hurts and I can hear the sound of feet kicking their way across the tiny stones. Have I left the window to my room open? Is that why I'm freezing? Why is my bed so hard? I prise my eyes open. Instead of the familiar landscape of my room – the poster of Leonardo DiCaprio, the corkboard of photos, dried flowers and invitations framed above my bed – all I can see is a wall of hard blue sky. I'm outside. Wearing last night's clothes. I put my hand to my chest and realise I don't have a top on. I clamp my hands over my boobs immediately. The background growl of my headache moves up a gear until my skull feels like it's throbbing. I move one hand and finger the left side of my forehead and find a lump. My teeth start chattering. This is bad. I look down. My arms and legs are covered in cuts and scratches. I feel like I've been run over. What the fuck has happened to me? I open my eyes wider, even though the light hurts, and take in my surroundings. I'm lying with my head against the bottom step of the chapel, a pool of foamy vomit like a halo around my head. My white vest, now shot through with black and red, is balled up by my right hand. I sling it over my chest. How the hell did I get here? The last clear thing I remember is heading to the bop. A pair of ducks pecks the grass near my feet but other than them, nobody else is around. I feel horrified; what if someone else has seen me like this?

I shift my weight to try to rearrange the waistband of my shorts. The safety pins fastening them are pressing into my skin. The effort of moving feels too much. But even in my fragile state, I know I can't stay here. It's disgusting enough to have woken up like this; it will be a thousand times worse if someone finds me. People have passed out around college before but not half naked, with their boobs out and no idea how they got there. If I don't move, I'm going to get hypothermia. I lift my head like an old dog trying to drink water. The pathway's deserted. It must have been the ducks I heard on the gravel. I can't allow myself to think it was anything else. I have to get home. I look over at the other side of the quad towards where my room is. The sun is barely peeping through the trees. It's early. The people I run into will be clutching their shoes and doing their own walks of shame. If I move now, I could get away with it. Speaking of shoes, why am I not wearing any? I look down. The skin between my toes is flayed and the tops of my feet are covered in dried blood. One of my shoes is lying to the left of my feet but there's no sign of the other one. I haven't got time to look. I need to get out of here.

I shrug my top on without bothering to try to find my bra and get to my feet. My legs feel stiff and heavy, like there's no bend left in them. I'm about 300 metres across from the staircase my room is on. The only thing on this side of the quad is the chapel and the library. Only scholars or sports stars like Will or Henry live on these staircases. I feel a jolt of recognition like an electric shock.

A series of recollections starts shuffling through my head, spitting out images like an out-of-control deck of cards. Lyla and Henry entwined on the dancefloor. Their faces twinned in horror as I drenched them with the Bacardi Breezer. Will drinking out of my shoe and the feeling I had when he kissed me. But there are big gaps between the images, like things on a shelf just beyond reach. The first one is: how the hell did I end up out here?

My lips feel raw and bruised. I must have come back to Will's. Then why am I outside? Did he bring me back to his room? Did he leave me out here like this? I thought he was going to look after me. Maybe I never made it back there? Then why aren't I wearing a bra? The questions are like a flock of migrating birds, beating their wings against the corners of my brain. I screw my eyes up so hard it makes the bridge of my nose throb. I remember Will scooping me into his arms. Then the tape goes black.

I feel dirty. I want to get under a hot shower and scrub myself until every pore squeaks. I look down the building, at the line of windows. I know Will's room is the fourth one along. I've been inside dozens of times, the four of us sprawled on his bed watching movies or crap TV. I've never found myself out here like this.

Will's curtains, like those of his neighbours, are pulled closed. I bite my lip, wondering why I'm not in there with him. It stings and I remember our teeth clashing. Did we have a fight? At least I know we didn't have sex; there's no way I would have been able to keep track of the safety pins if we had. I run my hands across the thin metal of the first pin. But why would he leave me out here? I thought we were friends. Then I think of him and Henry, so close they might as well be brothers. I should have known where his loyalties lie.

I grab my handbag, which has miraculously remained with me even though one of my shoes is missing, and cram the other shoe into the top. I start picking my way through the gravel, trying to avoid the tender spots on my feet. Cutting across the grass would be quicker and less painful but students aren't allowed to walk on it. Going that way would be a sure-fire way of drawing attention to myself. This way, I'll be less visible, but I'll have to go right past Will's window. In another world I'd go in and wake him but right now I don't want to see him. I've had nights with patchy recall before but something feels wrong about how much I can't remember. I didn't think I drank that much. And there's something off about the fact that he left me out here, without a bra on. It hints at something darker, something shameful. The more I try to piece together what happened, the sicker I feel.

I pass the first window, then the next, picking up my pace. By the time I reach Will's window, I'm sprinting, even though each step feels like pressing my feet into a thousand tiny knives. My lungs are burning by the time I get back to my room. I don't see a single person on the way. As I fumble my key into the lock, skin crawling with the need to get under the shower and hose off what happened, I allow myself to think I might have got away with it. Maybe Will won't say anything. What's in it for him? Even if he does, I've got two weeks left of university before I can cast this off and start the rest of my life. If Henry doesn't want me back, maybe I don't need him after all. Law school should be big enough for both of us. This is my chance to stand on my own two feet for once. I've always had someone to prop me up; first Helen, then Henry. Maybe that's what drew me to him in the first place; the idea that I didn't have to go it alone. Maybe law school is the time to really be me. As I cross the threshold and slide into my room, ready to get showered and then sleep it off, I'm thinking this whole episode could pass without making a ripple. How naïve. Because what I don't realise is that while I might not have seen anybody else out in college at that time in the morning, someone definitely saw me.

Sixteen

The wood-panelled toilet cubicle I'm in feels like a coffin. The walls are too close. I'm sitting on my haunches with my feet up on the lid so that if anyone does come in, they won't realise the cubicle is occupied. I want to beat my hands against the panels, smash them until the skin on my knuckles is a bloody pulp. I can't believe Liz would bring that picture. How cruel she would have to be to humiliate me in front of everyone like that. I gloss over what I'm planning to do to Henry, Lyla and Will. They deserve to have what they've done exposed. I can't let Liz derail me. If anything, seeing the photo flashed up in all its technicolour glory reconfirms I'm doing the right thing. I want them all to go down in flames.

My handbag vibrates. I look at my phone. Twenty-two missed WhatsApp notifications from Nick and several missed calls. He must be beside himself. He's never seen the photograph before. He was in his own bubble at college, barely aware of what was going on around him. His ignorance was probably the only thing that allowed our relationship to get off the ground. I never told him that I was with Will that night, about the gaps in my memory or what happened afterwards. Now I'll have to tell him. I can't bear the idea of seeing disappointment in his eyes.

The door swings open and two pairs of heels click in. I scrunch myself into a tight ball even though the door's locked. I'm being paranoid. It's the same when I reverse park; I hold my breath if I'm trying to get into a tight space. I remind myself the other cubicles are empty. Nobody will want to come in here.

Whoever has come in shows no sign of wanting to check the cubicles anyway. I hear the weight of a bag being stacked on the sink and a glass being set down on the side.

'Did you see it?' Lyla. Of course she would have brought her drink with her. She's scarcely had it out of her hand since we arrived.

'What was that? Why have you brought me in here?' It's Freja.

'The picture. Did you see the picture Liz Tripp put up?'

'All I saw was a picture of the college chapel, which while it's beautiful does not explain why you dragged me in here. Or Henry's reaction.' She sighs. 'Not that I understand much of what's going on with him these days. Men are from Mars, women Venus, as the saying goes.'

I think of one set of the photographs in my bag. If only she knew. She will soon enough.

'So you missed what was at the front of the shot?'

'Some litter?'

'You could say that.' Excitement crowds into Lyla's voice. 'It was a girl, one of our year, wasted and posing topless on the grass. It was quite the scandal at the time.'

'How sad.' Freja sounds disapproving. 'I feel sorry for this girl, though this is a very British story. I see it in Henry and the stories he tells. Even some of your friends tonight. The accountant who keeps stirring the drinks. In Denmark, we have a much more relaxed attitude to alcohol. I was able to drink with my parents when I was a teenager. One of the reasons I'm excited to go back.'

I'd almost forgotten Freja and Henry were moving. Turns out he wasn't the archetypal Londoner after all.

'She didn't do it because she was drunk.' Lyla's voice is sticky with pleasure. I think of all the times she used to come flying into my room, lips wet with the news of any scandal from around college. She's in her element.

'I don't follow.' Now curiosity creeps into Freja's voice. I feel a stab of disappointment. I hate how quickly women clamour to hear the worst of each other. Then I think of what I'm planning to do. I might not be intending to hurt her, but she'll be collateral damage. Who am I to judge her? I think of the promise I made Helen, the wheels we've set in motion. What I'm planning to do tonight will hurt Freja, who has done nothing to me.

Maybe we're all just crabs in a bucket, always trying to pull each other down.

'She was trying to win back an ex-boyfriend. Draw attention to herself. And you'll never guess who she was?' Lyla's too gleeful to wait for Freja to answer. 'It was Emily.'

'Who?'

'Emily Toller. Nick's wife. You met her back at the hotel.'

'The attractive one who seemed a little shy?'

'You'd be shy if you knew half the college had seen you naked. Anyway, she's always been like that. Not comfortable in her own skin. You don't have to feel too sorry for her, though. She's done pretty well. Happily married, husband's worth a packet. It all worked out for her. Turns out posing for a dodgy photo or two doesn't do you any harm in the long run.'

I push my fist so far back into my throat I almost gag. She of all people knows that photo wasn't posed. She's the one who took it. I picture her, stupid pink Nokia in hand, stumbling across me on her way back from Henry's room. That phone's memory was already jammed full of pictures of me. Of us together, getting ready, laughing it up in the bar, sprawled across the grass. I bet she couldn't believe her luck when she saw me lying there. Her chance to get her own back came practically gift-wrapped. My resentment threatens to combust.

I slide my hand into my handbag and finger the photographs as if to check and make sure they're still there. Do or die, as Helen would say. Freja is standing outside this cubicle, just as gift-wrapped as I was when

Lyla found me on the quad. I've got to take the chance; I can't be squeamish now. Anyway, she has the right to know what her husband's been up to. I slide the photographs out.

'Was he the ex-boyfriend she was trying to win back?'

'He wishes.' Lyla brushes past it. 'He's been in love with her since we were all freshers. Sweet, really.'

Her tone implies otherwise. How dare she patronise Nick, especially when she couldn't get enough of him outside. I can't believe how confident and self-assured she is, after everything she's done. She should be behind bars, not swanning around like she still rules the college. I can't wait to bring her down to her knees, destroy everything she's built up.

'It is hard to know what is going on in a marriage from the outside,' Freja says. 'I feel sorry for her. How hard it must be to come back and then have this happen to you.'

Second thoughts about what I'm about to do creep into my mind. I don't want to hurt Freja. There are kinder ways to deal with what I've found out about Henry. I should look into them. But I don't think I can let Henry walk away.

'I suppose.' I can hear the shrug in Lyla's voice. 'We'd better get back. Once more unto the breach and all that. Sometimes I don't know why I bother coming back. I can see the people I want to whenever I feel like it. Frankly the rest . . .' She trails off as if we're not worth wasting the words on. 'By the way, I would suggest going to the loo while we're here. Once the meal has started you won't be able to get up from the table until the head of the top table does. And Will likes to make people wait as long as possible. I believe it's his life's ambition to get someone to wet themselves.'

'You and your funny Cambridge traditions,' Freja muses. 'Being here is like being in another world. Or another time period at least. I will take your advice, though. Give me one minute.'

I wait for the sounds of both locks clicking. Then I take a deep breath and slide off my haunches on to the floor without making a sound. I feel like a silent assassin. I smooth down the edges of the photographs and push the weight into the toes of my shoes. There's something grubby about what I'm doing but I don't see that I've got any choice. I move each foot soundlessly and hold my breath as I slide the cubicle lock. I ease the door open, praying it doesn't creak and stand directly in front of it, eyeing the two occupied cubicles. I bend over slightly, wondering if I'll recognise which cubicle Freja is in by the shoes. I wish it were Lyla who would be hurt by these photos, not her. I push down my doubts and picture Henry's smug face, the way his eyes glanced over me dismissively at the hotel. I'm doing Freja a favour, even if my motives aren't altruistic ones. And at least this way she'll see these photos before everyone else does.

Unwittingly, Lyla helps me out.

'Is there someone out there?' she says imperiously from the middle cubicle.

She must have heard the lock. I freeze, photos splayed in my hand. I pull myself together and don't say a word. She's hardly going to come rushing out with her knickers around her ankles. I shuffle the photographs back together and run my finger along the top picture, trying to smooth out the creases. Not that it matters. Whether the corners are folded over or not, you can clearly see Henry's face thrown back in ecstasy, his hands pressing the head of the person on their knees in front of him into his groin. That person is definitely not Freja. And that's the least of his problems. I remind myself I'm doing her a favour. I step forward.

'Hello?' Lyla calls again. She sounds irritated now. 'Is someone there?'

I don't bother to answer. I thrust the stack of pictures under the door of the first cubicle, give them a good hard shove and mouth a silent sorry at the door. Henry's blissful expression glistening in the overhead lighting is the last thing I see before they disappear under the cubicle door.

'What is this?' I hear Freja ask. 'Lyla, did you pass me something?'

'No, why? Did you need something?'

'No, it's . . .' There's a sharp inhalation of breath and then her voice falls away. I hurry over to the door, not caring that my heels are ringing out on the tiles. As the door's sliding closed, I put my hand out to block it. I hear the sound of one of the toilets flushing as I lean back into the bathroom and flick the light switch. The room plunges into darkness and I hear Lyla shriek. She used to be afraid of the dark as a child. Sometimes knowing your enemy as well as you know yourself can only be a good thing. It's satisfying to hear the fear in her voice.

I squash down the flickers of guilt – it's not as if any

of these people spared me an iota of compassion back then – and straighten the creases from crouching out of my dress. Then I make my way towards the Great Hall. One down, two to go.

Seventeen

Then

The sunlight is already sliding through the gap in the curtains by the time I get back to my room. My mind is too churned up to sleep so I figure I may as well check my emails. I go over to my desk. The pocked wooden surface is covered in a light dusting of face powder and last night's bottle of Cava is open. Hardly conducive to the revision I need to do for Monday's exam. The smell of cheap alcohol makes me gag. I'm never drinking again.

I force the sash window up and tip the residue of the wine on to the gravel below. Then I pull the window shut and close the curtains. I hurl the bottle into the wastepaper basket and fire up my laptop, pressing keys at random to unlock it and studiously avoiding looking at my screensaver.

The desktop lights up like a switchboard. MSN messenger winks at me, letting me know who is lurking online and the number of emails coming in starts rising like a death count. By the time it calms down, the figure by the Outlook envelope is 433. What the hell?

I feel a tingle of unease. I bring up my Hotmail account. It predates my college days and not many people know I have it. Even this account has thirty-six fresh emails, bolded titles indicating they haven't been read. I scroll through the list of addresses. Some of them have the university's familiar @cam.ac.uk address. Most do not. I don't recognise a single name, except for the final one. Helen's work address. Why is my sister emailing me so early?

Dread mushrooms in my stomach. I can write off the other emails as some kind of college virus; some weird chain-mail circular. But I can't ignore Helen. She's all I've got left. I lean away from the laptop as though it's contagious. Then I click on the email.

'CALL ME,' it screams in bold letters. I go back over to my bed and fish my mobile out of my handbag. I haven't looked at it since last night. There are five missed calls from Helen and a series of texts that I don't have time to read. All before 7 a.m. I brace myself for bad news and dial her number.

She answers on the first ring. 'Have you seen it?'

'Seen what?'

'The link. You need to click on the link.'

'I didn't even realise there was a—'

'Check it.'

I look back at my laptop. My desktop has flicked back on to the screensaver I was trying to avoid; a picture of Henry and me by the pool in Tuscany. I can practically feel the sun on my back from looking at it. My smile is a mile wide. Lyla took it.

I click on the email and see the telltale blue link underneath the giant '**CALL ME**'.

I think about the last time Helen called me this early in the morning. To tell me that Mum had gone into hospital and this time she wouldn't be coming out. She didn't sound as serious then as she does now. 'I don't want to.'

'You need to.' Her voice brooks no argument. 'I'll wait.'

'But . . .'

'Just do it.'

My hands are quivering so much I have to click on the link twice to open it. When I do a huge image of the college grounds fills the screen, the chapel gleaming at sunrise. It's so beautiful it could be an advert for the college magazine. Except for the sack of flesh spilling off the bottom step on to the pathway. I take in my bare chest, the empty wine bottle, one red shoe off at an angle and the golden hair spilling across the steps. I don't need to zoom in to know it's me this morning. I slam the laptop shut as if it'll make the picture go away. But I know it won't. This is bad. Worse than bad.

'You see it?' Helen speaks into the void.

'I've seen it.' Any hopes that I could forget last night ever happened are vanishing. Where the hell did this picture come from? Did Will take it? I think of the footsteps on the gravel crunching away. It could have been anyone. 'Fuck.'

'Tell me in what universe did this seem like a good idea?'

'You don't think I knew this was being taken?'

'Well . . .'

I jab at the keyboard, trying to zoom in on the photo. 'You can't seriously think I'd pose topless in the middle of college?'

'Emmy, you were the front page of that bloody charity thing last year. What am I supposed to think?'

'I'm passed out. My eyes are closed. I can't believe you think I would do this.' My voice gets louder with each sentence. If my own sister doesn't believe me, what chance have I got?

'That's not what I'm saying,' Helen softens. 'I'm just giving you a worst-case scenario. So what happened?'

'I don't know.' I shake my head as if I can make it all go away. 'I got pissed, okay? Really pissed. And I did something stupid.'

'My sister, the master of the understatement.'

'Shut up, shut up.' I squeeze my eyes shut and bite down. 'I didn't know any of this was happening. I blacked out. I saw Henry with someone else and I threw a – anyway that doesn't matter. I started snogging . . . someone. We were drinking and laughing and then it got all hazy and I – I blacked out.'

'Did he take advantage of you?'

'Will wouldn't . . .' I stop.

'Will? This was Will?' Helen sounds incredulous. Then furious. 'He got you drunk and took advantage of you and then he took a picture to get off on it. I'll bloody kill him.'

'It wasn't like that,' I say, although I don't know it wasn't like that. I just hope it wasn't. 'He doesn't even have a camera. He hates taking pictures. He's always taking the piss out of Lyla and her camera phone.'

Things click into place so neatly I wonder I didn't see it the second I opened the link. I think of Lyla standing there, sticky orange liquid dripping off her like she'd been slimed. The one person I know that does have a camera on their phone. And I've definitely given her a reason to want revenge.

'I know who it was,' I say through gritted teeth. 'And it's not what you think.'

'I don't think you get it, Emmy.' Helen's got her victim-support voice on. I've heard her use it during multiple interviews. It's why she's so good at what she does. 'Will's taken this without your consent. God knows what happened when you blacked out. You need to report this. And –' she pauses '– you need to go to an STI clinic.'

'No.' I shake my head furiously. I'm mortified. 'We didn't have sex.'

'Don't be naïve.'

'I mean it. I know we didn't have sex. I was wearing these shorts and I was pinned into – anyway . . .' I'm too exhausted to go into it. 'We didn't have sex. Trust me.'

'Emily, he molested you and then took a picture of you to get off on it. You need to go to the police.'

'You aren't listening. He didn't take the picture.'

'I thought you blacked out. You don't know what happened. And you don't have to defend him, you know. This wasn't your fault.'

'I'm not defending him.' Except I am. I don't know why.

Maybe I don't want to face up to the idea that someone I thought was a friend could do that to me.

'Look, this is a shitshow either way. Do you want me to come up there? I can take you to the police station and you can report him for taking the picture at the very least.'

'No.' The last thing I want is for Helen to come here. I don't want to go to the police. I don't want to see anybody. I want to curl up in a ball until this goes away. Helen does not do curling up in a ball. 'I told you, he didn't take the picture.'

'Then who did?'

'Lyla,' I whisper.

If I thought Helen's reaction to hearing Will's name was extreme, this time she goes nuclear.

'Lyla. Lyla your friend. Lyla who has your back, dresses you up like a fucking doll, buys all your drinks, crashes your holiday.' I can hear her banging the desk, the way she's told me they do when people leave the newsroom. 'That fucking Lyla?'

'Yes.'

'But why?'

'We fell out. This is her trying to get her own back on me for something.' Even as I'm saying it, I start to feel better. 'I can sort it.'

'It doesn't look like that from where I'm sitting.'

From where she's sitting. The bubble bursts. I've been so busy wondering where the picture came from that I've missed the main point.

'Where *are* you sitting, Helen?'

'I'm in my office.'

I knew it. You don't get to be an associate editor on Britain's biggest paper at Helen's age, raking in six figures, without going into work at the crack of dawn.

'So how have you got this?' Horror pitches my voice higher than normal. 'Where has it come from?'

'It's come from your college intranet,' Helen says crisply. 'One of the student chat rooms.'

'What?' The bottom of my stomach falls out.

'Don't worry, I've got someone in IT trying to figure out the IP address so we can work out exactly where.'

'But why would they send it to you?' Even to my own ears, my voice sounds shrill.

'Emily, it's been sent to everyone. My news desk, the *Daily Mail*'s. The link's gone viral.'

Even to my own ears, the sound I make next sounds like that of a dying animal. It feels like the walls around me should be caving in. I know already this is something I can never come back from.

'Don't worry, we're not going to run it. And I can shut this story down before anyone else sees it. I've got a team on it already.'

'It's too late.' The reality of it all slams into me. 'I'm on the Internet. With my boobs hanging out. Everyone here will have seen it. Everyone.'

'Now, Emily, don't—'

'My life is over.' I hang up the phone and lurch back to the sink. I'm going to be sick. With any luck, I'll choke on it.

*

The sink is filled with watery bile that reeks of spirits. I'm slumped next to it. There's a gap between the unit it sits on and the floorboards. I picture folding myself into it and disappearing. The gutters are where I belong. My phone bleats in my hand. Helen has been calling me non-stop since I hung up on her. I don't answer. What is there to say?

Sounds outside my room suggest the rest of the corridor is starting to wake up. There are doors slamming and snatches of laughter as people get on with their usual morning routine. I wonder how many of them have seen the picture and what they're saying about me. Some of them will be going to the library. It's where I should be. I've got an exam on Monday. But how can I think of anything like that when my life is crashing down around my ears?

My hand vibrates as a text message chimes through. Helen never gives up. I click on the envelope, even though there's nothing she can say that will make me feel better.

> **Go and see college authorities.**
> **Get the picture taken down.**
> **We can contain this. xx**

I shake my head at the phone, like she can see me. As if. This genie is well and truly out of the bottle. The emails still pinging into my inbox prove that. The administrative offices are on the other side of the quad. How am I going to get over there without being seen? Who cares if the photo has been taken down, anyway? They've reached the national newspapers. It's only a matter of time before they surface somewhere else. Nothing ever dies once it's been online. Self-loathing courses through me. There goes law school. How can you be taken seriously as a lawyer if there are pictures of you with your boobs out on the Internet?

I kick my heels against the skirting board and feel the reverberation pulse through my entire foot. Good. I'm so disgusted with myself I want to cause myself physical pain. Just to feel something other than shame. I haven't even looked at the picture properly yet. I feel strangely carefree. I may as well. I'm at rock bottom. It can't get any worse.

I heft myself up against the desk and flip open the silver laptop. I stare at my desk while I wait for it to connect to the intranet. Prime ministers aside, how many students have worked on it through the annals of Cambridge's history? Have any of them ever fucked up as badly as me? I doubt it. Because any residual hope that the comments might not be as awful as I thought bleeds away the second I access the chat room.

The part of the college intranet that it's been posted on is intended as a shared space, for students to post study items for sale or share tips about the college at large, so anyone can add a photo or a comment. Usually, a post might get three of four comments. This one has hundreds. They're all obscene.

Underneath the photo, people are guessing my bra size and suggesting which lewd acts I've been performing before it was taken. The words 'pricktease' and 'asking for it' appear several times. There's a sidebox of suggestions about who the lucky guy was. Will's name appears among a cluster of other candidates that takes in most of our year group.

My eyes are smarting so much I can barely see more than a green and brown smudge. New comments are appearing every few seconds. They blur into each other until my eyes feel like they are burning. One user, big-bendingdong, suggests that, through the flash of my knickers on view, he can see that my vagina looks like a badly packed kebab. That comment scores him a congratulatory thread of its own, with people cheering him on. A couple of comments are defending me, saying I look too out of it to know what was going on but most people don't seem to care. The most popular comments zero in on features I've never even thought to be insecure about. My nose is crooked; I've got teeth like antlers; one boob is bigger than the other; I look like a man in drag. All of them are hidden behind aliases like Big Ben. More comments appear as I watch.

My head spins. I know I put myself in a stupid position but I don't know what I've done to deserve such vitriol. Henry and Will used to rank girls on breast size and ignore anyone below a C cup and Lyla struts around college thinking she's better than everyone. I might have liked the security of being part of their pack, but I've always tried to treat everyone as an equal. Do none of these people commenting understand what happened to me? How have I become such a target?

Ping.

I know where the picture comes from. I'm calling now. Pick up.

The phone starts ringing. I don't want to answer. I still want to crawl down the drain and slither away, but I know she'll keep calling until I do. I pick up.

'I narrowed down the IP address.' Helen doesn't even wait for me to say hello. 'J staircase. That's where that photo was sent from.' Helen can't keep the satisfaction out of her voice. She loves to get to the bottom of things. 'You know how each staircase has a computer in the lobby at the bottom? The college logs the addresses of all the communal computers. When we ran a search that one flashed up. Is J where Lyla lives?'

I feel an ache in my guts. I can see it all so vividly.

'Emily? Is that where she lives?'

'What?' I try to focus. 'No, no, she doesn't live there.'

'Oh.' Helen sounds disappointed. I may as well tell her. 'That's where Henry's room is.'

'What?'

I close my eyes.

'Henry lives there.'

'As in Henry, love of your life, thought you were going to get married, the one who dumped you and got you into this fucking mess?' Helen is a firework about to go off. 'That Henry?'

'Yes.' But Henry's crap with technology; he wouldn't have the first clue how to do it. Will would, though. I picture the three of them huddled over the tiny computer, Lyla's stupid camera phone in front of them. Will must have walked right past me to get over to Henry's room and still left me there. It would have been his idea – he's the one who likes practical jokes. And there was Lyla to supply the material. And then there was Henry, facilitating it all. I picture him standing over the other two like some sort of lord of the manor, providing the crappy ancient computer at the foot of his stairwell, their laughter mixing together. So much for a perfect square; maybe it was always them and me. For the first time, at the back of the shame and humiliation, I feel something else: anger. They shouldn't be allowed to get away with this. I may not have been to the same schools as them, or know how to play tennis or ski, but I do know how you treat friends. And it isn't like this.

The idea of setting foot outside feels like going off to war. But these people were supposed to be my friends. And they did this to me. I owe it to myself at least to ask why. It can't just be about me throwing that drink over Henry and Lyla. Even if it was, that's nothing to do with Will. In a funny way, his betrayal is the one that hurts the most. I thought I could be myself around him. I start looking around for some shoes and a hoodie. I'm standing up when there's a flurry of activity on the screen. It appears Hawkesmoreplease has something to add.

5/10. Could do better.

I feel like I've been kneecapped. Could do better. Three years with Henry, my entire university career, and that's what it amounts to. What was I thinking of? I can't go over there and have it out with them. I see Will's username appear and squeeze my eyes shut. Helen is still talking revenge fantasies. I open my eyes to tell her I've got to go and notice that Henry's comment has deleted itself. The comments above it are disappearing too. It must be a virus. I slam my own laptop shut. My whole life feels like a virus.

'You've been to college already, yeah?' Helen questions. 'You should tell them you know who's involved. Or are they launching their own investigation?'

Now the site appears to have crashed, there's no point in telling her I haven't told college any of this. Or that I don't intend to.

'I've got to go,' I mumble.

'Oh no no no.' Her voice is the equivalent of a wagging finger. 'Don't you do that. Don't you let them beat you. These guys that think they can do what they want because they went to public school and the old boys' network will protect them. You've got nothing to apologise for. It's them that should be sorry. Promise me you'll make them pay for what they've done.'

'Oh, Helen.' I feel teary and defeated. Hysterical from lack of sleep. I want to go to bed and not get up again. For someone who knows so much, Helen can be surprisingly clueless. In our first year, Henry's father threw a drinks party to make sure he was exposed to the right kinds of people. Half the Tory party turned up, and some minor members of the government. Doesn't she remember the name of the library? Doesn't she understand what I'm up against? I picture the three of them around the computer again, all so confident life's going to go their way and so quick to cast me aside. 'Get a clue. People like that never have to pay for what they've done. It's not the way the world works.'

Eighteen

Now

20.30

3½ hours to go

'Are you sure you're okay?' Nick asks again. 'We can go if you want.'

'Honestly, I'm fine.' Actually, I'd be more okay if he didn't keep asking me every five seconds, but I can't say that without hurting his feelings. When I got back from the loo, he was pacing up and down the hallway, looking for me.

'I'll bloody kill her,' he says as soon as he sees me. 'Spiteful little cow.'

I'm so distracted by what I've done to Freja that I've almost forgotten what Liz did. Nick has not. The collar of his shirt is all mussed up from where his neck's been bulging and he looks furious. I reach out a hand and straighten it, noticing a small pinkish smudge that looks like it might be red wine. Seeing him this angry is a new thing; normally he's so mild-mannered.

'She's not worth it.' I try to move him back towards the Great Hall. I don't want to run into Lyla or Freja.

'We don't have to go back in. We can go home now if you like.' Nick stops cracking his knuckles and gives my shoulder a squeeze. He's obviously expecting me to crumble.

'It's just a stupid photograph, isn't it? At least you know what all the fuss was about now. Does it make you look at me differently?' I try to sound flippant but I'm not sure if I pull it off because he looks at me kindly.

'Of course it doesn't. I'm sorry that happened to you. Then and now.'

If only he knew.

I lean into him. 'Now the worst has happened, maybe I can actually have a good time.'

'Do you want me to say something to Liz?'

'No. You'd have a job getting past her bouncer husband, anyway.'

'They're not married.'

'How do you know that?' I look at him curiously.

'I know everything.'

'Not still holding a torch for her, are you?'

'As if. Now, are you sure you don't want to go back to the hotel? I'll even let you choose what to watch on the box.'

'Honestly, I'm okay,' I say determinedly. 'I want to stay.'

'Then stick with me. I promise I won't let anyone you don't want to get near.'

'Thank you.' The idea of telling him flashes through my head. He certainly wouldn't be so comfortable chatting to Lyla or claiming to know Will better if he knew. Helen and I should have brought him in from the start. Then the dinner gong sounds and the moment passes. He'll know soon enough. There's an immediate scrum as everyone flocks to their seats. Nick and I are at the end of the second table, with a bird's-eye view of Will and his cronies up on the dais. Liz has positioned herself at the top table, on the other side of Henry to Freja. It's almost as if she thinks that by putting herself with what she perceives as the 'cool' gang, she'll be absorbed into it. It's amazing how strong the need to belong is, even after the best part of two decades.

On Henry's other side, Freja has her head down and is studiously avoiding talking to him. To be honest, I'm amazed she's still here. I wouldn't be. Henry's jaw is set and his face is getting pinker as he keeps trying to make her say something. Even from this distance, I can see the photographs have had the intended effect and that's before anyone else has even seen them. I should start thinking about the timing of that, how I'm going to get over to the screen without people noticing. How brave am I feeling? As I'm trying to figure it out, I notice Liz watching me. I can't help myself draping an arm around Nick, curling my hand around his collar as we sit down.

'Lint.' I brush off imaginary dust and resist the temptation to look and see if I've got a reaction. Then I take my hand away, embarrassed. I don't need to stoop to teenage pettiness. I've come here to reclaim myself, not try to engage in one-upmanship with Liz Tripp.

Nick introduces himself to the woman opposite him.

'Emma, isn't it?' he says, as though he's not reading her name tag. 'Am I right in thinking you were a medic?'

'That's right.'

'And you lived in York Court?' I wait for Nick's second fact. 'The only rooms with en suite bathrooms.'

Emma looks pleased to be remembered. 'That's right. They've all got them now. They're so spoilt these days.' She blushes. 'Now I sound about a hundred. You did engineering, didn't you?'

'For my sins. Are you practising now?'

'GP,' she says. 'For *my* sins. How about you, Emily?' I tense, wondering whether she saw what was on the screen. She gives me a sympathetic smile that tells me straight away she clocked the photograph. I press my teeth together, wondering what she's going to say. But she only asks, 'What are you up to?'

'Er . . .'

Nick intercepts. 'Em's a Jack of all trades. She works part time at our local school, spends more time than she should sorting me and the kids out and she's a keen runner. I can hardly keep up with her.'

'Have you met my personal cheerleader?' Nick sounds like he's filling in the gaps of a particularly patchy CV. I grab a bread roll from the basket at the centre of the table and attack it with the butter knife.

'I think it's sweet. I wish Dave would be as supportive.' She elbows the bald man sitting next to her. 'I'd love to take up running but I never find the time. Did you run while you were here?'

'Not at all. I don't think I even knew where the gym was when I was a student. Too busy eating takeaway pizza and drinking cheap wine.'

Her husband, who looks distinctly square-shaped, cuts in. 'Weren't we all? Looking back, I don't know how I managed to get any work done.' He leans forward and sticks his hand out across the table. 'Dave. I was actually at Oxford so I'm a bit of an interloper here.'

'The enemy.' Nick pretends to recoil and Dave chuckles.

'Only at Varsity Boat Race time.' Dave amps up the famed Oxford–Cambridge rivalry. Funnily enough, it's only the men who seem to take any notice of it. Perhaps us women are too busy elbowing the women around us out of the way to care about faceless competition.

'Nice to meet you,' I say.

I shake Lyla out of my mind. What I said to Nick was right. The worst has happened. And I'm still breathing. I glance over at the top table. Will's holding court while Freja stares into her glass and Liz peppers Henry with questions like some kind of celebrity fan. Will catches me watching and tilts his glass towards me. I snatch my eyes away. Getting the photograph off the screen doesn't make up for being part of putting it up there in the first place.

'I take it you two both went here,' Dave continues, gesturing at Nick and me. 'Were you college sweethearts?'

'As good as.' Nick takes a sip of the urine-coloured Chardonnay and rolls it around his mouth. 'I was smitten from the moment I saw her.'

'Aw,' Emma says, and I blush. I'm terrible with compliments but I appreciate Nick trying to give me a lift.

'How about you two? Where did you meet?' Nick nudges the bottle against Emma's glass then moves on to Dave's.

'On rotation. Dave was the registrar in my first hospital.'

'Sneaky.' Nick laughs. 'And I hear you guys are considering a move to the States together. That's exciting.'

I feel a pulse of remorse. Nick was about to be transferred to America when I got pregnant. The twins were a high-risk pregnancy so I wasn't allowed to fly. The opportunity passed him by and I've felt guilty ever since.

'It could be,' she says. 'The hospital that's offered Dave a role thinks they could find a position for me but I worry about the state of their healthcare system.'

'The NHS is in a pretty terrible state.' Dave's voice is weary enough to suggest they've had this argument before. I feel a wedge of gratitude that Nick and I are generally on the same page about these kinds of things.

'Because government after government keep hacking away at its funding.' Emma's eyes are flashing and her voice is getting louder.

I step in before Dave can respond. 'I know it's an emotive subject but shall we save politics and religion until after dinner?'

'Hear hear.' Dave laughs and holds his hands up. 'You should consider a career in diplomacy – or marriage guidance – if you ever get bored of teaching.'

'Actually, I'm hoping to get back into law.' The words pop out before I realise what I'm saying.

'That's exciting,' Emma says. 'What type of law?'

'God knows. I'm just playing with the idea at this

point.' I've painted myself into a corner here. I channel all the times Nick's colleagues have shut down when they've learned I'm a 'homemaker', or Helen's suggested I need 'something more'. I'm fed up with having nothing to show for myself. 'I'd need to go to law school and start at the bottom and I'm not sure I'd have the patience to do all that photocopying.'

Emma and Dave laugh. Nick hasn't said anything. I feel terrible for ambushing him. Then I think of all the brochures collecting dust in the top of my bedside cabinet, the half-completed application and the discussions Helen and I have had about my future. Do or die, babe. I cross my fingers under the table and then put one hand on top of Nick's.

'You'll have to excuse my husband's "deer in the head-lights" expression. My career got slightly poleaxed by the children. Having twins tends to do that. It's only now they're a bit older that I'm finally considering having something to myself. I'm presenting it as a bit of a fait accompli when I haven't actually applied yet. I might not even get in.'

'Of course you would, with a degree from Cambridge,' Emma says.

I tense again. This is the moment that, if Nick were more like me, he might pay me back for ambushing him by dropping in that I don't exactly have a Cambridge degree.

Luckily, Nick's not like me. He laughs and squeezes my hand. 'Deer in the headlights is about right.' He lets go and reaches for his glass. 'As I said, I can barely keep up with her. That's what will make her such a good lawyer.'

Nick finishes his drink and takes my hand again, plaiting his fingers in mine. 'You show me where to sign and I'll get the cheque book out.'

'And that's why I married him,' I say with a flourish, ignoring the fact that he's inadvertently mirrored Will.

Dave and Emma laugh again as if they're the audience to a comedy double act. At least they're getting along again.

'Thank you,' I whisper in Nick's ear, as a stream of waiters start laying down plates of beef carpaccio.

'Always got your back.'

I load a forkful of carpaccio into my mouth and look around the hall. For the first time since we arrived, I feel pleased to be here. Even the sight of Ollie and Hugo on the table next to me dropping pennies into each other's drinks to make them down them in one – 'pennying' as we used to call it back in the day – isn't enough to dent my good mood. Nick follows my gaze.

'Tell me how old your twins are,' Emma asks at the same time as Nick produces a copper coin of his own from his pocket. 'Our two are five and three. Tell me it gets easier.'

'Hmm . . .' I joke.

Dave and I cover our glasses but Emma's not quick enough. Nick flips the coin into her wine and we watch it sink to the bottom before she can fish it out.

'Penny for 'em.' Nick winks. 'For the queen.'

'Oh.' Emma looks at Dave in dismay. 'I hate this game. I don't think I can down it one. I was always terrible at this and I'll be worse now I've had kids. We just don't drink that much any more.'

Nick's normally so good at 'reading the room', as he calls it, I can't believe he's mis-stepped. Clearly the time he spent with the Odysseans at the bar has rubbed off on him.

'You don't really have to—' I start to say, but before I can finish Dave reaches over and grabs Emma's glass.

'For Oxford.' He tilts the glass in Nick's direction and then drains it without pause, rescuing the coin and with it 'the queen's head' as required.

'Touché.' Nick claps his hands together in appreciation. 'Now you've only got to beat us in the Boat Race. For the first time in six years.'

Dave groans, Nick laughs and I risk another glance at the top table. Henry has turned his chair away from Liz and is trying to get Freja to talk to him. The plate in front of him is untouched – he hasn't even picked up his knife or fork – he's too busy pleading with her. Obviously, I can't hear what he's saying but his face is twisted. Freja has a small, fixed smile but she's not saying a word, even as his face gets closer and closer to hers. I'd love to be that controlled. It's obviously winding Henry up because I see his cheeks darkening. He's never liked to be ignored. He picks up the glass in front of him and drains it, tops it up and drains it again. Freja flares her nostrils slightly but doesn't give any other sign she's noticed; I only spot it because I'm studying her so intently. I watch as she turns her back on Henry and begins a conversation with Will, who happens to be sitting on her other side.

Henry puts his hand on her shoulder, but she brushes it off like a stray hair. The sequence of what happens next occurs so quickly it's impossible to unpick what he did or didn't mean to do. As he finishes his drink and stands up, Henry lurches towards Freja and loses his balance. His hands flail and he cracks his fist straight into her cheek. She puts a hand to her face as Henry crashes on top of her. They fall to the floor together. The volume in the room drops away and half a dozen people – Emma, Dave and Nick included – immediately jump up and rush over to help. I can't move. I just sit there, feeling stricken. If I hadn't shown her the stupid photographs, none of this would have happened. It's all my fault.

Nineteen

Then

Brrring. I slam my hand on the phone to turn the alarm off. I set it with the intention of getting up and doing an hour's revision before this morning's final. I haven't cracked a book since the boat club party. I need to look through my notes. My brain feels like soup. I don't move. The spider above me in the corner where the ceiling meets the wall has been there since Friday. Normally that would be enough to send me squealing to the opposite side of the room and speed-dialling Will to come and vanquish it (Henry's always too busy on the river or the rugby pitch). Instead, I've just watched it, telling myself that I'll get up if it comes down the wall. It hasn't. So I haven't.

I should get up but I don't have the energy. I haven't eaten since the cheese toastie I scoffed before I left for the boat club bop. My stomach feels hollow. Yesterday, I took a sip from the half-drunk can of Diet Coke on my bedside table. I got a mouthful of ash and remembered I'd used it as an ashtray when I was getting ready. Nothing has passed my lips since, not even water. Right now, what I eat is the only thing I've got control of, and depriving myself feels good.

The alarm – the sound of an old-fashioned telephone – goes off again. My chance of doing any last-minute cramming is ebbing away. I need to get up. I experiment with pushing the covers down, inch by inch. The corridor's quiet. The PhD student next door brought someone home last night – I heard a series of low giggles and the bed banging against the wall – so he won't be up for hours. If I grab a towel and make a run for it, I could make it into a shower cubicle in the communal bathroom without seeing anyone. I haven't washed since it happened and my hair smells like a bog. I can't go into the exam hall like that. I was planning on showering last night after everyone had gone to bed but there was a knock on my door as I was getting my towel. I'm ashamed to say my heart actually leapt. I didn't stop to examine who or focus on the fact that the three people most likely to give a shit are the ones who did this to me. The person had gone by the time I got to the door. They'd left a piece of folded-up notepaper tucked under it. I unfolded it to see the word 'slag' diagonally scrawled across the lines. I got back into my bed and lay there, staring at the spider. I didn't sleep.

I look back up at it. Motionless. Maybe it's dead. Lucky thing. Who am I kidding? Even if I do make it to the showers, I've then got an exam hall full of people to face. The picture might have disappeared after the virus – I've been checking obsessively and it's not been put back up – but anyone could have seen it before that. I pull the duvet up to my chin and shuffle down the mattress.

Lying there, idling the minutes away, I consider jumping on my bike and pedalling down to the exam hall at the last minute. If I sling on a hoodie and keep my head down, people might not recognise me. I've wanted to be a lawyer since I read *To Kill a Mockingbird* as a child. I've never imagined doing anything else. How can I go to law school now? Whatever career I pick, I still run the risk of that photo surfacing. For the rest of my life, whenever I walk into a room, I'll have to wonder if anybody there has seen it. And I'll probably never know what went on that night. Are Will's hands going to be the only thing I remember about that night? How do you get past not knowing what happened to you? I sink deeper into my bed.

There are two other girls from my college sitting today's final with me. I wonder if either of them will notice if I'm missing. We've gone to all the other papers together, meeting at the p'lodge to walk down to the exam site as a group. Will they question my absence and come and get me? If they've seen the photo they probably won't bother. They'll think I'm a slut who deserves everything I get. That's what the chat room says.

I pull the covers over my head. They smell. I normally do Henry's and my laundry on Sundays but I didn't want to take my sheets without his last week. There was no way I was venturing into the laundry rooms yesterday. I'm still trying to tear myself out of bed when there's a rap on the door. My heart twitches in spite of itself. What if it's Henry come to apologise? Even as I think it, I know it's impossible. I don't think he ever apologised to me in three years of dating. This will not be him.

The rap becomes a bang.

'Emily, babe, open this door at once. I've been calling and calling.'

I cast my hand about under the covers, searching for my phone. Helen's missed calls are now in double figures.

'Emily.' Her voice is getting louder. 'I know you're in there. Are you going to let me in, or do I have to kick the bloody door in?'

My legs are weak from lack of use, but I hobble over to the door. I open it to find my sister in a pair of ripped jeans and a T-shirt that says, 'Fuck the patriarchy'. She doesn't look like a national newspaper editor; she looks like an anarchist. A pissed-off one, at that.

'You took your own sweet time, babe.' Her eyes sweep over my face appraisingly. 'And you look like shit, by the way.'

'Thanks.' I stand aside to let her in and then close the door as quickly as I can.

'It reeks in here.' She crosses over to the window and yanks the curtains aside so she can open it.

'What are you doing?' I try to pull the curtains back. 'Someone might see me.'

'You're not on *America's Most Wanted*.' Helen starts picking through my things, brushing the used tissues and the Diet Coke can off the bedside table into the bin. 'You can be seen, you know. Although . . .' She looks me up and down and waves her hand in front of her face. 'I can see why your pride wouldn't allow it. It's not the room that stinks; it's you. Why don't you go and jump in the shower before we go? I'll wait here.'

I can't believe Helen's come to escort me to my last exam. In spite of myself, I start to feel stronger, even though needing Helen to get me out of bed proves I'm totally co-dependent. I've always been able to cope with things better with someone by my side.

'Well, hurry up then, we haven't got all day.' Digging around under the sink, she pulls out an old can of Impulse body spray and starts squirting it, swiping her hand through the air in quick bursts. 'Ugh, I don't know how you can wear this stuff. Look, forget it, just throw some clothes on and you can have a shower at mine.'

'What?' I stare at her, feeling like I've entered some sort of alternate universe.

'I've come to take you home, you idiot. You've finished your exams, what are you hanging around for? We can always come back for graduation.'

I pause. I should tell her that I'm not finished yet. If she drove me down to the exam hall, I'd miss the crowd waiting outside, glugging on Rescue Remedy and sharing last-minute guesses about the questions. But the idea that she doesn't know about the exam starts to present a tantalising alternative.

'Shouldn't you be at work?' I look at the Apple laptop poking out of her handbag. I can't remember the last time she took a day off.

'The lads in the newsroom can look after themselves for a change. Now hurry up and shift yourself. I'll help you pack.'

I don't move. This is the moment to come clean. Then again, it's not my fault she's jumped to the conclusion I've finished just because English, which is what she studied when she was here, finished last week. I never said my finals had finished. It's only a lie by omission.

'If we both pack, it'll be much quicker.' Helen pulls a string of bin liners out of her bag and starts ripping them off. She puts one in each of my hands and takes a piece of folded paper out of her pocket. 'I've done a list. All you need to do is make a "keep it" pile and a "chuck it" pile and throw everything in these.'

It takes hardly any time to box up the contents of my life. Anything Cambridge-related – my college scarf, hoodie and ream of ball and college photos – I ball up and stuff into the binliner on Helen's left. The stuff I want goes on the right. I'm altering the parameters the entire time, telling myself I've still got time to make it. Helen and I can leave straight afterwards. I rip my posters down, leaving the walls pockmarked with Blu Tack that I have to prise off with my thumbnail, knowing I'm running down the clock. I need to tell Helen.

'What are you doing? Trying to leave a DNA sample?'

'I've got to get the Blu Tack off the wall or college will add it to my bill.' I hack at a particularly stubborn clump.

'Fuck the Blu Tack. I'll pay for it.' Helen looks at her own watch. 'Right, let's blow this joint. You sure you've got everything?'

I nod. Even as we leave the room, I'm telling myself I'll tell Helen about the exam. She'll be furious I've wasted all this time, but she'll still take me. If we jump into her car and peg it down Tennis Court Road, we'll make it. We're almost at the car park and I still haven't said anything when I see Lyla crossing the quad. She's got a stack of books tucked under one arm and a garment bag slung over the other shoulder. Even from this distance I can see her curls bouncing and her cheeks glowing. A crimson hem peeps out of the bottom of the bag. It's her ball dress for Trinity College's May Ball tomorrow night; my ticket is one of the first things I crumpled up and threw into Helen's bin liner. Lyla is carrying the same Badgley Mischka dress that Kate Winslet wore to the Oscars a couple of years ago. Not a designer rip-off like I was planning to wear. The actual dress.

I'm very aware that I'm wearing clothes that I slept in and a nest of spots has taken up residence on my chin. If possible, I actually look worse than I did the morning I woke up on the quad. Lyla starts to turn and I brace myself. But she's not turning for me. I watch Henry jog up and throw his arm around her. I pull Helen around the corner before I collapse. Not only have I lost him, I now have to see his relationship with the person I thought was my best friend playing out. I can't bear it.

'Let's go.' I step in front of Helen and start tugging at the door of her silver VW Beetle. She's parked it right next to Will's MGB. The sight of it is like another sucker punch to the stomach. I just want to get out of here. There is no way I'm telling Helen about the exam now.

'All right, speedy Gonzalez.' Helen points her keys in the direction of her car and catches me looking at the MGB. 'They're a fortune to maintain and spend their life breaking down. We did a feature on them a while ago. If one of your lecturers owns one, they're being paid too much.'

I nod, my eyes on the bonnet. I can't believe Will hasn't been to see me. More than ever, I want to get out of this place.

'In you get.' Helen opens the door and I clamber in. When we get to the p'lodge, she pulls the car around to the side next to the recycling bins. 'You run in the key to your room and I'll wait here.'

'Hels, I can't.' I burrow into the car seat. 'I can't go in there. I might see someone.'

'Emmy, you've got to front up to people one day.' Helen taps her hand on the steering wheel, making a fist and then releasing it. 'That picture was up for all of a couple of hours at the crack of dawn. Half the people here won't even have seen it.'

I don't tell her about the wall of hateful comments, the note under my door. 'I can't,' I say stubbornly.

'You've got to stop acting like your life is over.' Helen snatches the keys out of my hand. 'Nobody will even remember this by graduation. Which you are coming back for, by the way. I've already booked the day off work. I'll take you for supper at the University Arms afterwards, if you like.' She smiles. 'It's where Mum took me.'

I sink lower into my seat and don't respond.

'Fine,' she snaps. 'I'll do it. But only because I want to get on the bloody road.'

I stay low as I watch her march up to the porters' lodge. Once I'm sure she's gone in, I pull my hoodie over my face, scramble out of the car, scurry over to the bins and lob my mobile phone inside. I'm already back in my seat when Helen stomps back down the steps and gets into the car, slamming the door so hard the whole thing rattles.

'Done.' She guides the car out of the iron gates on to Regent Street, nearly taking out one of the lions as she goes. Helen doesn't do anything slowly. I can see shoppers going about their daily business. A woman is negotiating with a small child to get him to cross the road; a man's walking two schnauzers on one lead, calling them to heel to let a clump of teenagers past. Like it were any other day.

I think of the exam hall full of students, heads bowed over their papers. The yawning chasm of my empty seat. Everything I'm flushing away. I tell myself I'm doing the right thing. I couldn't have faced them.

'You know, you'll have to see them all when you come back for graduation,' Helen says, as if we're continuing a conversation. We're on Hills Road now; the cobbled streets of the city centre are already receding into the background. I check my watch. The exam has started. There's no way they'd let me in. College is far away enough that it's safe for me to say it.

'Actually, I won't,' I say as the lights shift to green.

'I know you don't feel like it now but you'll regret it if you don't. You've got to come back.'

'I can't come back.' I stare out of the window, watching as we leave the urban sprawl behind for a brief swatch of meadows before the motorway. I'll miss the beauty of Cambridge, since I'm never planning on seeing it again. 'I didn't sit my final exam. I won't be graduating.'

Helen whips her head around so fast the car moves with her and there's a chorus of beeps from behind. 'You what?' she says.

'It started half an hour ago.'

'I'll turn the car around.' Helen starts looking around for a turn-off. More beeping from behind as she raises her hand in a two-fingered salute to the rear-view mirror. 'Fuck you. Damn these bloody slip roads. We'll go back. You'll be able to explain and you'll start late.'

'You can't walk into an exam hall when it's already started.' I keep looking out of the window. 'Anyway, I don't want to. Even if you take me back, I'm not going in.'

'Emily!' Helen is almost hysterical. I've never heard her sound so out of control. I feel my own pulse speed up correspondingly. The reality of what I've done is starting to press in. 'What are you going to do?'

'I don't know.' I rest my forehead on the glass. 'I don't care.'

'Do you have any idea of what you've done?'

'Look, I'll get a doctor's note or something. I'll call college and explain.' I think of my phone buried among mounds of paper and cardboard. I have no intention of speaking to anyone. 'Worst-case scenario, I'll finish my degree somewhere else. It's not like I want to go to law school now anyway.'

'You'd better.' Helen's voice is dangerously quiet. 'Because if you thought your life was over before this, it sure as shit is now.'

She doesn't say a word to me for the rest of the journey.

Twenty

Now

21.00

3 hours to go

Henry gets up first. He grabs at the table setting to get his balance, knocking over a bottle of wine that instantly starts to bleed all over the white tablecloth, and staggers to his feet. Freja hasn't moved. My heart is in my mouth. I think of her inhalation of breath in the bathroom after I slipped the photographs under the door, how kind it was of her to tell Lyla she felt sorry for me. And this is how I pay her back. I crane my neck trying to see if she's moving but all I can see through the clump of people around her is one long, tanned leg sticking out of the crowd. I sink into my seat, feeling more and more scared.

At last, Freja's leg twitches. The crowd around her clears and I see her start to sit up. I'm giddy with relief until I see her face. The left side is swollen and there's blood running from the cut under her eye that Henry's signet ring made. I may as well have been pointing his fist. She gives a wobbly smile as Emma helps her to her feet.

'Freja!' Henry rushes towards her. His voice is too loud. He doesn't need to shout.

It's quiet enough for everyone to hear her hiss, 'Leave me alone.'

Henry looks like he's the one that's been hit as Emma helps her past.

I should feel pleased by this – I've got what I came for – but any satisfaction I might feel was hollowed out the second Freja hit the ground. For one crazy moment seeing her lie still, I thought he might have killed her. And it would have been my fault. My actions could have really hurt someone. I don't want to be this person. Sod the revenge; the email is enough. I want to get out of here. I slip out of the fire escape and walk round the side of the building. I'll call Nick from here and get him to come out. I can't imagine anyone wanting to stay around much longer anyway.

'Emily.'

'God, you gave me a fright.' Of all the people I didn't want to follow me, Lyla ranks in the top three.

'I know what you did.'

'I don't know what you're talking about.' Even to my own ears, my voice sounds false. With a few notable exceptions, I've always been terrible at keeping secrets. And she knows it.

'The envelope. I know it was you in the bathroom.

You're the one who slid it under Freja's door. I saw your shoes.'

My gaze drops guiltily to my shoes. They're nondescript black peep-toes. Regulation Chanel Rouge Noir nails. A dozen other women could be wearing the same ones. She's bluffing. It's what she does. She's not the only one who can read the enemy.

'I don't know what you're talking about.' I give a nervous smile.

Lyla shakes her head in a sanctimonious way that makes me want to smack her. 'Wrecking a marriage is funny to you, is it?'

I'm sick of Lyla pushing me around. I've never been able to stand up to her. Until now. 'I'm not the one who smacked their wife in the face.'

'You might as well have done.'

'How dare you stand here judging me after what you did?' I didn't want to take the bait but I can't help it.

'After what I did?' Lyla widens her eyes like the picture of innocence. 'Newsflash. You guys were broken up. And he came on to me. It was about five hundred years ago. Get over it.'

I can't help my mouth making a small circle. I still can't fathom that she doesn't feel any regret for betraying me. Then I think of the other secret that she's keeping. No wonder she doesn't feel regret. She's not capable of it.

'I know Henry hurt you.' Lyla sounds so condescending, I desperately want to wipe the smile off her face. 'But you didn't have to ruin his marriage and disfigure his wife over it. That cut might actually scar.'

'You'd know about scars,' I snap back at her and immediately regret it. I don't want my attempt to hold her to account to dribble out; the world deserves to know what she's done without her scrambling for excuses or a way to get out of it. Any thoughts I had about leaving evaporate. I'm not leaving until I've done what I came to.

'That's so typical of you.' The true meaning of what I'm saying sails past Lyla. 'Always looking for someone else to blame when perhaps the real reason you ended up in that mess is closer to home.'

Any resolve I had about staying calm disappears. 'How dare you.' The words scrape against my throat. 'Do you have any idea what it's like to live under that kind of cloud? Do you know what it's like to meet someone for the first time and wonder whether they might have already seen you naked? Do you know how violating that is? I've spent fifteen years being ashamed of myself. And I was the victim. You, Lyla –' I spit out her name as though I can't bear to have it in my mouth '– you're the one who should be ashamed. You ruined my life. So don't you dare preach to me.'

'I ruined your life? Hardly. I don't think you're doing too badly.'

She's like one of those serial killers who really believe they're innocent.

'I walked out of here with nothing because of you.'

'That was your decision. You can't lay that at my door.'

'Yes, I can,' I shriek. 'It was your candid camera that drove me out. That photo destroyed me. That's right, I know it was you. My sister found the IP address. I know it came from Henry's staircase. You were the only one with a phone good enough to take those kinds of pictures – you never stopped banging on about it. And Will was techy enough to put the pictures up.'

She opens her mouth but I draw in such a deep breath I can practically feel the oxygen hit my brain and carry on. I will not let her interrupt me. 'So don't try and wriggle out of it. Or tell me it was just a joke. If it were just a joke it wouldn't be a fucking crime.'

I've made a point of not swearing since I had the twins – one of the countless ways I've tried to be a good mum and delineate their childhood from mine. But it turns out swearing is like riding a bike; you never forget. And saying 'fucking' sounded so good, I think I'll say it again. 'You were supposed to be my fucking friends. And you ruined me.'

'Listen, I . . .' Lyla shakes her head.

'No, you listen,' I say firmly. I take off the silver Tiffany cuff Helen gave me and hold my wrist up so she can see the silver scar tissue underneath. 'I almost took my own life because of that photograph. And that's on you.'

Twenty-One

Then

I'm not really looking when I step out on to the road. The traffic's too loud and the smell of the tarmac is clogging my nostrils. Being in Canary Wharf is like living on a building site. Every day a new shiny tower goes up like a totem of success, while I sleep in my sister's spare room and try to work out what to do with my life. Most days I don't leave the flat but Helen's out of milk. I've been putting it off all day even though it's the least I can do since all I do is clutter up her apartment, drinking chocolate milk and eating buttered toast. I cram mouthful after mouthful down my throat but I don't even taste it.

All the people around me are dressed in suits and walking with intent. I'm wearing the hoodie I slept in. I keep my head down. I don't want to make eye contact. Each time I see a set of broad shoulders or flash of dark hair, I cringe. I know Lyla was planning on working in the City and that Will scored a place on a coveted graduate banking programme. I ricochet between wanting to bump into one of them and being terrified of it. It's never them.

The daylight is hurting my eyes. I close them briefly and step out, Tesco bag in hand. There's a screech and a cacophony of swearing as a guy on a motorbike comes skidding by. He swerves to avoid me, the whole bike dipping to touch the ground.

'Are you trying to kill yourself?' the driver screams, sticking his finger up at me as he roars past.

I mumble an apology but he's long gone. I feel shaken all the way home, even though he didn't even come that close to me. When I get back to the flat, I unpack the groceries in a daze, leaving the milk on the side and putting the bread in the fridge before I realise my mistake. There are a hundred things I should be doing this afternoon. Helen's circled some job adverts for me and there are mounds of washing and ironing I could do to help. Instead, I just sit on the sofa, flicking through daytime TV. There are a couple of old quiz shows, horse racing and a terrible American made-for-TV movie that doesn't hold my attention. It's all so pointless. I feel like I'm wasting away. I think about the man on the motorbike shouting and how my first reaction when I heard the tyres was one of disappointment.

The movie finishes and I feel overcome by the urge to do something. If I wasn't so unfit, I'd go for a run – Helen likes to jog around the Limehouse Basin on Saturday mornings – and run until my lungs burn. I don't have the energy. Right now, I'm barely existing. I drift into the kitchen to cut myself some of the bread I bought. If

I can't run, I might as well eat. Some days I like to cram the insides of a loaf into my mouth until my cheeks are full. Something about the sensation of chewing is comforting.

When the bread knife slips, it genuinely is an accident. It's so blunt (judging from the dust on her skirting boards, Helen's not really into domestic upkeep) that it bounces off the top of my thumb without leaving more than a scratch. It smarts a bit though and it's that feeling – the short sharp sting and the release that comes with it – that makes me reach into the drawer and take out Helen's paring knife. It's the sharpest knife in the kitchen – Helen peels apples with it. I think of her expertly turning the knife and taking off the skin in one long strip. Then I hold the blade to my wrist and scrape it across, pushing it in so deep it practically grazes the bone.

There's more blood than I expected. It sprays all over Helen's industrial steel counter. I stare at it in shock. My wrist feels like it's burning. I have no idea what I was thinking. It feels like my rational brain is observing me from outside my body and wondering what the hell I'm doing. But underneath that I feel a spurt of satisfaction. I've been carrying around this pain that nobody can see for months and now at last there's something to show for it. I pick up the knife again. I genuinely don't know what to do next. If the bread knife hadn't slipped I'd still be thinking about watching *Countdown*. Do I want to cut myself again? To replace my mental pain with the physical? But if I start hacking away at myself, will I be able to stop? I don't get the chance to find out. There's a clattering at the door and Helen comes in, laptop case in one hand and handbag in the other. She dumps them both by the door and comes bustling down the corridor into the open-plan kitchen.

'You'll never believe the day I've . . .' Her eyes take in the knife in my hand and the blood on the counter. She freezes. 'Emmy, what are you doing? What the fuck?'

I let the knife fall on to the counter. 'I'm sorry.' I squeeze my eyes shut like a child playing hide and seek who wants to disappear. 'I don't know what to do.'

Helen becomes a dervish of action, rushing over to me and yanking me over to the sink. She runs the cut under the tap and starts rummaging through the kitchen cupboards for bandages.

'Bandages, bandages, where the fuck are they? Where the fuck is anything in this house?' She's trying to sound casual but really she sounds scared.

'I'm sorry,' I say again. 'I don't know what I was thinking. I'm such a mess.'

'You're not a mess.' Helen finally locates an unopened packet of gauze. She rips through the plastic and presses the whole roll against the cut.

'It's pretty deep.' She chews on her lip. 'I think I might have to run you to casualty.'

'No. I'm fine, honestly. I'll be fine.'

'You're patently not.' She watches the gauze turn from off-white to pink as the blood seeps in. 'Is that doing anything?'

She turns back to the cupboard and starts pulling more things out. 'Here. At last.' She grabs a massive cloth bandage from the time she sprained her knee a few months ago and grabs my wrist. 'This'll do.'

She wraps it around my wrist like a turban, turning the material over and over and pulling it tighter. Then she secures it with one of the safety pins hanging off the end. The sight of it makes me think of the denim shorts I was wearing that night and I clench my fists, trying to shut it out.

'Emmy.' Helen's voice is soft now. 'What were you doing?'

I sink to the ground, sliding down her kitchen units, holding my injured wrist in front of me like a paw. 'I don't know,' I say. 'I don't know.'

'Were you trying to . . .' Helen stops, as if she can't bring herself to say it. 'Was that a – were you trying to hurt yourself?'

'I just wanted to feel something.' I let my head fall forwards. 'I'm sad and tired all the time. I wanted to feel something else for once.'

Helen slides down next to me. 'I'm not going to pretend to know what you're going through,' she says. 'But I'm going to help.'

'You can't. It's hopeless.'

'What's hopeless?'

'I see them everywhere I go,' I spit. 'I think about them all the time, wondering why they did that to me, what they're doing now. I think about them all being so successful and how I've fucked everything up. I'm such a loser. I've thrown it all away. Everything.'

'Now, you listen to me.' Helen sounds fierce now. 'You're not a fuck-up. You're amazing. You're kind, you're funny, you're clever. You've got so much to offer. You can't let people make you feel like you're nothing.'

'I am nothing.'

'No, you're not. Look, we're going to beat this. I'll scale back at work and be around more. We'll get you some help and you'll be back on your feet again.'

'With no degree and no prospects.'

'So, you'll do another degree. Or you'll go back and you'll finish.'

I shrink away from her. 'I can't do that. I can never go back there.'

'You can make it through this. We can make it through this. This is not your fault.'

I look at her. 'Yes, it is.'

'No. It is not.'

'I'm the one who put myself in that position.' I feel a spurt of anger. I don't know where it comes from. I'm not angry with Helen.

'You did nothing a hundred thousand other people aren't doing up and down the country every bloody weekend. It was them.'

'It's not fair.'

'No, it's bloody not.' Helen grabs me by the shoulders. 'So get angry. This is not your fault. And the sooner you realise that, the better.'

I don't argue with her. Maybe she's right. Not that it really matters. Whether or not it was my fault, I've still messed everything up.

'Why don't you see about getting a job?' Helen says. 'Something to keep you busy. All this navel gazing isn't helping. I'll speak to some friends. I know someone who runs a restaurant. You've done waitressing, haven't you? We'll get you a counsellor. Find you somewhere to live. We'll get you out and about. You'll feel better. We're going to make this right.'

'Sure,' I say, because it sounds like it's what Helen needs to hear. Not because I actually believe it.

'And one day they'll get what's coming to them. We'll do it together.'

'Sure.'

'Don't fob me off like that. You've got to say it like you mean it.'

'Say what?'

'That you'll make sure they get what's coming to them.'

'Fine. I hope they get what's coming to them.'

'Not hope, Emmy. It's not enough to hope that karma catches up with them. You've got to make it happen.'

'Fine.' I look back down at the bandage. The material's getting pinker. Perhaps Helen's right and it will need stitches.

'Promise me.'

'Okay, I promise,' I agree, although I have no intention of sticking to it. I just know what Helen needs to hear.

'Good. Now get up and get your things. I'm taking you to casualty.'

Twenty-Two

Now

22.00

2 hours to go

'In all that drama, you've missed dessert,' Nick says when I get back to the table. 'I saved you a bit of mine.'

I look at the dessert plate in front of him; the dark smears across them suggest brownies or some kind of fondant.

'Thanks, but I'm not that hungry.'

Nick misinterprets my anxiety. 'Freja's going to be fine. Dave saw her into the ambulance. These facial injuries always look worse than they are.'

He looks at me expectantly. Normally we'd be discussing this at length – I've always loved that Nick can gossip like a girl – but right now there's no time.

'Where did everyone go?' I notice the spaces further

down the table. I glance to my right; the other table is similarly deserted.

'After what happened, a lot of people have left.'

'But what about the speeches?' I try not to sound plaintive.

'I guess they're not doing them.'

'But you said . . .' My mind starts to race. I need people. I want them publicly exposed. Caught like rats in a trap.

'I guess these reunions aren't for everyone.' Nick shrugs. 'I think the mood's been well and truly killed. Speaking of which, should we make like trees and leave?'

'What? But it's not over yet. We can't go.'

'Come on.' Nick puts on the fatherly 'own up' voice he uses on the twins. 'You obviously don't want to be here. You've barely sat down all evening. So why don't we just put both of us out of our misery and go back to the hotel? Order ice cream and watch a movie.'

'I'm fine. Really.' I look over his shoulder, measuring the distance. I have to get to the screen. 'I don't want to leave yet.'

'Then why have you been up and down every five seconds? You haven't been in your seat for more than a half-hour stretch at a time. You've been gone so long Emma was wondering if she should go and check on you at one point.'

'I'm sorry. Weak bladder. Blame the twins.'

'Are you sure that's all it was?'

He's not a stupid man, my husband. He must know something's up. If I tell him what's going on, he might be able to help. But he's always counselled the children to turn the other cheek. He's spent hours sitting with Artie in the last few weeks, telling her not to react to the bullying; that if she stoops to their level, she'll regret it. I think of how much he enjoys coming back to this college. If I involve him, it'll change things for him. It's not fair. And from this point, it's not difficult. All I have to do is plug my phone into the screen and press play. I can do it on my own.

'I'm sure.' I curve my mouth into a smile. I need to throw him off the scent. For his own good. I'm not going to be able to do this if he's watching me like an overprotective parent. 'Let's stay. There're only a couple of hours left of this thing, anyway. Let's wait till the bitter end. They might even take photos of people who made it to closing, like they did at all the balls.' I click my fingers. 'They had a name but I can't think what it was.'

'Survivors' photos, you mean?' Nick's a pub quiz obsessive (and borderline know-it-all) – I knew he wouldn't be able to resist the opportunity to win at college trivia. I think of the ball I didn't get to 'survive', and feel my resolve harden.

'That's it. So, who's still hanging around?' I start flicking my eyes around the room, using the comment as an excuse to do an inventory. Will is standing between the stained-glass window and the dark curtain marking where the founder's portrait normally hangs, posing with a bunch of sycophants who all want to have their picture taken with him. Booze has obviously reduced people's inhibitions and upped his fanbase. For now. Wait till they find out what his business empire was really built on. I turn my attention back to Nick. 'Who do you think is going to be the last one standing?'

'Well, certainly not Lyla, if that domestic's anything to go by.' He scratches his nose and uses his index finger to point over to where Lyla and her date are locked in what from the expression on his face looks like an argument. 'To be honest, I was surprised she brought anyone at all. Normally she comes alone.' His eyes linger.

'How cosy for you.' I don't like how often our conversation seems to pivot back to Lyla. I think of the mark on his collar and mentally chide myself. Lyla's lipstick is bright pink, anyway, and *Nick's* not a cheat.

'Don't be silly. You know I've only got eyes for you.'

I shift on my feet. Nick's interest in Lyla heightens my desire to get this whole thing done so we can get out of here before these people infect us any more. I glance at the clock. It's now or never. 'Are you going to be all right on your own for a couple of mins? I just need to pop to the loo again.'

'Again?'

'I need to retouch my face. I'll be five seconds.' I present it as a fact. With Artie coming up to puberty and her insecurity about everything from her dimples to the shape of her eyebrows, Nick knows better than to argue with the inner workings of female beauty regimes. 'Are you going to be okay on your own?'

He rolls his eyes. 'I've been coming to these things on my own for the best part of ten years. I'll be fine. In fact, I'll go and talk to Lyla and get the dirt on that domestic. Looks like her date's ditched her as well. Come and find me when you're done.'

He kisses the top of my head and slips away. I watch

him go, the shadows from the candlelight dancing across his face. I think of the way he greeted her in the hall. What if she tells him what happened outside, what she suspects I did to Freja? And he seems to know an awful lot about her love life. I think of the mark on his collar again. How sure am I that it wasn't lipstick? I force myself not to look over. From the very first moment he came back into my life, Nick's never given me a reason to doubt him. I can't let my past insecurities colour my present. I park my concern on the increasing stack of things I'll deal with later and make my way towards the screen. I've got a presentation to upload.

Twenty-Three

Then

Table 12 has been given the wrong order; Table 4 is kicking off because the three under-twos on it have been given the complimentary ice cream and the sugar has gone to their head and the teenagers on Table 6 have asked for another bottle of wine. I should be on my break but I'll be lucky if I get to sit down once this shift. The advantage of my job at this popular local pizza restaurant is that I scarcely have any time to think; the disadvantage is that I hate it.

When I say 'local', I don't mean to me. This pizzeria is in leafy Dulwich Village; everyone in here probably lives in a multi-million-pound house and goes to one of the plethora of exclusive public schools in the area. A far cry from my flat-share up the road in Brixton, where I have to alternate the nights I wash my hair with the two other girls because there isn't enough hot water to go around. They're both nice enough; they know each other from uni and, when I first moved in, they kept asking me if I wanted to go to the pub at the end of the road with them or to see a film at the Ritzy on Orange Wednesdays. I never said yes – I wanted to keep my time free in case more shifts came up – and eventually they stopped asking. I'm saving to get a flat on my own, ideally closer to Helen, but for the moment, greasy hair and a bedroom the size of a broom cupboard will have to do. Given the state of me, the trio of glossy mums sharing a cheeky Prosecco at Table 4 would die of shock if they knew that I'd been to Cambridge University. So would the people I work with; I'm too embarrassed to tell them that I went to university at all. It's not like I've got anything to show for it.

It's been almost five years since that night – 1,814 days to be precise – but who's counting? I still wake up sometimes in the early hours, sweating in a tangle of covers and wondering where my life has gone, why I'm still treading water. I'm not a struggling writer or an aspiring actress; it's no longer acceptable to be doing a job I don't enjoy for little more than the minimum wage. I should be trying to formulate a way forward, but I find thinking about the future almost as difficult as thinking about the past. Helen keeps trying to talk to me about it or offering to lend me money. I won't let her. She's done enough. But the higher she climbs at work, the more worried she gets about me. I'm seeing her later and I'm already dreading the latest interrogation. I can't believe I used to be as ambitious as she was.

'Excuse me?'

I hope it's not one of the teenagers chasing the wine. I

look up briefly, trying to convey that I'm extremely busy. It's the guy from Table 12. I flush and start scrolling through the order tabs to try to work out what his table actually asked for.

Table 12 isn't even my table, but Tiffany, who waits that section, is snowed under with the toddlers who have simultaneously thrown their ice creams on the floor.

'I'll be right with you. I'm just trying to locate the source of the problem and reorder your dishes. At no extra charge, of course.' I look up and try to give him a reassuring smile.

'Oh my goodness, Emily. Emily Wells. Is that you?' He leans right over the till and I instinctively shrink back. He's got dark, curly hair, twinkly brown eyes like chocolate buttons and he's wearing a neatly pressed polo shirt. I have no idea who he is. The fact that he's pronounced all his Ts and doesn't have a face tattoo means I probably didn't go to school with him. Which means he must be from Cambridge. The cheap acrylic of my striped T-shirt feels itchy against my chest.

'It's N-nick. Nick Toller.' He points his finger at his own chest like I'm deaf and he's signing it. 'From . . .' He names our college.

I knew it. I still don't have a clue who he is. I don't want to. I nod and press my teeth together into what might pass for a smile. Then I turn back to the till. I hope he'll get the message.

'You don't remember me, do you?' he persists. 'I shouldn't be surprised. We ran in pretty different circles and I guess I've changed a lot.'

There's something so humble about the way he says this that I spare him a second glance. I squint for a second.

'Your hair!' I say without thinking. 'It's all gone.'

'I no longer look like an Ewok.' He runs a hand through his close-cropped locks self-consciously. 'Or Brian May,' he adds and I flush guiltily. I never realised he knew we called him that.

'I . . .' I don't know what to say. I barely remember Nick – I think he did engineering – but even the sight of him is enough to make me feel awkward. I immediately wonder if he's seen the photograph. The more time that passes, the more I wonder whether it was as significant for everyone else. Probably not. Which in some ways makes it even worse – I threw away my degree for nothing. Either way, it doesn't answer the question about whether or not he saw it. I goggle at him unattractively and unsurprisingly he backs away.

'Anyway, I'll let you get back to it. You look busy. I'm over there with my parents – dutiful son duties on Mother's Day and all. But I wanted to come over and say hello. So, hello.'

'Hello.'

'It was nice to see you.' He flashes a smile and ducks back through the tables towards the older couple I can see sitting with a younger woman by the window.

I send Tiff over with a bottle of wine as an apology for the mix-up, ignoring the way she waggles her eyebrows at me as she goes. It's not restaurant policy so I take the money out of my portion of tips for the day – I feel bad about the whole Brian May thing. Even though I don't go over, my eyes are drawn to his table for the rest of my shift. I'm not sure why. Am I trying to see what life looks like when you do graduate from Cambridge? Helen's stratospheric success makes her a bad basis for these kinds of comparisons. Nick and his father playfight over the bill, while his mother and the younger woman, whose frizzy hair implies she might be a sister, look on. They seem happy. I wonder if I'd have handled things differently if I'd grown up with both parents around. In a bright checked Ralph Lauren shirt, Nick's dad looks like the kind of big, blustery man who'd kick up a fuss about things if he needed to. I shouldn't complain. Even when my parents were alive, they lacked the air of polish that Nick's family gives off, but I've got Helen. She would have kicked up a fuss, if I had let her. Sometimes I think she lives to challenge authority. But at the time it was the last thing I wanted. Even now I'd rather forget about it.

I feel a weird stab of disappointment when Nick's table pays the bill and gets up, even though his presence makes me feel self-conscious. I watch them walking down the quaint high street in pairs, past the designer clothes shop and the pub, with a feeling akin to regret. I have no idea why. I should be proud. Being able to have a relatively normal conversation with someone who was there at the time means I'm moving on with my life. That's progress – albeit five years too late.

The end of my shift is approaching and I'm clearing the table under the stairs where the teenagers were sitting when I hear the bell over the door tinkle. My heart sinks. Even though I can have a (hot) shower at Helen's apartment, I was hoping for the chance to freshen up before I left here.

'Table for one?' I hear Tiff ask in a flirtatious tone. I don't know why she bothers.

'Actually I wanted a quick word with Emily.'

I look up so quickly I bang my head on the underside of the stairs. It's Nick. Ignoring the throbbing in my head, I make my way over to the door.

'Nick, what can I do for you? Did you forget something?'

'Er, no.' He sticks his hands in his pockets and looks down at the floor.

'I'll go and finish clearing up your table,' Tiff tells me with a wink. I don't know her that well; I'd certainly never confide in her, but we look out for each other where we can. That's probably the closest thing I've got to a friend these days. She sashays across the restaurant and we both watch her go. She's got waist-length braids that click together with each wiggle. She's sexy – far sexier than me. Especially today: last night was not a hair-washing night. I'd never have let myself go out looking like this at university. I'm also about a stone heavier than I was last time Nick saw me. I'm surprised he even recognised me. I look at him and he looks so stomach-churningly awkward that I think for a horrid moment he's going to say something about the photo. My brain spirals down a rabbit hole of horror. Finally, after what seems like an hour but from the look of Tiffany's table wiping is really only about thirty seconds, Nick clears his throat.

'I know this is, er, a bit, er, out of the blue. And I'm sure you're very busy, but I thought I'd ask whether you'd like to go for a drink sometime. With me.'

'Er ...' I don't know what to say. Other than a couple of random snogs in bars when I've been out with Helen, I haven't had a date for five years. I always scarper if any of the guys wants to take it further. I don't think of myself that way any more.

'Stupid idea, really.' Nick scuffs his feet against the black and white tiles. 'But you can't blame a guy for trying.'

I think how brave it was for him to come back to the restaurant to ask me out. It wouldn't be that difficult to say yes. But I live in a city of eight million people. Do I really want to go out with the one person who went to Cambridge with me, who knows exactly what I want to forget?

'Er ...'

'She'd love to.' Tiff appears from nowhere, cloth in hand.

'Tiff, shut up.' I glare at her. I've been wary of female friends since university, but I thought I could trust Tiff. I don't know what she thinks she's doing. 'I'm so sorry about her.' My face feels as red as the jars of artisan pizza sauce we sell.

'I was kind of hoping you agreed with her.' Nick's eyes twinkle. 'How about one drink? If you hate it, you can phone her and bail on me halfway through.'

I bite my lip. After misjudging Will and Henry so badly, I swore I'd never get involved again, but I'm tempted to say yes.

'Go on.' He makes a puppy-dog expression, pulling his

lips down and widening his eyes. Behind him, Tiffany makes smoochy faces.

'Okay.' At the very least, it will shut Tiffany up.

'Okay you'll hate it and you'll bail halfway through or okay you'll come?'

'Okay I'll come.' I smile.

'Great. What time do you get off?'

'I can't do tonight. I'm going to my sister's.'

'Of course.' Nick gets out his phone. 'Well, let me take your number. I'm flying to Aberdeen tomorrow, but I'll be back at the weekend. I'm out on Friday night but maybe the Saturday?'

'I work Saturdays.' Perhaps this is a sign. I cast my eyes around the restaurant. It's significantly quieter but there's always work to be done. 'Speaking of which, I should get back . . .'

'Look, why don't you come with me on the Friday, then?' Nick suggests. 'I'm meeting a few people from uni for a couple of drinks. A bit of an informal reunion. We could drop in and then go on somewhere together. Could be fun.'

I fight back a shudder. 'No.' I shake my head and try to remember how the therapist Helen had me see a few years ago coached me to handle this. 'I don't tend to socialise with people from back then. Nothing against anyone who does but I prefer to look forward rather than back.'

I wait to see if my trotted-out refusal will evoke any memory of why I might not want to. He must have seen that photo. Everyone did.

'No problem,' he says easily. 'I'll sack it off. Let's go out together instead.'

'I don't want you to miss out on my account.'

'Those uni things tend to get old fast. Also, my ... ex organised it so it's probably as well if I give it a miss. Things will be quite raw for Liz.'

'I'm sorry to hear that.' I can barely remember who Nick dated at university.

'Don't be. We should have broken up ages ago. We're completely different people now.'

'You can say that again,' I say without thinking, unable to quite conceal the bitterness in my tone. He looks at me curiously. Now I've done it, I think. *This* is the moment he's going to ask me why I don't want to see anybody from college, where I was at graduation and why I'm working as a waitress when the rest of my year are probably pulling in six figures. He doesn't say anything. I could let it slide. I look over at Tiff. She's giving me such a wide smile I can see her wisdom teeth. I dig my thumbnails into the palms of my hand. My heart is beating double time. I may as well get it out into the open. 'Thing is, when we were at uni, there was this photo and it got put up and ...'

Nick looks pained. I've blown it. I'm surprised by how disappointed I feel.

'I know the one you're talking about.' He looks me straight in the eye without blinking. 'I never saw it. Never went on those stupid message boards. Too busy being a geeky engineer. Anyway, there's a great little wine bar near where I work. So, what time do you want to meet?'

In the background, Tiff has graduated to making

full-on kissy faces. As we fix a time, I allow myself the smallest sliver of hope, like light under a door, that what happened then might finally have stopped affecting what happens now.

Twenty-Four

Now

22.30

90 minutes to go

Up close, the screen gleams like a sheet of metal. I feel stupidly intimidated. I remind myself it's an inanimate object. Then I reach out and touch the switch at the bottom. There's a bank of speakers at the top; they're what you roll the screen around when it's time to pack it away because they're the only part that doesn't bend. They're also the most powerful on the market. The on button moves from red to green. My pulse jerks. All I have to do now is open the right file and touch my phone to the screen the way Will and Liz did and then melt away. Nobody need even know it was me. I'm so close.

It's amazing how much information can be contained on one tiny phone. I suppose that's what got me here in the first place. The idea that everything we've found out about Will, Henry and Lyla can be distilled into a single file that will play on the very screen that made Will's fortune is mind-boggling.

I start tabbing through my phone for the presentation. I've already got my body inclined towards the screen so I can swipe the phone against it in a single movement. I feel my muscles straining like a sprinter at the starting blocks. All I need to do is find the file.

'Gotcha!'

I drop my phone. What is Nick doing here? 'You scared me half to death.'

'Sorry. What are you doing back here? I thought you were in the loo.'

'I was. I came back but I couldn't find you so I thought I'd sit down.' I pick up the phone and try to subtly scroll through the icons on its screen. I made such an effort to bury the presentation in case anyone looked at my phone that now I can't find it when I need it. Who exactly did I think was going to be going through this phone anyway – the secret police? I flip through faster, no longer caring if Nick notices. I go past Words with Friends, Spotify, Paperless Post and about a hundred other apps that are absolutely no use to me now. Where's the bloody file?

'Anyway, a group of us are planning on blowing this joint and heading down to Cindies for old times' sake. What do you reckon?' Nick smiles. 'Will's going to head early, see if he can throw some cash around and make sure we get in without having to queue.'

I nearly drop the phone again. This whole thing means

nothing if Will's not here. 'He's going to what? But he can't.'

'Why not?' Nick's voice sharpens to a point. 'Why are you so fussed about what Will Jenkin's up to?'

I'm on the edge of a precipice. I think of all the times Nick's rescued me. I can see that, finally, long after it should have done, his patience is running out. I jump.

'Because he's the reason I was out on the quad the morning of the photo,' I blurt. 'He took me back to his room and then he took my bra off when I was out of it.' I shudder, remembering Will's hand. 'He left me out there. On my own. And then he walked right past me and helped them put the photo up. So I'm not leaving this room until I've made him pay for it. Until I've made them all pay.'

Nick's face drains of colour. He looks stunned and I feel desperately guilty that I've kept him in the dark. Then he reacts.

'Will Jenkin did what?' He starts looking wildly around the room. 'I'll kill him.'

'Don't,' I beg. 'Look, I don't even know what happened. And it wasn't just him. They're all involved; Henry and Lyla too.' I rush the words, like getting them out of my mouth will distance me from them. I wonder if Nick will make the connection to me wanting to punish Henry and his wife lying on the floor. I still feel terrible; it's the lowest thing I've done. I need to find out which hospital she's at and check she's okay. I stumble on. 'She's the one who took the photograph and then she went back to Henry's staircase and they uploaded it together.'

'How do you know all this?' Nick has gone from red to

green. Finally, he must understand why I haven't wanted him to spend time with Lyla.

'I've always known.' The quicker I get the words out, the easier it will be. 'Helen tracked down the IP address at the time. She made me promise I'd do something about it. That's what I've come here to do.'

'And I'm hearing about this now?'

'I'm sorry.' And I am. 'There never seemed to be a right time to tell you. All I wanted to do was forget about it.'

I could point out that he's never asked. Perhaps things would have turned out differently if he had. But I don't want to make him feel bad. There are three people here who should feel ashamed of themselves. He's not one of them.

'I don't understand. What changed?'

'Nothing changed. Helen always said I shouldn't let them get away with it—'

'This was Helen's idea?' The confusion in Nick's eyes has given way to pity. 'It's all very well for her when she's—'

'Don't you dare criticise her!'

'I'm not trying to criticise her. Don't you see this isn't the right way, Em? You should go to the police and get Will charged with a crime. I'll take you to the station tomorrow.'

'It's not a crime to leave someone outside in the cold.' I shake my head. 'And I can't remember anything else.' I push the image of his hands taking off my bra out of my head. 'It's not about what happened that night. It's about the photo. They all did that. And it ruined my life.'

Nick looks like he's been slapped.

'You know I don't mean you and the kids. But everything else I could have done. Could have been. Gone.'

'But you're going back to law school. It's not gone. You can go anywhere you like. Oxford if you must!' He waits for me to acknowledge the joke. I can't. I know he's on my side but I'm tired of being dictated to. 'We're behind you,' he says pleadingly. 'The kids and I. Don't let's do anything tonight. Come on, let's go home. We can go to the police in the morning.'

'It was two decades ago. They'll only wonder why I haven't come forward sooner.' I shake my head again. 'It's not as if I'm a reliable witness.'

'So, let me take you home. We can sort it from there.' My husband, the pacifist.

'You don't understand. I can't walk away from this.'

'What do you mean?'

'I found out this stuff about all of them. Bad stuff. I'm going to broadcast it on that screen. On Will's screen.' I smile bitterly. 'See how they like having their dirty secrets aired.'

'What kind of stuff?'

'You'll see in a minute. And I'll tell you everything afterwards, I promise. But I've got to be quick. I'm running out of time. Please, I need your help.'

He looks me in the eye and for a split second it's like we're back to that night in the pizza place. Not the one we met in, but where he proposed.

'Okay, I get it. Tell me what to do.'

Warmth spreads through me like honey. 'Okay, all the

stuff that I found out about them is on my phone. I need to get it on to that screen before everyone leaves. I should only have to swipe it and it will play. But I can't find it.'

'Give it to me.' He holds out his hand and his wedding ring flashes in the light. 'It'll be quicker if I do it. We've got these screens in the boardrooms at work.'

'Thank you.'

I toss him the phone, vowing that when all this is over I'll be a better wife to him. Maybe we'll make it to Houston after all. Have a fresh start. No more secrets. I don't know if I'm distracted and fumble the pass or Nick fumbles the catch. But somehow my phone slips through his fingers and lands face down with a sickening crack.

Twenty-Five

Then

I take the pregnancy test in the toilet of the McDonald's on Clapham High Street. Two teenagers are squaring up to each other outside and the floor has got muddy footprints tracked into the tiles. Against a backdrop of increasingly irate female voices asking, 'Am I bovvered?' I pee all over my hand as I'm trying to hit the stick. I don't have to wait the full three minutes. The blue line darkens within seconds. It feels like an arrow straight into my heart.

How can I have been so careless? Nick and I have only been seeing each other a few months. He's got a job in America. I've finally been looking into going back to uni and making something of myself. This will ruin everything. I think of Helen with her crisply ironed silk shirts and pencil skirts, her perfectly ordered penthouse and wonder how we share DNA. Her life seems perfectly in order. She's invincible. I'm a disaster.

I feel a surge of desperation bubbling up in the back

of my throat. It's hard not to feel like I'm being punished for something. Why do I keep screwing things up? I've just saved enough money for a deposit on my own flat. Rental, of course. Unlike the rest of my Cambridge cohort, I can't appeal to the bank of Mum and Dad. I could have asked Helen but I wanted to be independent. For once.

How on earth can I look after a baby? I've only just started looking after myself. I look at the graffiti scratched on the cubicle door to distract myself. 'Beth loves Callum'. 'Call Shaniqua for a good time'. 'U R a bitch'. The idea pops into my head that I could make this pregnancy go away. It's super early. I only bought the test because my period's never late. That and the fact that Tiff pointed out how much bigger my boobs were looking. I stare at the stick. It's so unfair. Nick always wears a condom. I've been on the mini-pill since a bout of acne when I was in sixth form. I picture the pill packet sitting on my nightstand. I don't *think* I've missed any, but it only takes once. How can I be so unlucky? I feel a nugget of dread. Poor Nick. How can I do this to him?

The sanitary bin is overflowing with dirty nappies and there's no room to jam the test in, so I have to stick it in my handbag next to the printouts about law courses I got from the library. Courses that will mean nothing to me now. Outside, the teenagers have gone, leaving an empty fag packet and a tidemark of orange makeup around the dingy sinks. Who am I to judge? I'm the one who's just screwed herself over. Again.

I think about what I'm going to say as I march out of the

McDonald's and down Clapham High Street. I can't drag Nick into this. It's not fair. He doesn't deserve to have the rolling five-year plan he's had since he was about twelve disrupted because I screwed up. What's the alternative? I ask myself the question that's become my default setting over the past five years: what would Helen do? On past the bookies and the charity shops, I roll it around my mind. If she wanted a baby, she'd find a way to make it happen. And I know she'd support me. But do I actually want this? I'm not stupid enough to think a baby is something to love or something to make its father love me. I think of all the mistakes I've made, all the things I'd like to have been protected from. This is my chance to do it right. It's not like I've got a career to give up. Other than Nick, there aren't too many sacrifices that I have to make. It could be me and this child against the world. By the time I've passed Waterstones and crossed on to the more illustrious Northcote Road, with its artisan bakeries and butchers, I know what I have to do.

Nick's waiting for me in his favourite pizza place. I suggested burgers but he loves this place. It's a busman's holiday for me, given where I work, but I can have salad. The closer I get, the heavier my steps feel. It wasn't as if I thought I was going to marry him. But things were going well. Until this.

The terrace of the restaurant is teeming with people. It's one of those hot summer days where the whole country collectively whips their tops off and heads outside. I can see several pairs of red shoulders and bad tan lines already. Nick is sitting at a table by the sliding doors that open from the restaurant on to the terrace. The best of both worlds. For a moment, I consider what it would be like to take the other option, to sidestep this pregnancy and go on living the life of a normal, unencumbered 26-year-old, meeting her boyfriend for a pizza, just because she can. Nick's wearing a navy suit and a pale pink shirt and thumbing through his swanky work iPhone, a bottle of Peroni sweating on the table in front of him. Then I think of all the times Helen's saved me. Now's my chance to put someone else first. My mental picture evaporates. I'll have to tell him things are over. I can't ruin him. I grew up without a dad and it didn't do me any harm, I tell myself. So did Helen. She's a bit more of a poster child for success than I am.

As if he can feel my eyes on him, Nick looks up. A smile spills across his face and I feel even worse. But what other choice do I have? We've only been dating a few months. He didn't ask for this.

'Em,' he says, standing up. 'There you are.'

I glance self-consciously at my watch. 19.17. 'Sorry I'm late.'

'Don't worry about it.' Nick sits down and pats the seat next to him. 'What can I get you to drink?'

'Diet Coke, please.' I put my handbag on the floor, checking to make sure the lid is firmly closed. With another 26-year-old, the soft drink might be a clue. But I very rarely drink these days.

'Diet Coke, Alberto.' He flags down the waiter, who gives him a wink and bustles off. Nick knows everyone.

'So how was your day?' He turns back to me, all ears.

'Fine.' I shift in my seat. I don't want to look at him. 'How was yours?'

'Amazing.' He spreads his arms expansively. 'How can it not be? The sun's shining, the project I'm working on got the go-ahead in Houston and I'm sitting here with you. What's not to like?'

I squirm like I'm sitting in wet sand. I've never had to break up with anyone before. I don't know how to start. He doesn't notice. The waiter's come back, carrying a plastic tray with another Peroni, a can of Diet Coke and a bottle of San Pellegrino on it. I watch him unloading them and fight the temptation to grab the beer bottle, put it to my lips and glug it until all my problems are swept away. I remind myself that my problems tend to start, not finish, at the bottom of a bottle.

'Emily,' Nick says.

'Yup?' I'm watching the bubbles fizz in the bottle. I can practically taste it. I take a swig of Diet Coke instead.

'I've got something to ask you.'

'Oh?' I tear my attention away from the bubbles.

He looks uncharacteristically nervous.

'I know this might seem quick, but I wondered whether you'd consider coming with me?'

I'm so busy working out whether I should tell him about the baby and then break up with him or just break up with him that I'm not concentrating. 'Where?'

'To Houston.' He gives me a funny look. 'I know it's a big ask but what do you think? Fancy an adventure?'

'You want me to come with you?' It seems insane that we could be thinking on such different trajectories. Perhaps that's the way break-ups are. I certainly never saw Henry dumping me coming. I start picking at the skin around my fingernails. Nick's offer makes this harder to do.

'I've already talked it through with HR and they reckon they could get you a visa. Or you could use the time to study. Have you looked into all that teaching stuff yet? What do you think?'

Law, I mentally correct him, even though I know I won't be studying anything now. If only he'd asked me this a month ago. 'I can't.'

'If it's the distance from your sister, my company pays for flights back twice a year. And I'm sure we could scrape together more if you needed.'

'You don't understand.' I feel grimy. I haven't felt this sickened at myself since the night I woke up on the gravel. It's such a beautiful offer, but I can't take it.

'What don't I understand?'

'I'm not good enough for you,' I say in a low voice. 'I come with so much baggage. You'd be much better off without me.'

'Don't I get to be the one that decides that?' The dent in Nick's smile disappears. 'You're perfect.'

The Diet Coke threatens to repeat itself on me. 'I'm not perfect. Not by any stretch of the imagination.'

He takes my hand across the table. 'Emily, what's wrong?'

His kindness undoes all my good intentions. 'I'm pregnant.'

I screw my eyes up. I can't bear to see his face. Silence. Is it me or have all the tables around us fallen quiet too? We're crammed in sardine-like enough that I'm sure they've heard every word. I open my eyes, cringing. Nick is not at the table. This is even worse than I expected. Then I hear him clearing his throat. He's on the ground in front of me. On one knee. Holding out the ring pull from the Diet Coke can.

'Emily,' he grins. 'Will you—'

'What the . . .'

Of all the outcomes, I did not see this one coming.

'Nick, get up.' My face is so hot it feels like it's melting. I try to pull him into his chair but he won't shift. Everyone must be staring. 'What are you doing? This isn't the 1950s. I'm not going to be sent to an Irish laundry without you. You don't have to—'

'I know I don't have to, so shut up and listen.' He clears his throat again, like he's about to begin a long speech.

I squirm again. I hate public displays of affection. 'Please will you get up?'

He slides into his seat as if abandoning his romantic gesture is no big deal. But he hasn't given up. 'If you think about it, getting married now is simply saving time. I've known we were meant to be together since you cocked up our order on Mother's Day. Probably before that, come to think of it. And you know I'm always right.'

I don't laugh. It's like he lives in a parallel universe to me. One where nothing knocks you down and problems are always surmountable.

'How are you not terrified?' I say in a low voice. 'This is massive.'

'It's only as big as you make it.'

I look at him uncomprehendingly. What kind of a world

does he live in when a surprise pregnancy is not a big deal? I wish I had that kind of confidence.

He sees my expression. 'Yes, having a kid is a big deal. But so is anything until you do it. Weren't you bricking it when you went to Cambridge? I was. My first day at work, I was sick on the way to the Tube. But I got through it. Just like we'll get through this. Together, if you want to.'

'What about America?'

'We'll still go. We'll have a little Yankee Doodle baby and say diaper and crib instead of nappy and cot.'

'I feel like I'm ruining everything for you.' I feel like a fisherman trying to free something that refuses to leave the net. Why won't he listen to what I'm saying?

Nick looks horrified. '*You* could never ruin things for me.'

'You had this perfect life and I've come in and messed it all up. I haven't even met your parents properly.'

'They'll love you as much as I do.'

'There's so much you don't know about me.'

'I know everything I need to. You're pretty awesome.' He winks. 'Just don't tell anyone.'

His certainty starts to cloud my doubt, like ink in water. I think about how nice it would be to feel part of something bigger than myself. I remember being at Cambridge, the safety and comfort of knowing I belonged to Henry, Lyla and Will.

'Anyway, you're forgetting something.' Nick tilts his head.

'What?' I force them out of my head.

'You haven't said yes.'

I look at his happy, unguarded face, wide open. Being

with him feels easy, the way love is supposed to. It's different from how it was with Henry. Safer. But that doesn't mean it can't be better.

'You really want to get married, when we've only known each other about five minutes?'

'I really do.' His smile is a mile wide.

There's a final moment when I think about backing out of this and sticking with my original plan. But his enthusiasm is contagious. When I say 'yes', every table on the deck breaks into applause.

Twenty-Six

Now

22.45

75 minutes to go

'No,' I lunge for the phone, almost ripping my dress in the process. When I turn it over, there's a spider's web of broken glass down the centre and a huge chunk missing from the corner. I stab at the keys. Nothing happens. I keep pressing, trying to access first PowerPoint, then WhatsApp, my email, anything. The whole thing's frozen.

'I think it's broken.' I feel my face crumpling like the screen. 'What am I going to do now?'

'I'm sure I can fix it.' Nick crouches down next to me and puts his hand on my shoulder. 'Let me have a look.'

I hand him the phone and sit on my haunches while he tries to bring it back to life. I watch his square fingers confidently jab at keys. If anyone can fix it, Nick can. But after a couple of minutes, he shakes his head. 'I'm afraid it's dead. This model's notoriously fragile. I should have upgraded you when I did mine.'

'There must be a way. Can't we pull the file off it and send them to your phone? Isn't that what the cloud is?'

He shakes his head. 'I can't even get it to turn on and I can't get the SIM out. You'd need to be able to log on to iCloud on a Mac. My laptop's back at the hotel.' Nick slips the phone in his pocket. 'I'm so sorry.'

He sounds like he's pronouncing a dead on arrival.

'Are you sure there's nothing we can do?' I can't bring myself to give up.

'I really am sorry. I think we'd better go back to the hotel, get a good night's sleep and see where we are in the morning. There are plenty of other things we can do. If Will committed a crime, we can report it. And I'll kick the crap out of him on my way out if you like.'

I don't bother to point out that Will's twice his size. It's not about Nick kicking the crap out of Will, even if he could.

'I could have got a first, you know,' I say. I need him to understand what I lost. 'I know it doesn't matter now and you shouldn't say you could get a first-class degree unless you actually get one but that's what my professors said I should aim for. It's what I got in Part One. Like Helen.'

Nick looks pained. 'I know you could have done, Em. You can do anything you put your mind to. You still can. But—'

'Except this.' I explode. 'This whole night has been one

disaster after another. And now I can't even do the one thing I set out to. The one thing I promised Helen.'

'She'd understand.' Nick holds up his hands. 'You must know she . . .'

'Must know that she what?' I rage. 'You can't speak for her. That's the whole fucking point, isn't it? We don't get to know what she'd think. Of any of it. Because she's dead.'

Each time I say that it feels like dropping a fresh bombshell, even though she's been dead for months. This is the kind of loss I'm never going to get used to. My words make Nick recoil, as though they're driving a stake through his heart, not mine. He prefers flowery euphemisms, like 'slipped away' or 'passed on'. Tonight, I don't want to pretend. 'Passed on' sounds like leaving one function in favour of another. And Helen didn't slip away; she fought tooth and nail. Like she always has. Like she wanted me to. I think of her tired face, imploring me to turn my life around.

'I didn't mean to . . .'

'This is the one thing I promised her I'd do. And I can't even manage it.'

I think of my beautiful sister, lying there at the end. Of course, her final wish would be for me. I can't flake and crumble, like I usually do. Tonight I have to stand tall because she can't.

'Emily.' Nick's tone has graduated from pity to concern. 'I know you're upset about Helen. Of course you are. But I promise you, a file on your phone is not going to fix things, no matter what's on there.' He closes his hand around my wrist, tethering me to him. 'The phone's totalled. You're much better off coming back with me. We'll sleep on it and figure out a plan in the morning.'

'I don't want to figure out a plan in the morning.' I wrench my hand from his grip. 'I'm so sick of doing the right thing all the time. Being sensible.' I square my shoulders. 'Helen was right. I need to stand up for myself more.'

'What are you doing?'

'What I always should have done. I'm going to get up there and I'm going to stand on that stage and I'm going to tell everybody exactly what happened. It's like what you said. It's not about the stupid file. It's what happened then. It's my chance to clear my name.'

'That's not what I meant.'

'I know it isn't. But you were right.'

I leave Nick standing there and march towards the stage before he can stop me. I almost trip on the first step. Falling flat on my face would be one way to get everyone's attention. I regain my balance and keep going, shaking my shoulders out. This dress is so tight I have to take pigeon steps. My palms are sweating. I hate public speaking. Not that I've had much cause to do it in my non-career. I see notice Lyla already snaking her way over to Nick to see what's wrong and I don't even care. Will and Henry are talking intently by the window. I didn't realise Henry was back. It says a lot about him that he hasn't even gone with his wife to the hospital. I mount the final step like a scaffold. In a room full of about sixty people, I'm going to struggle to find a single friendly face. I pause. I could still back down. Nobody has noticed what I'm doing, except Nick and he's rooted to the spot. But the second I put one foot on the stage I'm committed. Do or die. I think of Helen and I step forward.

'Excuse me.' My voice sounds croaky. A couple of heads turn, but most people ignore me. I'm not deterred. I'm not as nervous as I thought I would be. From this height, I can see bald spots and sweat patches. Nobody down there seems better than me any more.

'Excuse me,' I call more loudly. More heads start to turn. Will and Henry's are not among them. They're still arguing in the corner. I'm not important enough to warrant their attention. I put my fingers to my lips and let out a wolf whistle, the way my dad taught Helen and me when we were little, before drink tore our family apart. The single note splits the air. At last people start turning around. A few smile when they see it's me. Some frown. I sneak a glance at Henry and Will. They've stopped arguing. Will looks mildly curious at the sight of me up on the stage; Henry looks as furious as he did when Freja left. But it's not about them any more; it's about me.

'Can I have your attention?' At last my voice comes through for me. Loud, confident and determined. 'There's something I need to say.'

Twenty-Seven

Then

I am standing in our kitchen cramming garlic bread into the oven when she tells me. The twins are sitting cross-legged in front of the TV in the family room, Nick is outside doing something complicated with a thermometer on the Weber barbecue and Helen is sitting with her elbows on the kitchen island, one cheek resting on her open palm.

'So, depending on the biopsy results they'll go in and lop it off, blast me with a few rounds of chemo and possibly radio and then I'll be good to go.' She dips a finger of pitta in my homemade hummus as if she's delivering a punchline. I stare at her in disbelief.

Her deciding to leave the national newspaper she was editor of to go freelance should have been the first clue. Helen's always been so driven; it didn't fit with her personality at all. But I was so delighted at the idea that she wanted to spend some more time with me and the kids that I didn't stop to question the motivation.

'Come on, babe. Cheer up. You know I've always wanted my boobs done.' She reaches out a hand to rub my arm. I jerk away.

'It should be me comforting you, not the other way round.'

'Plenty of time for that. I'm not going anywhere.'

'Mum, can I have some crisps?' Xander's voice precedes him as he comes charging down the hall. He digs his hand into the bowl of crisps before I can respond. 'Are there any Pringles?' He waggles his eyebrows hopefully.

'No.' I can barely get the words out. I can feel tears behind my eyelids.

He pauses mid-crunch. 'What's wrong?'

Helen gives me a warning look.

'Oh, nothing.' I make an effort to pull myself together. This isn't what Helen needs. 'I've been cutting onions for the burgers and you know they make me all weepy.'

Luckily, Xander's not observant enough to notice the chopping board is completely clear and the onions are in a bowl wrapped in cling film in the fridge. Artie wouldn't let me get away with such a weak excuse.

'Is it nearly ready?' Xander scoops more crisps out of the bowl.

'Dad will put the burgers on when Nonna gets here. Where's your sister?'

'In her room.'

'I thought she was watching telly with you?'

Xander shrugs. 'She said she wasn't in the mood. Told me to leave her alone.'

I frown. That doesn't sound like Artie. 'What did . . .

oh never mind.' Today I don't have time for adolescence. 'Just go and tell her she's got to come down when Nonna gets here.'

'Sure.' Xander lopes out of the kitchen, leaving a trail of crumbs behind him. Normally I'd be itching to sweep them up before they hit the floor but right now I turn straight back to Helen.

'Thanks,' she says. 'I don't want them treating me any differently.'

'They wouldn't,' I say, though I don't know that for sure. My two have been starved of life's tragedies. Cancer's never been in their orbit before.

'I still want to be their cool aunt.'

'You'll always be their cool aunt.'

I try to smile at her, but she looks away. Her evasiveness sharpens the situation. No matter how bright a face she puts on, I'm terrified. She's already had the biopsy done. She makes out like it's because she's so efficient, but I know Helen. She's the type of person who would avoid the doctor unless some part of her was practically falling off. She'll have left this to the last minute. She's had the biopsy done because it's serious.

I'm trying to find a way to ask the hard questions, the ones that I don't want answers to, when my mother-in-law bustles into the kitchen.

'I used my key.' Despite being told she need bring nothing to a small, family barbecue, she starts unloading bread, crisps, dips, a punnet of strawberries and two more of blackberries out of her recyclable hemp Waitrose bag.

'Now I know you said not to bring anything, dear, but

245

I couldn't resist. You know my Nico loves my crumble so I whipped one up before we came. It needs forty mins at one sixty.'

Luci's grandfather was Italian, a heritage she never tires of drawing attention to. In addition to insisting on being known as Nonna and having the waistline of someone who enjoys pasta a little too much, she's the only person who ever calls Nick 'Nico'.

'That's so kind of you, Luci. Thank you.' I feign a smile. On the surface, Luci and I get on well but I know she's never forgiven me for getting pregnant so early in our relationship. She doesn't even know I don't have a degree; Nick thought it would be too much for her.

'Helen.' She gives the name an Italian pronunciation, elongating the vowels. It makes me want to punch her. 'It's lovely to see you. How are you?'

'I'm doing well,' Helen lies, but Luci isn't listening. She's already turned back to me.

'Now, where's that handsome husband of yours? Have you set him to work already?'

'He's in the garden.' I wave vaguely towards the French doors, not taking my eyes off Helen.

'And the children?'

'In the TV room.' Normally at this point, I'd call them in to greet her. But right now I can't bear her presence and I know if I don't, Luci will bustle out to Nick.

'I suppose I'd better not interrupt their screen time,' she says after a pregnant pause. 'I'll go along and see to Nico, shall I? Give him a hand. He must be tired after a long week.'

'That was a bit rude,' Helen says after Luci's safely ensconced on the patio with Nick. 'You didn't even offer her a drink.'

'There's a wine cooler and glasses out there. Nick will sort her out. Since when did you care about her feelings, anyway?'

'*I* don't. But you should.'

There's something final in the way she says it that makes me want to cry. I latch my tongue to the top of my mouth and blink hard.

'Sorry,' I say, as if I've dropped a glass or said the wrong thing. 'I'm being stupid.'

Helen gets off her bar stool, comes around the kitchen island and folds me into a hug. I can smell the mint of her shampoo and the Ponds face cream she always uses. I bury my head into her shoulder and she winces slightly. 'Bit sore.'

I rear away. 'Sorry.'

'You can stop saying sorry, babe.' Helen strokes my cheek. 'What are you like? First thing you can't apologise to your mother-in-law, now you can't stop apologising to me.'

'The old bat's never liked me anyway.' I see what Helen's trying to do. If she wants to keep things light, I'll keep them light. I'll google the answers to my questions later. 'Do you remember when I first went round there, there were pictures of Nick and Liz still up?'

'I wonder if she and Luci are in touch.'

''Spect so.' I take the conversation and run with it. 'The photos would probably still be up if Nick hadn't specifically asked her to take them down.'

I look out of the window to where my husband is pouring his mother a glass of wine. Standing side by side, you can see the similarities in the aquiline nose, the dark, chocolate-button eyes (though Luci's aren't nearly as twinkly) and of course the hair. Helen and I don't look at all alike. I wish we did.

'It was almost worse when she did finally take them down,' I babble. Anything to drive the silence out. 'She could have put pictures up to replace them, but no, she left the walls bare so you could see the patches where they'd been.'

'Be kind. You're going to be a mother-in-law one day, god help you.' She doubles back. 'Do you ever think of people like that? People like Liz. From university, I mean?'

'Not if I can help it.' I don't look at her. 'Nick goes back for the opening of an envelope, but I tend to avoid those things. Why?'

'I see my year all the time.' Helen says it so casually that I know she's planned this conversation. 'We're a fairly well-scattered lot but most people are travelling all the time and there's a big bunch in London. It's not fair you missed out on all that.'

'We had very different university experiences.' To think I once thought she might be jealous of mine. I go over to the fridge and take out a bottle of rosé. Then I head to the cabinet above the sink and pull out two fresh wine glasses. I fill both to the top. 'Cheers.'

'Steady on,' Helen says. 'Since when did you start drinking again?'

'Since right now.' I tilt my glass against hers but she takes a sip before our eyes can meet.

'Fair enough.'

Helen picks up the topic again when Nick's walking Luci home. She lives two roads away but tonight I'm grateful he's such a devoted son. The twins are sprawled upon a sofa each in the family room, their earlier disagreement forgotten, and we're back in the kitchen. I'm stacking the dishwasher. Helen tries to help but I won't let her.

'There's no point in treating me like an invalid yet.'

'That's exactly what you ... fine, forget it.' I know better than to argue with Helen. 'Rinse these.' I hand her a set of glasses and angle the tap at them for her.

'About what we were saying earlier ...'

'Which bit?' I stiffen. Is now going to be the time I can ask the difficult questions? I start shuffling through them.

'About university.'

'Oh. I'd rather not go into all that. Why don't we talk about—'

'It's not only my year group I've run into.'

I start putting the glasses I've already rinsed in the dishwasher.

'I've run into some of your contemporaries once or twice.'

I take two bowls out that are lying flush and rearrange them so there's enough space between. Helen waits for me to ask. I don't say anything.

'You know exactly who I'm talking about. I've seen that delightful ex-boyfriend of yours strutting around as if

249

he's some sort of demigod. He can't wait to stand up after dinner and make speeches about the law. As if he didn't break it at university.'

One of the bowls slips through my fingers to land on the floor, where it smashes.

'Oh shoot.' I stoop down to pick up the shards of china, shutting out Helen's words. 'I said I didn't want to—'

'It's called revenge porn now, just so you know.'

One of the fragments of bowl embeds itself in the end of my finger. 'Crap. Keep your voice down.' I put my finger in my mouth and start sucking the wound.

'From shoot to crap in one fell swoop.' Helen arches an eyebrow. 'I'll have you swearing by the end of the evening. As I was saying, it's called revenge porn and it carries a custodial sentence.'

'Keep your voice down. The kids are next door.'

'They're watching *Hollyoaks*. They can't hear a word I'm saying and you know it. It's you who doesn't want to hear it.'

'Because I've moved on.' I get up and close the dishwasher more forcefully than necessary. Then I set upon the kitchen surfaces with a wet cloth.

'Have you?' Helen snorts. 'Yet you've never been back.'

'I've got a different life now.' I concentrate on sweeping stray crisp crumbs into the palm of my hand.

'Yes, I can see how fulfilling you find being class mum, year rep, volunteer numero uno, parent representative and whatever the fuck else you do.'

'Why are you being so horrid?' I flip the lid of the Brabantia and pour the crumbs in. I reach for my glass of rosé and take a large gulp. 'I don't understand why you're attacking me.'

'Oh, babe, I'm not attacking you. I'm defending you.'

'How do you work that one out?'

'I'm not saying that what you do isn't brilliant. It is. Those kids are a credit to you. They're brilliant and I'm so glad I get to hang out with them more now. But once upon a time you were going to be a lawyer, travel the world and God knows what else.'

'Helen. I'm a mother of two. I wanted to be a brown crayon when I was five. Sometimes you don't get to be what you want when you grow up.'

'It's not the same and you know it. You could be a lawyer. If you did something about it.'

'We don't exactly have a spare ten grand lying around for me to do a glory degree,' I say. 'Times are tight in the oil world. There's a chance Nick will be made redundant in the next few months. Now's not the time for me to be getting any big ideas.'

'I'd lend you the money in a nanosecond. I'll put it in your account first thing.'

'It's not about the money.'

'Then what is it about?'

'Look, it was all such a long time ago. I'm happy as I am.'

'So it doesn't bother you that they're all just getting away with it?'

I swallow the hard lump at the back of my throat. 'I don't think about it if I'm honest.' It's not really a lie. I try never to think about what happened. Usually I'm successful. I've built my marriage and my family around me like a protective shell. Very occasionally, I'll wake at night, my mind tangled up with images of hands grabbing at me. But it doesn't happen that often and I know how to handle it.

Helen's eyes bore into me. 'I don't believe you.'

'That's your problem.'

'Don't let them get away with it. You promised me once that you wouldn't let them get away with it.' She grabs my arm across the marble and for a moment I think she's going to look at the scar. She doesn't. She just squeezes my hand. 'Even if I'm not around, I'll do everything I can to help. I've actually started looking into—'

'Helen, you're scaring me. You said you were going to be fine.'

'I am. But you need to start taking charge of your own life. Don't live it around Nick or the kids.'

'I don't.'

'Okay. It's only ... I want the best for you, whatever happens. I always have.'

'I know.' It's the ease with which she gives up the argument that scares me the most. In all the time I've known her, Helen has never backed down.

'You would have made a great brown crayon, by the way.' She flashes me a sad smile. 'Come on, let's get out of here. I promised Artie I'd watch *Strictly* with her.'

When Nick comes back from dropping Luci home, he finds Helen and Artie on one sofa, Xander and me on the other. There's a bucket of spilled popcorn on the carpet and the TV is blaring. It's apparent from the hyped-up state of the kids that none of this weekend's homework will be completed tonight, as planned. To his credit, Nick flops on to the edge of my sofa, nudging Xander to one side with his legs.

'Room for one more?' he says. 'What's Craig Revel Hallwood up to this week?'

'Dad, it's Horwood, not Hallwood. Get it right.' The twins groan at exactly the same time. There's a moment when we all burst out laughing, whether at their weary correction or Nick's cluelessness, I'm not sure. But I hold on to it afterwards, anyway, because Helen dies six weeks later.

Twenty-Eight

Now

23.00

60 minutes to go

'I'm sorry to interrupt everyone's evenings.'

Nick looks like he's watching a car crash. I ignore his pained expression – he'll come around – and adjust my stance, shifting my legs wider apart so I'm standing like a gunslinger. Then I find them in the crowd; the three people whose actions have so defined me. Henry is stabbing away at his phone, teeth grinding. I look at the clock. Only an hour to go until the email drops. If he thinks it's bad his wife saw the photos, think how he'll feel when everyone else does. But I don't need to think about the email now. Now is about what they did to me *that* night, not what's happened since. Will's murmuring in Henry's ear, trying to calm him down. Only Lyla is staring at me, her eyebrows raised as much as the Botox will allow. I think of all the times in our friendship that she took centre stage. This is my 'Nobody puts Baby in a corner' moment. At last. Lyla was a mad *Dirty Dancing* fan. She had the DVD at uni and we used to watch it hungover on Sunday mornings. I only have to hear the opening notes of 'The Time of My Life' to think of her, like some obsessive ex-boyfriend. Funny how the end of a friendship can be like the end of a love affair.

'Actually, scratch that, I'm not sorry. Sorry.' It's late in the night and the people left have had a skinful. I need to start talking quickly. 'I want to talk about the photo that Liz Tripp was so kind to put up on screen earlier. The one of me with my boobs out lying in the middle of the quad.'

A guy at the back puts his pint back on the bar and a couple having what they think is a discreet domestic stop mid-conversation. It's amazing what the word 'boobs' will do to a conversation.

'It probably won't matter to a single one of you, but I need you to know that I didn't know that photo was being taken. I know most people thought I posed, but I didn't. I had nothing to do with it being taken and nothing to do with it being put on the Internet.'

All these years I couldn't find the words; they were there the whole time.

'Some of you might be wondering why I'm bothering. It was all such a long time ago. We were different people then.' I take a breath. 'But I promised someone I'd finally stand up for myself.' I close my eyes briefly, thinking of Helen. Then I open them and stare straight ahead. Any sense of shame falls away. 'And that photo ruined my life.'

Will and Henry have stopped talking and they're both staring at me with expressions of horror. Good.

'These things have a habit of catching up with us, even if Liz hadn't been so sweet as to provide us all with a visual recap. Thanks for that, Liz. I wouldn't be up here without you.'

Liz bunches her mouth up like she's sucking a lemon and I feel a grim satisfaction. Helen was right. I did need to let go of these demons. I hope I'm making her proud.

'So why am I up here making a fool of myself when you all just want to bugger off to the bar?' A ripple of laughter encourages me. 'I said earlier that these things have a habit of catching up with us. It caught up with me. I left college three days after that photo was put online. I couldn't stay with that hanging over my head. I worked my arse off to get here and then slogged it out for three years but I didn't even graduate.'

Another ripple goes through the crowd; this one of surprise. Nick was right. All these years I've let myself be held back by it and most people didn't know.

'That's right. I left Cambridge with nothing and I've beaten myself up about it for years. I blamed myself for getting into that position. For getting so drunk that I trusted the wrong person and he took advantage of me.'

I look directly at Will. His olive skin darkens.

I look back at the room, deliberately taking them all in. Most people look sympathetic, though there are some judgy faces. Ironic when I can see people I came across face down in ditches or hunched over toilet bowls. My voice gets stronger. 'How many of you haven't once got so drunk that you've done something you regret? I know for a fact that two of you at the back used to down pint glasses of your own vomit.' That wipes judgement off a couple of faces. 'I might have got myself so out of it that I put myself in that position. But I wasn't the one taking the picture or the one uploading it. And I wasn't the person who left me in the quad on my own in the middle of the night. It's taken me fifteen years but I finally get that it's not my fault. And you know what? The people who did all that are all here tonight. Walking around as if nothing happened. Well, it did.'

People start glancing around like I've announced someone in the room is carrying a weapon; they're all trying to work out who it is. I won't leave them in suspense.

'So why don't you stand up and take a bow, Will Jenkin?' I spit. 'And know that letting you take me home that night is one of the biggest regrets of my life.'

Nick puts his head in his hands and there's a cracking sound as Will slams his glass on the windowsill and leaves the room, with Henry hot on his heels.

'She did not just say that,' I hear a linguist with bright red hair and a face full of freckles say to the woman standing next to her.

'Oh yes she did. And did you see the way he stormed out?' Her friend's voice is rippling with the scandal.

'I'm nearly done, I promise.' I feel strangely giddy. I'm aware that if I stay up here much longer I'll risk being written off like a drunk commandeering the mike at a wedding. 'I can't lay this all on Will. He had some help in putting that picture online – the kind of six foot three-inch lawyer help that just followed him out the door. Cheers, Henry.' Again, I see heads whip around. Someone even appears to be holding up their phone and filming. How ironic. 'And, of course, he didn't take it. He wasn't the one with the camera phone.' I can see Lyla advancing on the stage. Why is she coming closer instead of legging it like Henry and Will? How can she be so brazen? I start speaking faster.

'That honour goes to Lyla Miller. She's the one who stood over me and decided to take a picture rather than help me out. So much for girl power. Anyway, I've said what I came to say. I'll let you all get on with the dying embers of the night. I hope you choose your friends better than I did.' I walk off the stage with my head held high. I just need to collect Nick and we can get out of here. And I never have to come back.

'I didn't take that photograph.' Lyla's waiting at the bottom of the stairs.

'So someone else with a grudge and a camera phone on their way to bang Henry Hawksmoor just happened to walk by?'

'I've gone over it a thousand times in my head. I should have helped when I walked past and saw what was going on. But I was too angry. I wanted you to get what was coming to you. But I didn't take that photo.'

'Yeah, right. Pull the other one, it's got bells on.'

'Emmy, I'm telling you the truth. It's about time someone did.'

'What are you talking about?'

'That picture wasn't taken on a phone. It was taken

on a digital camera. I thought you knew.' She pauses for effect. It's like watching an actress at work. 'You've got to believe me. Otherwise I'd have said something before you got married. I swear I thought you knew.'

'What has me getting married got to . . .' I stop talking. Dozens of images are tumbling through my mind. The beautifully posed pictures of our children that stretch from the top of our house to the bottom. All taken on the digital camera Nick has had since university.

With a dull thud, like a heavy weight falling, pieces start to shift into place. I swing my head to where he's standing, hoping against hope there is a different explanation and that seeing his face will give it. But a girl who studied veterinary science is standing where he was. Nick has gone.

Twenty-Nine

Then

I find the envelope when I'm sitting on Helen's bed, sorting through the drawers in her bedside cabinet. It's A4, metallic blue and has the name of a small children's clothing brand on the corner. Remnants of one of the many gifts she's bought Artie and Xander over the years. There's a white label with my name scrawled almost illegibly on it, stuck to the centre. Her neat print is normally so recognisable. This version looks like she could barely control the pen. I think of how much pain Helen must have hidden from me in the past few weeks. I've been setting anything personal aside to read later, when it hurts less, but seeing my name written like that, and the effort gone into it, makes me open it straight away.

A series of bank statements falls out. Not what I'm expecting. She's already told me I'm her sole benefactor. And she put the ten grand in my account even though I told her not to. She should know I couldn't care less how much money she had. I'm about to toss them into the large bin liner at my feet when I see the bright pink Post-it note on the final page.

Consider this a jumping-off point to start negotiations.

Clueless. Helen took me into London to see the film at Leicester Square; we quoted it at each other for years afterwards. I let the memory sit for a while, then I flick back to the first page. Which is when I notice that the cash payments on the page have more zeros than Helen could ever have access to. The transactions are over three years old and all the account names are things like Turgenev and Litvinov. Why was Helen getting payments from a bunch of Russians? And why does she want me to know about it? I flick to the account details on the top of the page. The spot where her name should be reads 'Jenkin's Junkins'. I drop the pages. What's Helen doing with Will's financials?

I get up off the bed, leaving an indent in Helen's top-of-the-range memory mattress and start pacing around the room. Already, I don't think I want anything to do with this. Through the window, the light on the top of Canary Wharf Tower is winking at me. I go and sit back down, the mattress dipping to receive me. I pick the financials up and shake the rest of the envelope's contents on to the bed. Even for a financial disaster area like me, the bank records tell a pretty straight story. Around the time of the last General Election, which his company was working on, Will's accounts received several generous injections from Russia. Months later, he announced the prototype for his screen. It's not concrete proof of wrongdoing but, as Helen, quoting Alicia Silverstone, said, 'a jumping-off point to start negotiations'.

I think of Helen lying in her bed at the hospice, wasting away, still putting this together, and feel a bolt of something I haven't felt for years: resolve. I'm rifling through the accounts again, brain whirring, when the buzzer to Helen's flat goes.

'It's me,' Nick's voice booms out when I press the button. 'Sorry I'm late. Mum wanted to chat and then it took me ages to find a parking space. I'll be up in two secs.'

I'd forgotten he said he'd drive over and check how I was getting on after he'd dropped the twins at Luci's. I buzz him in and keep looking at the envelope in my hands. What has Helen done?

'What's that you're holding?' Nick tosses his car keys on to Helen's mirrored side table and nods at the envelope.

'Just some old bills.' I stuff the financials back in the envelope. Until I know how I feel about this, there's no point involving Nick.

'You ready to grab lunch?' Nick flicks his thumbs under his belt loops and rocks on his feet.

'Sure.' I'm about to tell him about Helen's favourite

sushi place, with the best crab rolls in London, when he adds, 'I'm starving and there's a Browns around the corner.'

I walk over to the sofa where I've left my handbag and stuff the envelope in. I'm not hungry anyway.

I go straight to my bedroom when we get home and let Nick pick up the twins on his own. I suggest they might want to grab an early supper with Luci and he agrees. He's been treating me with kid gloves since Helen died, offering to put a wash on, suggesting takeaways instead of cooking. I should have at least an hour.

I pour the contents on to the duvet cover and flip through the pages of the statement again and notice that Helen's made notes, her writing varying from the print I know to be hers to loops that I can barely read.

There's one that reads 'sources', with a jumble of Russian names I imagine she was planning to approach for corroboration. I know if Helen were still here, she'd have gone to the papers with this. There's reference to the Bribery and Corruption Act and some other stuff I can't read. Clearly, she was halfway through looking into this when she died. My brain starts to press in on me, like it's too big for my skull. I don't know if I'm ready to be the person Helen wanted me to be. I'm not a journalist, I don't know how you go about writing a story like this. I don't even know if I want to.

I pick up all the loose papers and shove them back into the envelope but I can't get it to close. There's a sheet that's somehow got crumpled at the bottom. What I pull out is what starts the tears. It's an application to read law, with my details filled in by Helen's shaky hand. Stuck on to it is another Post-it note with Henry and Lyla's names on them. Scrawled underneath in writing I can barely read are words I recognise: 'You promised.' At that moment, I know I won't let her efforts go to waste. She spent enough of her short life mopping me up. It's time I stood on my own two feet. And I made her a promise. Now I need to find a way to keep it.

Ironically, it's Luci who gets the ball rolling. She comes over for supper a week later, cock-a-hoop because she's caught her cleaner stealing. While for most people this would be bad news, my mother-in-law is beside herself with pleasure because she's employed the services of a PI to catch this poor Latvian woman attempting to pawn one of Luci's old rings.

'You can't trust anybody these days,' she says, remarkably cheerfully after her third glass of wine.

'I quite agree.' Normally I detest this kind of griping, but Luci's pettiness has inadvertently opened up a new world for me. I try to sound casual. 'How did you find him?'

'Who?'

'Your private investigator.'

'Oh, it was a piece of cake.'

'I suppose you used the Internet?'

'Don't be silly,' Luci scoffs, 'you don't know who's lurking online. I used the good old Yellow Pages.'

I didn't even know they still made them. I do know that

Nick is militant about making sure we don't receive any unwanted mail (our phone number is unlisted) and I'm pretty sure the Yellow Pages would fall into that category. I can hardly ask Luci if I can borrow hers. Then inspiration strikes. 'One of the mums at school is having exactly this issue with her tennis coach,' I lie smoothly. 'I don't suppose you could give me the details to pass on to her?'

Luci reaches inside the Radley handbag 'the twins' got her for Christmas. 'As long as she isn't intending on using my name to try and get a discount.'

Two days later, I'm meeting the guy in a business village near the Asda superstore in Clapham Junction. He doesn't look anything like a PI. With his close-cropped bald head and designer trainers, Greg could be any of the dads at school, or one of the guys Nick occasionally plays football with. I suppose that's the point.

'I don't really know what I'm looking for,' I fumble after he's explained what kinds of services he offers and I've explained there's not one person I need investigating, but two.

'You don't need to worry about that,' he says reassuringly. 'That's my job.'

'Do you often handle cases . . . like this?'

He shrugs, as though he doesn't want to break confidentiality, and I feel stupid. Stupid that we're using police terminology like 'cases' and 'jobs' and stupid for what I'm trying to do. He must see something in my face because his folds into a smile.

'I do custody battles mainly, or cheating spouses. But

it takes all sorts. The other day I had an old dear who wanted me to trail her cleaner.'

I shift in my seat. 'So what happens next?'

'I take these –' he gestures at the pictures of Henry and Lyla that I've pulled off the alumni website '– and see what I can dig up.'

It doesn't take him long. Either Henry is worryingly indiscreet or Luci has a knack for picking PIs. Much as I'd like to credit my mother-in-law, I imagine Henry's built-in arrogance allows him to be indiscreet. Within a week, Greg calls to tell me he's caught Henry having sex in a car parked down a backstreet, near a well-known gay bar. With a boy who barely looks old enough to drive. I struggle to believe it, until he emails the photos over. Watching the image of Henry's face thrown back in an almost animalistic pleasure while what's obviously a teenager fellates him in an alleyway pixelate in my Outlook, I feel a funny sort of judder. All that heartache – each tiny action we took that led irrevocably to that night – was for nothing. I think of his taste in music, his obsession with plucking his chest hair and the missing weekends when we were at university. Am I surrendering to cliché or were the signs always there? I think of his poor wife – Nick often talks about how nice she is – and for the first time since Henry dumped me, I don't feel like I missed out on a better life than I would have had. What kind of life can he offer anyone when he can't even live with who he is himself? I feel a pang of sympathy which I quickly squash down. He wouldn't spare me the same consideration.

What Greg finds out about Lyla is much worse,

although when I stop to think about it, it's typical Lyla. She always did try to wriggle out of responsibility. Greg says as soon as he got the assignment, he went to do a routine check of the area around her house and realised she was no longer parking the Mini that was her pride and joy on her driveway. Closer examination – I didn't ask him exactly what this meant – revealed that the Mini was stashed in her garage under a tarpaulin. When he lifted that up, he noticed the right headlight was damaged and there was a dent and some scratches on the paintwork around it. He wouldn't have thought anything of it if she hadn't covered it up. He took photographs then and there, which turned out to be fortuitous because when he went back for another look a few days later, the car was gone. By that time, a police appeal for witnesses to a hit-and-run by a drunk driver a few nights before had been on the radio. When he shows me the photographs, which he printed in his own darkroom to avoid a paper trail, Greg tells me that as the woman Lyla hit is likely to make a full recovery, he'll sit on the photos for sixty days as a courtesy to me. Then he'll take them to the police.

I almost have second thoughts at this point. Will's crime seems impersonal and all Henry is really guilty of is cheating on his wife, but Lyla's crime has a face to it. I debate going to the police straight away but the woman she hit is already out of intensive care. I know I could do something more with them. It doesn't make me feel great morally – to be honest none of this does – but I'm not going to break my promise.

I look at the photographs and the financials most nights.

I know I have to do something with them, but I don't know what. The obvious thing to do would be to go to the police myself. Although the woman who was hit was not badly injured, Lyla needs to pay for her crime. Will too. But I haven't followed up Helen's leads on Will and the evidence against Lyla is circumstantial. Who is to say with a smart lawyer they might not get off with little more than a slap on the wrist? It doesn't feel personal enough. I want them to know the creep of dread when you realise the one thing you didn't want anybody knowing about is being brought out into the open. To know that blink of a moment before your whole life implodes. There must be a way. I might not be as resourceful as Helen but I can find it. And when the stiff, ivory, gilt-edged reunion invitation drops on to our doormat a few days later, I can't help thinking it's almost as though she's organised it.

Thirty

Now

23.45

15 minutes to go

'I don't believe you.' I shake my head. But even as I'm saying it, I'm thinking of how Nick's been happy for me to skip the reunions all these years, how close he's stuck to me all night, how nervous he was about me coming. All these things I mistook for concern could have been him covering his tracks. I don't want it to be true.

'I thought you knew. When you got married, I thought you'd made your peace with it because of the other ... benefits.'

The sympathy daubed across her face makes me feel worse. 'Why should I believe you? How do I know you're not just trying to fuck up my life again?'

'Because I saw him.' And there's such finality in the way she says it, I know it's true.

'How?'

'I'd forgotten my contact lens solution. I was on my way back to Henry's and I saw him standing there and—'

'So, you actually saw him take it?' I demand.

'I know I should have done something, but I was so angry with you about that stupid drink.' She shakes her head. 'He was standing over you with the camera. I'm sorry.'

'He might not have been the one that uploaded it.'

'What?'

'You didn't see him do that, did you? It's not like he even lived on that staircase. Maybe someone found the camera.'

'Emmy, I saw him there later that morning when I woke up. That girl with frizzy hair he was dating lived there. I'm so sorry. I swear I thought you knew.'

The condescension in her tone hardens me. 'Do you really think I'd have married him if I knew?'

'But he, you, he said . . .'

'Spit it out, Lyla. What exactly did he say in all your little chats? You've certainly had enough of them. Do you know what, you're so tight with him maybe you should have married him?'

She tries to hide it but Lyla's lip curls.

Even now, given what she's done, she's so sure she's better than me. 'If he's so beneath you, why are you cosying up to him every five seconds?'

'That's business.' Lyla looks baffled. 'What with the new clinic—'

'Oh yes, the new clinic. La-di-da. Lyla conquers the world again. Well, Nick's hardly your target audience. We've got kids. We don't need you marketing yourself like the fucking Mother Teresa of the fertility world. I know what you're really like.'

'What do you mean?'

Forget the email, I've had enough of this charade. It's time to call her out on what she's done. I need to see her face. 'I know what you did.'

'We've been through this.' Lyla's starting to look bored. 'You know I didn't take that picture.'

'I'm not talking about me. I'm talking about what you did to that woman. On Daglish Road.'

'What are you talking about?' Lyla darts a looks over her shoulder. She needn't bother to be cagey. The whole year will know what she's been up to when that email pops into their inboxes.

'I know you were involved in a hit-and-run. And I've got photos to prove it.'

'What?' Even the Botox can't stop her forehead creasing into a worried frown.

'Yeah, that's right. Turns out the right photos can fuck up your life, can't they?'

She starts looking around more wildly now. If it wasn't all so sordid, I'd feel triumphant. 'I don't understand.'

'Unfortunately for you, I hired a PI to tail you a couple of weeks after the crash. He saw the damage to your car and put two and two together. Just like the police will after I go to them.'

'You don't have any proof I did anything. My car could

have been damaged by any number of things.' She folds her arms but her self-assurance has gone.

'I'm sure it won't take the police long to find some. The marvels of modern science. As you'd know.'

There's a long pause.

'The clinic will fold without me,' Lyla says defiantly.

'Remind me why I should care.'

'If my clinics go under, you and Nick lose your investment.'

'What investment?'

'The seed investment?' I know Lyla is registering my blank look by the grin that spreads across her face. 'I couldn't have done it without Nick. Didn't you wonder why I called it The Artemis Group? Frankly I'd have called the latest clinic the Nick Toller Appreciation Project, given that he stumped up close to half a mill for it. I won't be the only one ruined if the clinics fold.' She looks at me closely. 'You did know, didn't you?'

'Of course I knew,' I snap.

Of course I didn't know. I've always left the finances to Nick. It's only with Helen's money that I've even thought of myself as having any right to our savings or the money he makes. Another realisation lands like a boot in my chest.

'When you say half a million pounds . . .' It pains me to ask. 'What exactly do you mean?'

'Four seven five.' Lyla rattles it off like it's pocket change. 'He wasn't sure if he was going to be able to come up with it with everything that's going on in the world, but he came through a couple of weeks ago. Family money, wasn't it?'

The bottom falls out of my stomach. Even with everything I'm discovering about Nick, taking Helen's money is a new low.

'I want it back.'

'Sorry?'

'That money wasn't Nick's to lend. I want it back.'

'I don't think you quite understand. It wasn't a loan; it was an investment.'

'I'm not an idiot, I understand what an investment is. But that wasn't Nick's money to invest. It was mine.' I put extra emphasis on my final words. 'And I want it back. Now.'

'And as I said, that's not possible.' Her tone matches mine. 'You're all in. For a lot more than four seven five, given what Nick's put in over the years.'

'How long exactly?' I'm not even sure I want to know.

'About ten years. Pretty much your whole marriage.' Her eyes are bright like a bird's. She thinks she's won. I think of my happiest times with her, lying on The Backs while the boys rowed, sipping Pimm's so sticky it attracted a swarm of wasps, and wonder whether our friendship was ever anything but a competition.

'Why him?'

'What?'

'Why did you go to him for money? You could have asked your parents. It's not like you guys were friends at university.'

'Well, I knew—'

'I'll tell you what you knew,' I interrupt. 'You knew what he'd done. You saw him taking that picture and then you sat on it and waited until you could make use of it. Just like you always do. You asked him for money, because you knew if you didn't get it you could always threaten to let slip that it was him who took it. Your whole fucking empire's built on what he did to me.'

'Don't be ridiculous. I told you I thought you knew.' But she's looking everywhere but me.

'But you didn't bother to check.'

'It's not my job to check who you're dating—'

'No, you're right, it's not.' I look at her standing there, pink sapphire earrings swinging, face still as lovely as ever, and feel contempt rather than competition. 'I've spent fifteen years thinking you betrayed me taking that photograph in the heat of the moment. What you did was worse.' I shake my head. 'You should have come to see me at the time and told me then. That's what a real friend would have done. But we were never that, were we? So forgive me if I don't really care what happens to you. I'm taking the evidence I've got to the police first thing tomorrow. I don't care what happens to your clinic.'

I walk off without giving her the chance to reply. I can see everyone staring but nobody approaches. I obviously look like an unexploded bomb. Or else they all want me to go so they can start gossiping about me again. For once, I don't really care either way. I need to find Nick. Even though the thought of seeing him makes my skin crawl, I have to know why he did it. Before I can make it out, Liz sidles up.

'Emily, please can I have a word?'

'I don't really have time for a half-arsed apology, Liz.'

I see Dave and Emma among a crowd shrugging on their coats. Emma lifts a hand and waves. I can't believe I felt that Nick and I were superior to them when they were squabbling over the NHS.

'There's something I need to say.'

'Let me guess,' I reel off. 'You're sorry you put the picture up tonight. You thought I knew. That I'd love to be reminded of the worst night of my life and that I get off on posing in my underwear.' I pause. I can't bring myself to ask if she knows that Nick took the photograph. It's too humiliating.

'I'm sorry.' She hangs her head.

'You should be.' I look over her shoulder but there's still no sign of Nick. What am I even going to say when I do find him? 'Was there anything else?'

'I thought I was going to marry Nick, you know?' she says earnestly. 'Back then. We talked about it at university and after we graduated. We were going to move in together, we were talking to his parents about a loan and then out of nowhere he wants time on his own. I was having pizza with his mum and dad one minute, the next he's telling me he wants to be young and single. He married you about five minutes later. How do you think that made me feel?'

'I'm not your therapist. I don't care.' It's bitchy but she deserves it after what she did tonight. She doesn't react.

'That's not what I wanted to talk to you about.'

'What else could there possibly be to say?' My brain can't even begin to process what Nick's done. It keeps flipping between him taking the photo and him stealing

Helen's money, without getting any further, like a CD jumping between two tracks.

'There's something else I need to tell you.'

'Look, Liz, whatever it is you have to say, I don't care, all right? I just want to—'

'I spiked your drink that night.'

'You did what?'

'It was supposed to be a joke.' The horror I'm feeling is reflected on her face. She rushes on. 'I was jealous of you. I thought if you got really drunk and made a fool of yourself, you'd be a bit more human. It would bring you down a peg or two.'

'I was never anything but nice to you.'

'That made it even worse!' Liz exclaims, then puts her hands to her cheeks. 'I'm sorry. What I did was horrible, but just imagine for one second what it's like to be around someone that seems to have it all. It all seemed to come so easily to you. I could see the way Nick looked at you whenever you went past. I thought if I could just bring you down to our level, give you something that would make you make a fool of yourself, you wouldn't be so perfect.'

'Me, perfect?' I don't have the energy to explain to her how much my world was imploding already that night, how hard I worked to get into Cambridge, how out of place I felt until I got together with Henry. Looking back at the fragments of that night that I remember, it starts to make sense. That's why I was so out of it. It really wasn't my fault. I almost smile but I don't want to let Liz off the hook.

'What did you give me?'

'It was ketamine. Only a very small dose. I made sure of that.' She rushes on as if the amount can justify what she did. 'My brother's an obstetrician,' she says urgently. 'So I knew it was pure, that it wasn't cut with anything. I told Jamie it was for me. Something to cut loose after finals. I put it in the alcopop you were drinking. I didn't know what was going to happen. When you disappeared, I thought you'd gone to sleep it off. I had no idea you hadn't agreed to that picture being taken. I didn't even make the connection until tonight.'

'When you uploaded that very same picture? Yeah, right.'

'I mean it. I wish I could take it back.'

I look at Liz, the person who unwittingly kicked this whole thing off, and I want to punish her.

'I'm sure you do. Your brother will, too, when I report him to the medical board.' I have no idea whether there is a medical board or how you go about reporting someone to it, but it's worth it to see the look on her face. Helen would know, I remind myself. The thought of her makes me stronger.

'You wouldn't?' Her face drains of colour.

'Really?' I raise my eyebrows. 'He should be ashamed of himself supplying medical drugs to students.'

'You can't.' She puts her hand on my arm to beg me but I shake it off. I know this is misplaced anger, that it's Nick I'm really furious at, but it feels good.

'What's going on?' The tall burly guy I saw Liz with earlier comes over.

'Swapping stories of happier times.' I give him a wide fake smile.

'Liz?' he asks.

'Oh, Dom.' She melts into him like some sort of helpless female. My dislikes of her congeals. 'I'm so worried about Jamie. She says she's going to . . .' She breaks off and collapses into tears.

'What's your problem?' He glares at me. 'You've been making trouble all evening.'

'See you around, Liz.' I give her a wave. 'Give my best to your brother. Jamie, wasn't it? James Tripp. One of those names you don't forget.'

'Please don't do this,' Liz begs. 'I'll do anything.'

'She's not worth it, Liz. Stuck-up cow like that, she'll get what's coming to her,' Dom says.

I ignore him. I think of Helen again and what it is to lose a sibling. I'm not going to tell anyone about what Liz's brother did. But she doesn't have to know that. Let her know what it's like to live in fear for a bit.

'Just tell me one thing.' At this point, I don't care about losing my dignity in front of Liz. Hers is long gone. 'Was Nick there when you did it? When you spiked me?'

Her eyes widen but she doesn't say anything. The pause is more damning than any words. Any last bit of affection I had for Nick starts to wither.

'After all this time, you're still protecting him?'

'Please, I'm begging you, don't say anything about my brother. I'm sorry.'

Another jigsaw piece of the picture of a husband I don't know at all slots into place. I turn away.

'So am I.'

Thirty-One

Then

'Nick?' I'm in the alcove off the family room, trying to access online banking on our ancient family Mac, when I hear the front door open and close.

'Uh-huh.' He comes up behind me and starts kneading my shoulders.

'Do you know how long the bank takes to clear things?'

He takes his hands off my shoulders and leans forward to look at the screen. 'What do you mean?'

'The money from Helen's estate.' I hate reducing my sister to 'an estate'. 'The solicitor who was doing probate said it should come in sometime this week.'

'Hmm . . .' Nick nudges me to the side of the swivelly office chair and sits down next to me. 'What are you looking at?'

'I'm trying to access the joint account but I can't see it.'

'Are you sure you're putting in the right password?'

'I know what my password is.' At least I think I do. To be honest, so many things seem to demand the kind of password that looks like a mouse ran across your keyboard, now I'm not sure.

'Do you want me to try? I can log in on the app.' Nick gets out his phone. 'When did you last check it?'

'This morning.'

He stops what he's doing and gives me a hard look.

'What?' I say.

'A watched pot never boils. Isn't that the expression?'

'You sound like your mother.'

'Don't pout. Right.' He starts scrolling through the account so quickly that all I can see is a series of numbers swimming in front of me. 'No sign of any large deposits. Worse luck. How much was it again?'

'Four hundred and seventy-five thousand pounds.' Even though this house is worth almost four times as much, the figure sounds huge. Possibly because it's the first time it's come from my side, rather than Nick's.

'Nope, no sign.' He puts his phone face down on the computer table and gives me a sympathetic smile. 'Why don't I call the bank in the morning? Sometimes these big deposits get held for a few days until they clear. Anti-money laundering and all that.'

'Don't worry, I can do it. I'm not at school tomorrow. I'm free all day.' Actually, I promised Tiff I'd swing by the new restaurant she's managing but I can work around that. 'I can even go into the branch if needs be.'

'Now, don't take this the wrong way, but don't you think going into the bank might be too much for you? This whole thing has really knocked you for six. Understandably.' He holds up his hand before I can protest. 'Losing Helen has been devastating for all of us. Especially you. I worry you going into the bank to have to rehash the whole thing while it's all so raw might be too painful. Better to wait ... or let me do it for you.'

'I'll be fine.'

'Let me be the judge of that. Come on, I'm happy to help.'

'If you're sure?' The idea of not having to dig around in Helen's finances is tempting.

'You know I want to look after you. Leave it to me.'

'Thank you.' I press myself against him gratefully.

'What did you want the money for, anyway?' He leans over and closes down the computer over my shoulder.

'Nothing major.' I stand up. 'Thought I might treat myself to some new clobber for the big reunion and wanted to check I had the cash.' Less clobber, more armour. If I'm going to have my day in court, so to speak, I want to make sure I look good.

'What reunion?'

I look at him in surprise. Nick's back and forth from Cambridge so often I joke they should give him frequent flyer points. How can this have slipped his mind?

'The fifteen-year reunion? The one with the champagne reception Will Jenkin's sponsoring.' I force myself to speak naturally, even though I can't stand the sound of that name in my mouth.

'Oh, that.' Nick shifts on his feet. 'I guess I'd forgotten.'

'You'd forgotten?'

'I've had quite a lot on my mind.' He sounds defensive and I feel bad. He's been carrying a lot of the burden since Helen died.

'Sorry.' I reach out and rub his shoulder. 'Anyway, don't worry, I RSVPed for us both. We're in. We just need to book a hotel.'

'You're sure you want to come? It won't bring back too many bad memories?'

'Maybe it's time to make new ones,' I say determinedly.

'Maybe you're right. We can stick together. I tell you what, I won't leave your side. And I promise we'll have a great time. I'll book somewhere nice, away from college. Don't bother to wait for that money. Put your dress on my credit card. Treat yourself. I don't want to see you in anything you can get on the high street.'

'Are you sure?'

Nick's firm continues to make worrying noises about mass redundancies. They call it restructuring but Nick says it isn't looking good. The uncertainty is one of the reasons I wanted to use my money to buy the dress.

'I'm sure. If a joint university reunion isn't grounds for a joint account purchase, I don't know what is!' Nick tugs at the end of my ponytail. 'You should get your hair done, too. Really push the boat out. See if they can fit you in this weekend.'

'It's not for a little bit yet.'

'So . . . ?' Nick kisses my neck.

'I don't think you understand much about women's hair.'

'Probably not.' Nick trails kisses from the back of my neck around to the front of my throat. 'Where are the kids?'

'Xander's at football. Artie's at swimming.' I hold my

arm up so I can see my watch face. 'I need to leave to pick them up in about ... twenty minutes.'

'I'll be quick.' Nick pulls the neck of my sweatshirt down and bites my shoulder.

'I haven't had a shower today. I just got back from the gym,' I warn him.

He slides his hands around my waist, his fingers almost meeting as he pings the waistband of my leggings. 'You know I like you dirrrty.'

I allow him to work the leggings down my legs until I'm standing there in the sweater, my underwear and a pair of socks.

'I feel like I'm in some eighties workout video.' I laugh as he sits down on the swivel chair in front of the computer and pulls me on to his lap.

'Stop talking,' he mock-growls, burying his face in my chest. He pulls the sweatshirt over my head and I try to get myself into the mood. I can feel him hard against my thigh.

I kiss his lips, his eyelids and his face, reminding myself how lucky I am to have him and how supportive he's been since Helen died. His hands are inside my jumper, toggling my nipples like he's trying to find a radio frequency, but there isn't time to remind him I prefer to be touched gently. He's been so stressed at work I know he needs this. I manoeuvre myself so he can slide my underwear aside and push himself inside me. I feel a jolt of pain because my body isn't ready but I tighten my legs and ignore it. There's only a limited time before I have to leave the house so I can't tell him to slow down. I remind myself how lucky I am as, with a huge convulsion, I feel him climax. 'That was amazing.' He buries his head in my shoulder. 'Did you want to . . . ?' He walks his fingers up the inside of my thigh. I wriggle out of the way.

'You can do me next time.' Oh, the glamour of married sex.

I'm hopping around on one leg trying to put my clothes back on when I realise he wouldn't normally be back at this time. 'You got let out of school early?' I say as I shimmy back into my leggings.

He's on the swivel chair, reading the sports results on the BBC website with his back to me.

'Nick?'

'Uh-huh?' He clicks on to another page.

'How come you're back so early? I thought you were trying to put in as much face time as possible at the moment.'

'I am.'

'Sooo . . . did you get let off for good behaviour?'

'No.' His hand pauses on the mouse.

'I feel like I'm conducting the Spanish Inquisition here?' His ramrod-straight posture is starting to make me feel on edge. 'Is everything okay?'

'If you must know, I got made redundant.' Hurt pride makes him sound like a sulky child.

'Oh my God, Nick, are you okay?' I fly towards him but he bats off my attempts to put my arms around him.

'I'm fine.'

'What happened?' I try to moderate my tone. He doesn't need to deal with my worry on top of his own.

'They're closing the London office. They had a big

town hall meeting and called us all in and then top brass in Houston told us they could no longer make a business case for it. Turns out there's not much oil in London. Who knew?'

'What are we going to do?' I'm careful to say 'we' rather than 'you'. I don't want him to feel alone. It's times like these that make me realise how little I contribute and how much Nick has to carry. And how much my not being able to go to America held him back. I dig my thumb into my palm, worrying at the inside of my knuckles. I wonder if he ever regrets marrying me. 'There's always Helen's money.'

'Don't be ridiculous.' Nick stands up. 'I don't need a handout from your sister. It's nothing to worry about. I've got a three-month notice period anyway and I've been there for the best part of eighteen years. That's one hell of a redundancy package.'

'Are you sure? I could ask school if there are any paid positions going, or . . .'

'Don't worry about it. I've got plenty of other things going on apart from oil. Some lucrative investments to tide us over even if I don't find something else. Which I will.'

'Are you sure?' I don't want him to see that I'm worried. I wish I could wear problems as lightly as Nick does. It's a skill.

'I'm sure.' He kisses me on the head. 'Now, don't you have some children to ferry around? I'm going to have a beer. I think I've earned one. Shall we have a takeaway for dinner?'

I watch him pad down the hall towards the kitchen.

I wonder whether I should wind back my plans for the reunion in light of his redundancy. But he doesn't seem fazed. And I need to do this. Then we can get on with the rest of our lives. I grab my coat from the bottom of the banisters and hurry to the car. There's less time than I wanted to pick the twins up. Halfway to the local leisure centre, I realise I've forgotten to pack snacks for them to have in the car. I'm so busy debating where I can stop to pick up something en route – will the deli on Half Moon Lane be open or should I swing by Whole Foods? – that I'm barely thinking about Nick's redundancy by the time I pull into the car park. And I'm not thinking about Helen's money at all.

Thirty-Two

Now

Midnight

'Are you okay?' I feel someone touch me on the arm. I look around to see Emma and Dave, their heads tilted at matching angles. I'm not sure which one of them touched me. I wonder whether Nick and I were ever that in step. How can you be when the foundations are rotten?

'I'm fine.' I muster a smile. 'Just getting some air and thinking about grabbing a cab.'

It's too humiliating to tell them that I'm looking for my own husband. If I'm honest, I don't even know if I am any more. I think of all the lies he's told. I think of Helen's money. Lies he's still telling. I've spent years thinking I didn't deserve Nick and being grateful to him for never pressing me to tell him what happened that night. I never imagined it was because he already knew. I can't believe I never guessed. I feel as though every single framed photo in our house was mounted to mock me.

'Can we give you a lift somewhere?'

'That's so kind, but I'm waiting for someone.' I'm desperate for them to leave me alone.

'I think we're the last.' Dave follows my gaze back towards the Great Hall. 'If that helps.'

'Cheers,' I say, hoping they'll get the hint. Dave does. He gives Emma a squeeze around the shoulder and lumbers off. She stays put. I wonder if she knows that it was Nick who took the photo. She must be wondering where he is, why I'm on my own. I catch the thought before it balloons. If tonight's proved one thing, it's that people really only think about themselves.

Emma grinds her heel into the gravel. 'I wanted to say I'm sorry about what happened to you. You were really brave up there.'

'Thank you.'

'I'm sorry I wasn't there for you.'

She looks like she's about to cry, which somehow makes me feel worse. The idea that Emma, who I never hung around with at college, might think that she could do something proves how poorly I chose the people to surround myself with. I think of Nick, the man I married. Still choose poorly.

'I never realised any of it. I always thought you and Will made such a great couple.'

'We never dated.'

'No, no, I know.' She looks mortified. 'I'm so sorry, I just mean, you know, whenever I saw you together. You

288

were always laughing. And he seemed so proactive afterwards, getting the picture taken down and getting rid of any printouts.'

'There were printouts?' Of course there were.

'Not many,' she scrabbles. 'I just meant he dealt with all that fallout. Deleting all the comments, putting up the firewall, making sure people couldn't access the photo. You'd never have guessed what part he played ...' Her voice falls away. 'I'm making it worse, aren't I?'

'You're not.' I smile stiffly. 'But I could use a bit of time on my own.'

'Of course.' She leaps back like I'm contagious. Maybe I am. Nothing good seems to befall those who get close to me. 'I'm sorry.'

I close my eyes and listen to the sound of the gravel as she hastens to catch up with Dave. I'd want to get the hell away from me too if I were them. I have the opposite of the Midas touch – everything I touch turns to shit. Is this my fault? Have I done this to Nick? How did I not know? All these years together and I never realised what kind of person he was. I need to find him. I don't think I can stand to be in the same room as him but I need to find him. To find out why.

I think I feel Will before I see him. Some people have that kind of presence. Romantic heroes. Evil spirits. Anyway, something makes me turn. There he is, standing next to a clump of ivy and glaring. Guilt churns with dread. I remind myself that whatever else happened, Will left me lying there on the grass and took off my bra without my consent. I might not remember anything else, but I remember his hands. That much I know.

'Quite a shitstorm you've stirred up in there.' His expression is so cold it's unrecognisable. Normally he's smiling or laughing. It's a shock to see his face so still.

'I . . .'

The chapel clock strikes midnight. Nick's got my phone but I imagine screens across the campus, stuffed in pockets, lying next to people who've already gone to bed, all lighting up as my grenade of an email drops into their inbox. At the very least, I should warn him.

'Will, I—'

Someone huge and blonde comes barrelling around the side of the building before I can finish.

'Have you seen it?' Henry's tuxedo is torn and he's panting. Will turns to him and they exchange a meaningful look. Out of nowhere a scene from some horror movie I watched when I was a teenager springs to mind. When there was not one killer, but two. It's only the three of us outside. Other than the dull glow of the old-fashioned lamp posts that mark the corners of the quad, the only light is coming from one window of the porters' lodge. That's at least 500 metres away. The bar is closed and all the accommodation is on the other side of the grass. College has never felt emptier.

'It was you, wasn't it?' Henry starts to advance, jabbing his finger through the air at me. 'You sent that email. You gave my wife those photos. What are you playing at?'

I notice the skin under his fingernails is dirty. Where's he been? I shrink back against the wall. It's hard to let go of the idea that Henry uploaded the photo. I've held on to it for so long. I'm still afraid of him. I used to see his decisiveness as a sign of confidence, rather than control. I think of his 'five out of ten' comment and all the other times he put me down, his hand striking Freja's face. He was a bully at college; he's a bully now.

He steps closer, right into my face. Up close, his eyes are bloodshot. The features I once held above others are all wrong. His cheekbones are too sharp; his nose is too long. His hairline's a centimetre further back than it should be. I smell booze on his breath. 'Why would you do that?'

'Leave it, mate,' Will interjects. 'This isn't the way.'

While Henry's voice is smudged by alcohol, Will sounds crisp, like he's sober and rational. But I saw the look in his eyes. And I know what he's capable of. Or perhaps I don't. And that makes it worse.

'You haven't seen it, have you? She's sent the whole fucking college an email.'

'What?' Will turns sharply.

'You need to look at it, buddy. Now.'

'It doesn't matter.' Will dismisses it. 'I can scrape the server.'

'Buddy, you need to look at it. It's got details of those Russian deals, it makes me look like some kinds of paedo and there's some shit about Lyla in a car. It looks bad.' He scrabbles around in his pocket for his phone and holds it up to Will's face. 'It says it's from a "wellwisher" but it's blatantly her. She's not even denying it. See?'

Will grits his teeth and pulls his phone out of his pocket, ignoring Henry's. His eyes scan the screen.

'I told you.' Henry is dancing on his feet like a pugilist. 'I fucking told you.'

'And I told you, it's not a problem.' Will taps furiously at his phone then smiles and puts it away. Memories of other times Will covered for Henry push their way to the front of my mind; the elaborate excuses he always offered to explain Henry's Saturday-morning absences; the time Henry urinated on the steps of the library after a huge fight with his dad and Will took the rap. He's always cleaned up after Henry. Like Helen did for me. It's for her that I stand taller. What are they really going to do to me, anyway? This is reality, not some film. We're in the middle of a Cambridge college. All I have to do is scream.

'Not a problem?' Henry roars. 'Freja's gone. I've got nothing. And if that email gets out, I'll lose my job, my reputation . . . every damn thing.'

It says a lot about Henry that he thinks being outed as gay will ruin his life. If he'd shown one iota of humanity tonight, I'd feel sorry for him. But I don't. Now he knows what it's like to be stripped of things he holds dear. Whatever he did or didn't do, he kept me in my place for three years. Being with him made me a lesser version of myself. I still lost something. Satisfaction must show in my face because Henry grabs me by both shoulders, knocking one of the straps of my dress.

'Don't you fucking smirk at—'

Will hauls him off. 'I told you; I've got it covered. It won't get out. Those emails are being recalled as we speak. I've got a team on it. Go home, sort things out with the missus, sleep it off. I'll tidy up.'

He and Henry lock eyes like two lions fighting over a kill. There's something creepy about the way Will said 'tidy up'. It makes me think of quicklime and buried bodies. I tell myself I've read too many Stephen Kings. All the same, I find myself slithering down the wall away from them.

'You stay where you are,' Will barks.

I freeze. I didn't realise he'd seen me.

'Go,' he jabs his fist at Henry. 'I've told you I'll take care of her.'

'Enjoy,' Henry says unpleasantly and starts to lumber off, his shirt hanging out of the back of his jacket and the bottom of his trousers covered in mud. When he's rounded the corner, Will shucks off his jacket and rolls up his sleeves. I tense. Is he going to hit me? But instead of raising his fists, he holds the jacket out.

'Here.' It flaps in the breeze. 'Take it. You're shivering.'

'I'm fine.' I wrap my arms around myself again. I'm not taking anything from him. I look around as if Nick might suddenly appear. 'I've got to go.'

'Suit yourself.' He shrugs back into it. 'Nice and toasty. So here we are again. This time, I'm a fucking date rapist, am I?'

'I never said that.'

'As good as. And now there's this email.'

'You can't prove I sent that.' I press myself against the wall.

'Doesn't matter. I've shut it down. Didn't happen. Nobody's seen it. It's not true, anyway.' He steps closer. 'What I want to know is why you were coming for me, after everything I've done for you.'

'You left me outside on the quad in the middle of the

night,' I explode. 'You took my clothes off. I thought you were my friend.'

'What are you talking about?' He looks appalled. 'Don't you remember—'

'That's the whole point.' Tears of frustration threaten to muffle my voice. I cough angrily. 'I don't remember. All I know is that one minute I was fine, the next I was waking up outside your room in my underwear. And your hands . . .' I shake my head. I never have been able to get the image of those hands out of my mind. 'I thought we were friends. But you dropped me like I was a piece of crap. And you never once—'

'You really don't remember a thing?'

'No.' But now, standing here staring at him, I'm no longer sure if that's quite true. It feels like a swarm of memories are hovering just out of reach. If I could just reach for them. I no longer know if I want to.

'I need to find my husband.'

He kicks at the gravel and swears under his breath. 'There I was thinking you were just being a bad sport about it.'

The words buzz in my ears. I've heard him say them before. He's still kicking the gravel and swearing under his breath, but the ground has started shifting beneath my feet. The buzzing gets louder.

'Well, sweetheart, this is your lucky day,' he says. 'Or not, depending on how you look at it. Because I remember every damn second.'

The air feels loaded and heavy, like it does right before it rains. I can still feel the hurt and humiliation, but behind it, for the first time, there's something else. I shake my head. 'I don't want to know.'

'Too bad.' Will grabs my arm and tries to pull me up the stairs. 'You don't get to choose any more.'

'I'm not going anywhere with you.' I try to shake him off but he's too strong. All the while, the swarm is getting closer.

'I'm afraid you don't get a say.' He heaves me up the stone stairs, through the medieval archway and into the building. Gripping my arm, he throws open the door to the room I've been avoiding all night. The swarm descends. The smell of damp umbrellas and stale comestibles brings it all rushing back. Even before he pushes me over the threshold and throws the lock behind us, I know. None of it happened the way I thought I did. I've been wrong this whole time.

Thirty-Three

Then

There's something soft against my cheek. My arms and legs are pinned down but it's not uncomfortable. I half open my eyes and look around, trying to get a feel for where I am. The first thing I see is a picture of Britney Spears in her iconic school uniform, shirt tied at the waist exposing perfect abs, leering down at me.

I snap my eyes open. There's a college scarf slung across the open wardrobe door and a pair of dirty rugby boots strewn across the floor. Next to Britney on the wood-panelled wall is a signed poster of the winning English Rugby World Cup side. I know instantly that I'm in Will's bedroom. My hands fly to my shoulders, which are bare. I start giving myself a subtle police brush down, trying to work out what I'm wearing. The last thing I remember is bumping into him in the anteroom. And throwing the drink over Henry. I close my eyes again. What have I done?

'I only took your shoes off. Scout's honour.' I can hear

him but I can't see him. There's an open door between the wardrobe and the chimney breast, leading into a separate study area. I shuffle forwards and crane my neck around it. Will is sitting at a desk by the window drinking a can of Coke.

'I doubt you were ever a scout.' I feel disorientated and embarrassed. My head feels tight, as though there's a migraine waiting in the wings. Or one hell of a hangover. How much did I drink tonight?

'You'd be surprised by what I can do with a knot.'

His words hang in the air like they're supposed to mean something else. I twist uncomfortably. Did something happen between us earlier tonight? Why can't I remember?

'I should get back.' I straighten my clothes under the covers, feeling relieved to discover that he was telling the truth and that my clothes all appear to be intact. There's something about this situation that I don't trust. I want to get out of here. I pull back the quilt and half tumble out of the bed on to the floor.

'Classy.'

'Says a guy with Britney Spears on his wall. Do you know where my shoes are?'

'By the sink.' He points. 'I had to rinse them out after you made me down drinks out of them. They're a bit wet. You might want to wait a while for them to dry out.'

I wrinkle my forehead at the vague recollection. 'I didn't make you. Wait, if my shoes were wet, how did I get back here?'

'I carried you.'

Embarrassment flares again. 'Oh.'

He gets up from the desk and comes over to the doorway, his broad frame filling the space. 'You were quite funny, really.'

His use of the word 'quite' makes me cringe. It's so patronising.

'I'm sorry.' I press my teeth into my bottom lip. It stings. I touch my finger to my mouth. It feels swollen. I look up at Will, leaning against the doorframe. A memory flutters. Did we kiss? It's hardly something I can ask.

Will takes another sip of Coke, then crushes the can and flicks it neatly into his wastepaper bin. 'You were bouncing off the ceiling when I first got you back here,' he says, even though I haven't asked. 'Making all kinds of crazy suggestions.'

I put my head in my hands and squeeze my eyes tight shut. I wish I could remember something. Anything. Even if it was bad. The only positive about this situation so far is that I'm still wearing my clothes.

'Quite a set of pipes you've got, too. Kept singing "Hungry Like the Wolf" and howling. Of course that was before you jumped on my bed and . . .' He raises his eyebrows suggestively.

I adjust my fingers across my face, creating a slat that I can see him through. 'Did we . . .' I squeeze the words out.

'What do you take me for?' Will laughs. 'I'm a gentleman, you know.'

'So nothing happened?' My voice is tinged with relief. I hope he doesn't notice.

'You were pretty much all over me before we got back here,' he says. 'But you were too out of it to know what you wanted. So I put you to bed and came out here. You snore pretty badly, you know. Hawksmoor never let that one slip.'

I feel a blaze of shame. There's something locker room about the way he's talking. He's obviously trying to embarrass me. It's working. I stand up. If only I'd gone back to my own room last night. I walk over to where he's standing and try to duck under his arm. 'I think I'll grab those shoes now.'

He reaches out a hand and blocks the way. 'Come on. You're talking to someone who regularly sees guys set fire to themselves for fun. I'm unshockable. Don't be a bad sport.'

Of course, he would use a sports analogy. This isn't a game.

'I'm not. I need to get back.'

'Sure you don't want to stay? I won't tell if you won't.'

'I . . .' Two seconds ago he was rejecting me. Now he's propositioning me. I don't get him.

He shrugs and lets me through. 'Your loss. There's a hairdryer in my desk drawer if you want to dry the shoes out. I would have stuffed 'em with newspaper but *Varsity*'s not out until tomorrow.'

'My sister used to write for *Varsity*.'

'No offence. Do you want the hairdryer?'

'You've seriously got a hairdryer?'

'This barnet doesn't style itself.' He tugs on his fringe. 'Do you want it or not?'

'Sounds good.'

I follow him over to his desk and watch as he flips

open the drawer. The hairdryer is lying among a tangle of belts, cufflinks and collar studs. I spot a pair of enamel cufflinks, embossed with the college's crest. I look at the twin lions snarling out of their magenta background.

'I gave a pair of these to Henry for graduation.'

'I know. He, um, passed them on to me.'

He hands me the hairdryer without looking at me. I feel even more of an idiot. Why did I waste my time or my money? I did the graveyard shift at the supermarket every night for two weeks to afford those.

'Like I said, he's not worth it. You're worth ten of him.'

Will's standing close enough that I can smell his after-shave. I don't know if it's that flash of humanity, the fact that he wears Allure, just like Henry, or just the need to escape from the idea that Henry really didn't care about me at all, but I drop the hairdryer and reach up and pull his face down to mine. It's the only way I can think of to get my dignity back. I can tell from his breathing that he's into it so I pull away to yank my top over my head. It's at this point he steps back.

'We can't.'

'What do you mean?' I reach for him again, but he sidesteps me.

'You know what I mean. We can't do this.'

'Why not?' I reach a hand behind my back to unhook my bra. It's the kind of bold move Lyla would make, not me. But we've all seen how well being myself has worked out for me. He puts his hand on my elbow, like he's apprehending me.

'I'm not saying I don't want to but you know this isn't a

good idea.' He stoops down and picks my top off the floor. 'Here. You better put this on.'

I feel a cold wash of humiliation. I snatch the top off him and hold it against my chest. 'Have it your way.'

'Don't be like that.' He shrugs like it's a simple disagreement over what film to see or whether it's time to go to bed.

I turn my back on him like he's a creepy PE teacher trying to perv on me in the changing rooms, not someone I was contemplating sleeping with, and try to wriggle into my top. The zip's jammed. 'How do you expect me to be?'

From behind me, I hear a sigh.

'You don't have to be so fucking patronising.' I whirl around with the top held against my chest. 'You asked me to stay. And you didn't have a problem being all over me earlier. I practically had to fight you off.'

I have no idea if that's true but he winces.

'So, I'll just get my shoes and be on my merry way. I won't trouble you or your "conscience" any more.' I fire off every word like a 'fuck you' and stomp over to get my shoes.

'Emmy.' Will comes up and hovers behind me.

'Don't call me that!'

'Fine. You don't have to go all radio rental on me.'

'Stop talking like that. You're not even cockney.'

'Fine. You're not being mental.' He sighs again, sounding even more put upon. 'But you know I'm not doing this to hurt your feelings. If things were different . . .'

'Spare me.' I try to push past him.

He puts his hands on the top of my arms. 'Listen—'

'Get your hands off me. I'm sick of people like you trying to make me do things I don't want to.'

'Hold on—'

'No, you hold on. I'm only here tonight because I got too out of it to know any better. Now I'm going to go back to my room and forget this ever happened. I can't wait to get out of this shithole. I hope I never see you again.'

'I don't think you should be walking home alone.'

'It's a bit too late to act like you give a shit.'

'It's dark out there. Let me grab my coat.' My words are rolling off his back as if they mean nothing. It makes me even angrier.

'You'd like that, wouldn't you? Another chance to get me alone in the dark. Sicko. Well, no thanks. I'm fine on my own. I always have been. Now get out of my way.'

I mean to push him lightly, to get him to move out of the way, but somehow he ends up stumbling back and falling on the bed. His head smacks the wall.

'You need to calm down.'

'Fuck you, Will.' I turn at the door to his room. 'Don't tell me what to do. And just so you know, I was thinking of Henry the whole time. I wouldn't even look at you if I were sober. Because you're always trying to be something you're not. You're a loser. And everyone knows it.'

'Fuck you, Emily.'

At last, I've got him. Now he knows how it feels to be humiliated. I jam my feet into my wet shoes and slam the door shut behind me. I stomp back into the entrance foyer and yank the door open, my feet squelching the whole way. A wave of cold air slaps me in the face. It's so dark that I can only make out the vague shape of the trees. Up towards the entrance to the college, the porters' lodge is glowing like a beacon but this section of the grounds is dark. I tuck my top into my bra to hold it in place, put a foot out towards the path and promptly fall flat on my face. I put my hands out to break my fall but my reactions aren't quick enough and I smack my head on the ground. The left side of my face takes the impact. My cheek burns from the scrape of the gravel. Nobody comes. I lie there for what feels like ages. Will's light goes out. My ears are ringing and what I can see in front of me is blurry. I give up and raise myself on to my knees. My head is banging like a jungle drum and what little I can see is blurred. One of my shoes has come off but I'm too exhausted to grope around for it in the dark. Hatred and resentment make me push my knees off the ground and press my feet into the gravel, wincing as it digs into the soles of my feet. I half limp, half hobble forward. I don't stop until I reach the steps of the chapel. I sink on to the top one. I feel dizzy and wonder if I'm concussed. Henry says you have to shine a light in your eyes to see if your pupils contract, but where am I going to get a light from? I'll be fine. I'll stop for a few minutes, until I'm strong enough to get up again. I bow my head against one of the chapel pillars and let my body slump down until I'm sprawled across the steps. Perhaps I'll have a quick rest before I move again. I close my eyes, even though the sun's starting to seep in, turning my vision red. I'm on the cusp of consciousness when I feel the hands around my waist. At first I think Will's come back to help me up. I wonder if he's got a light. I try to open my eyes but strong hands stroke them shut. I feel hands at the back of my bra, fumbling with the clasp.

'Wait,' I mumble, not sure if this is reality or the edge of a dream.

Then there's a flash. Is it outside or is it something to do with my blurry vision? I have no idea what's going on. It seems easier to let sleep claim me than worry about it now. My last thought before I drift off is how much I hate Will Jenkin.

Thirty-Four

Now

12.15

'Let me out.'

Will is standing against the door with his arms folded across his chest like a bouncer. 'Do you still need me to tell you what happened?'

I can't stop looking at his hands. His fingers are slender and tapered. The hands I remember were bigger, squarer. Hands I know well. I think of the flash of light. The kind a camera might make. The person who took the picture is the person who undressed me. Nick. I start shaking. This time Will does not offer me his jacket.

'So you've got there at last?' His eyes are burning with injustice.

'You didn't take off my bra, did you?' But I already know the answer.

'No.' He looks disgusted, either at the thought or at me for thinking it. Maybe both.

'Then it was ...' But I can't bring myself to voice the thought.

'Nick's the one who took the picture, isn't he?' I don't know if he's asking me a question or giving me an answer. I think of all the times I've willingly let Nick undress me. Those same hands manhandling me, creeping over my body without permission. I feel overwhelmed by the desire to vomit.

'How did you find out it was him?' I whisper. 'Was it Lyla?'

'Lyla?' Will snorts. 'Get real. She can't even turn a computer on in case she breaks a nail. I clocked it from the IP address.'

'What do you mean?'

'I had to have the IP address the shot was sent from if I was going to bury it. When I saw it was J staircase, I put two and two together. It was hardly going to be Hawksmoor, was it? He's far too self-centred to give a shit about what anyone else was up to. I thought it might be the girl for a while, Liz. But Toller spent his whole life on that staircase, hanging outside Henry's room trying to get eyes on you. Don't even think you knew he was alive. That's why I was surprised when you guys got hitched. Especially after the photograph. I figured you must have been a more forgiving person than me. And I was hardly in any position ...' He breaks off. 'You made it pretty clear it wasn't my place.'

'What do you mean, *you* buried it?' I swallow. I don't

want to think about Nick being obsessed by me. 'Helen was the one that stopped it going in the papers.'

'I'm sure she did.' Will half-shrugs. 'But I'm the one who wiped it off the web. I was sorry to hear about what happened to her, by the way. Cancer's a bitch.'

'You wiped it?' I brush past the reference. I don't need his sympathy. 'What do you mean?'

'I mean wiped.' Will's starting to sound annoyed. I don't blame him. 'Totally buried. Come on. You must have wondered why if you type your name into Google nothing to do with you comes up.'

'I never type my name into Google. I've always been too scared.'

'You should.' Will fishes out his phone and starts keying in. 'Even if you type in "Emily Wells" and "debauched Cambridge students run wild" or some other *Daily Mail*-style headline, you'll never see anything to do with it. The picture is gone. See?'

He brandishes his phone at me. A screen full of tiny images of Emily Wellses appears; not a single one of them is me. I look at the rows of thumbnails of different hair-styles and faces and wish I were one of them. I still don't understand what he's done.

'What did you do?' I peer at them.

'After I wiped them from the college servers, I planted so many fake Emilys – images and identities – that any-thing to do with that picture dropped off the algorithm. You'd have to go forty-two pages down a Google search to find anything to do with you.'

I put my hand to the back of my neck and start pinching

the skin. I've spent years thinking the Internet had something hanging over me like the sword of Damocles. Now he's telling me there's nothing there. All this time, the threat was much closer to home. 'Why would you do this?'

'Felt guilty, I suppose.' Will snorts again. 'I should never have let you go off in the state you were in. Mind you, I'd say you got your own back tonight.'

'I'm sorry.' I genuinely am. I don't know how I got it so wrong.

Will shrugs. 'I buried that email, so I guess we're quits. I did a lot of shit I wasn't proud of back then. I probably deserve it. I came to see you, you know,' he says. 'Afterwards. A couple of days after I saw the pictures. I should have come sooner, I know. But I was angry with you. By the time I got there, you'd already gone.' He gives a sad laugh. 'The bedders were all outside your room bitching about the Blu Tack on the walls. That's how I knew you weren't coming back. I tried to message you a few times, but you never replied.'

'I got rid of my phone,' I say absently. I think of Will banging on the door and me being already gone. Someone did care, after all.

'So can we talk about the elephant in the room now?'

'I don't know what you mean.'

'What happened afterwards ...' He looks at me meaningfully.

I curl my toes into my feet. Of course he couldn't just leave it at that. I have no interest in rehashing what happened afterwards. I need to cut this conversation short. Fast. 'I was hammered. I didn't know what I was doing.'

'Oh no, you don't get to use that old chestnut.' Will shakes his head. 'You can tell yourself that if it makes you feel better, but you weren't that pissed and you know it. Not then.'

He's obviously not going to drop it. I don't want to hurt him but there doesn't appear to be another way. I need to hit him where it hurts. 'Fine. If you really want to know why, it was because I wanted to get my own back on Henry. I thought you might tell him and he'd know how it feels when someone you care about shags your best friend.' It's thin but it might work. In my experience, if you dig deep enough into any friendship you'll find an insecurity. 'Now, can you please let me out? I need to go home.'

'It was more than that. You and I had a connection and you know it.'

If I didn't feel so anxious about this conversation, I would marvel at what it must be like to automatically assume everyone likes you. 'I was hammered, all right? Like I told you. I was trying to get the better of you, be the one who got to walk away.' Then, just to make sure he drops it, I go for the jugular. 'Come on. You didn't think it was because I actually liked you, did you?'

He looks like I've slapped him. I feel a moment of remorse but it's too late. His face has closed down. 'After all this time you're still a bitch.'

He grabs the iron bolt to the door and levers it up so hard the sound echoes around the room.

'I hope you get what's coming to you.' He walks out and slams the door behind him.

*

I don't know how long I stand there. Damp from the wall I'm leaning against has seeped into my bones. For someone who hates this room, I certainly seem to spend a lot of time in here. I don't know where else to go. I can't go back to the hotel. I feel sick to the stomach. My fight with Will has brought everything to the surface. There's such a strong parallel to what happened that night that when I hear the scrape of the door, I fully expect it to be Will coming back. But it's not Will at the door. It's Nick.

The skin around his eyes is starting to pouch the way it does when he's tired and there are lines around his mouth that weren't there before. He looks like he's aged about a hundred years. I know every plane of his face but I feel like I'm looking at a stranger.

'Emily. There you are.'

'Here I am.'

There's so much I want to say to him that I don't even know where to begin. There are so many questions I don't have the energy to ask. It's like pulling a thread. I want to know why and how he could do what he did but I don't think I can bear to be in the same room long enough to hear his answer. There's a pause then we both start speaking at once.

'Look, I'm sor—'

'Can I have the car keys?' I hold out my hand. 'I want to go home.'

'They're back at the hotel.' Nick dismisses the suggestion. 'I don't think you're in any state to drive.'

'And I don't think you're in any position to tell me what

to do.' I curl my hands shut. 'I'll go back to the hotel and get them, then.'

'Now, I know this has been an upsetting time with everything that's been going on but you're being irrational.' Nick is using the 'drawing matters to a close' voice he uses when he's telling the twins it's time for bed. The thought of all his lies swirling around them drives me on.

'*Irrational*? I'm being irrational, am I? Oh, silly me.'

'I think with everything that's happened with Helen, you're grieving. And that's making you blow things out of proportion.' Nick sounds like he's swallowed a self-help book. 'I'm not saying we don't have things to work out but the main thing is—'

'That's the best you can come up with? You know what, Nick? You should have crawled in here on your hands and knees. I don't even know what's worse; that you took that awful photo and put it online or that you kept it hidden from me for all of those years? That's not even touching on all the crap with Lyla and her clinic and the money you stole. But no. Instead, you come in here and have the nerve to tell me I'm fucking grieving.' Nick winces at the pro-fanity. I redouble it. 'Of course I'm fucking grieving. Only now I'm grieving for my marriage as well as my sister.'

'Just wait a—'

'Do you know you haven't even said sorry? Not once. For any of it. I can't stand to have you near me. Even breathing the same air as you is making me sick.'

'Emily, I *am* sorry. If you let me explain . . .'

'Go on then, explain.' I bark out a laugh. 'Only I don't think there's a sorry big enough to cover this.'

'I never meant for that picture to end up online.' He crinkles his eyebrows together beseechingly. It's learned behaviour. Xander does it. He uses it to get away with stealing biscuits out of the tin or reading an extra book after lights out. Not quite in the same league as explaining away a crime. 'I was waiting for Liz to get ready and I was fooling around on the computer and I pressed the wrong button ...'

His lie is laughably weak. 'You just happened to have the cable to connect the camera to the computer with you, did you? Quelle chance.'

'Honestly, it was an accident.' But Nick's eyebrows have dropped and his eyes are darting around the room. 'I didn't mean to hurt you.'

'You took my bra off!' I scream at him. One look at his face erases any last traces of doubt. 'That's right. I remember now. Everything. I was out of it. You should have woken me up and helped me. Not ...' I don't even have the words to finish the sentence.

'I'm sorry.' Nick's voice starts to thicken like he's on the edge of tears. I feel nothing but revulsion. This man is the reason I've felt like a victim for my entire life.

'Why?' I want him to make me understand. 'Why would you do it? I never did anything to you.'

'Because you didn't know I was alive,' he snaps. 'Do you know what it's like to know that the person you're meant to be with doesn't even know you exist? I tried everything.' It's like he hasn't heard me. 'I left notes in your pigeonhole, chocolate, I always offered to buy you drinks in the bar, I even tried to help you that night. And what did I get in return? You and your mates laughing at me behind my back.'

'We didn't laugh at you.'

'You called me Brian May,' he screams. 'Believe me, you laughed at me.'

'So this was your revenge, was it?' I take a step back. His anger's frightening. 'Public humiliation on a global scale.'

'I never meant to humiliate you.'

'What were you trying to do, then? Launch my career as a page-three girl?'

'I didn't even realise you were there.' He's pleading again. 'I was taking pictures of the college, I didn't even know it was you until I got closer. I didn't mean you any harm.'

'You stripped me and then took a picture.' Now I'm the one shouting. 'And you posted it online. How is that not meaning me harm? That's a fucking crime, Nick. Why did you do it?'

'I don't know.' He looks wretched but I don't feel an ounce of sympathy. I don't feel anything but disgust. 'I wasn't planning on doing anything with the picture. I was just going to keep it. But then I had this big fight with Liz and she said you'd never be interested in someone like me. And I thought of all the times you'd passed right by me and I wanted you to know what it felt like. The computer was right there. I wasn't thinking. I took it down when I realised it had got out of hand.'

'Out of hand?' I think of him holding my hand in the delivery suite of the hospital, his face sweaty and proud as first one twin then the next was passed to him before they were rushed off to the NICU. This man has wiped my tears; seen me sweat; made me come. Every intimate act now feels like a violation. I twist up my face. 'You ruined my life.'

'Emily . . .' He holds up his arms like he's trying to tame a wild beast. 'You said yourself it was just a photograph. You said yourself we've all done things we regret—'

'How dare you use my own words against me.' I feel bile building at the back of my throat again. 'You. You're the thing I regret.'

'Don't say that. We can go home, see the kids and—'

'I want a divorce.'

'Now you're being silly. If you'll let me—'

'I'm not letting you do anything again.' I think of all the decisions he's made for me, all the ways I've let him be in charge of my life. 'I'm going back to the hotel and I'm going to get into that car and I'm driving back to London. I suggest you take the train. By the time you get back, I will have packed you a bag.'

I feel a tug of my old self. The person I was before I came to Cambridge in the first place. I think of the money Helen put into my account and picture her standing on the sidelines, cheering me on.

'And what are you going to tell the children?' His need to be in charge has always run like a central vein down our marriage; me taking control is starting to rile him up. 'You might remember they're currently with *my* mother.'

'Don't worry, I won't let *Nonna* know that her son's a sexual predator.'

'Don't throw words like that around.'

'You undid my bra, Nick. When I was passed out. Not to mention putting that picture online. That's sick. If you'd done it now, you'd go to prison.'

'You'd struggle to make charges stick when you can't even remember what happened,' he blusters. 'That's before we've even got to the matter of the lawyer's bill.'

'Which I'd be able to pay if you hadn't stolen my sister's money.' My whole body pulses with hatred. 'How do you think the twins would take to finding out you're a common thief?'

'You leave my children out of this.'

I think of that hazy summer evening on Northcote Road when I told him I was pregnant and he spread the future out in front of us like a blanket. It seems to belong to another lifetime.

'They're not your children.' The words are out of my mouth before I can call them back.

'Don't be ridiculous,' he snaps.

I could pretend the words were said in rage and paper over them. But I don't want to. 'I mean it.' I say it slowly and clearly so there's no room for misunderstanding. Each word must be a spike through his heart. 'You're not their father.'

Thirty-Five

Then

I'm in a bar in the City waiting for Helen when I see him. It's one of those pretentious places that used to be a bank so it's all high ceilings and chrome lighting, full of braying City workers. Just the kind I hate. Helen's late, which annoys me. I rushed from a busy shift and schlepped up here on the Thameslink without even stopping to change. I normally avoid the City – I only agreed to meet her here because she's been promoted (again) and wants to celebrate. I'm drumming my fingers on the brushed-metal bar and wondering if I've got enough cash to order another drink when a shadow falls across me.

'Emily.'

A voice I'd hoped never to hear again. Every cell in my body stands to attention. I don't turn around.

'It *is* you,' he continues. 'I saw you from across the bar and I wasn't sure but I had to come over. Damn, are you a sight for sore eyes! I haven't seen you in for ever. How the devil are you?'

I finally bring myself to stop studying the surface of the bar. There he stands, all 6 foot plus of him. Apart from the spokes of laughter lines around his eyes and a new, sharper haircut, he looks exactly the same as he did the last time I saw him. Untouched. It doesn't seem fair.

'I'm with a couple of the guys from college.' If he thinks it's weird that I haven't uttered a word, he doesn't show it. He sweeps a hand towards the other side of the bar. 'Come join us?'

Even the way he says it isn't a question but a command.

'No, thanks.' I fold my arms over my chest. 'I'm actually waiting for someone.'

'Still the lost sheep.' He's talking like he's an old friend, rather than someone who betrayed me. 'Don't you keep in touch with anyone?'

Now's the moment to tell him about Nick, but I don't. He gave up the right to hear about my personal life years ago.

'Not really.' I've thought about him so much over the past five years, imagined bumping into him when I'm looking my best, the way most people do with their exes. Of course, it had to be now, when I'm sitting on my own, in an ill-fitting white shirt with a tomato stain on the right boob, looking like I've been stood up.

'Shame. We had some good times.'

I look at him incredulously, wondering if he and I are thinking of the same things. He wouldn't be standing here acting as though we're taking a pleasant trip down memory lane if we were.

'It was a long time ago.' My words rap out harder than I intended. I've worked hard to put university behind me. Seeing him brings all of the darkness flooding back.

'I think perhaps I owe you an apology.' He's obviously picked up on my froideur. It's more than just an apology that he owes me.

'Forget it.' I make an effort to unclench my fists. 'Water under the bridge. But don't let me keep you. Tell everyone I say hi.'

'Emmy . . .'

'Please don't call me that.' I turn back to the bar and flag down the barman. 'Glass of red wine please. Make it a large.'

He tries again. 'Emily . . .'

I don't turn around. I hear him sigh.

'It really is good to see you.' He leans in to drop a kiss on my cheek. The smell of him is olfactory overload. Allure. Too many memories. 'I really am sorry that things ended the way they did.'

He walks away.

'Here you go.' The barman brings over what looks like a fishbowl of wine. 'I was a little generous with the measure. Thought you could use a top-up.'

'Thanks,' I manage. I can't concentrate on his face. All I can think of is how low I sank back then, how small I felt. I need to pull myself together. Helen's paid for enough therapy. All the hours I've spent talking over a box of tissues with a woman who seemed predominantly to steeple

318

her hands together and nod has to count for something. I've worked through this. I don't need to see her any more. And I'm not going to be undone now.

'Ex of yours?' The barman nudges me out of my reverie. I notice he's got flesh tunnel piercings in each ear. He's totally at odds with the City bar he works in. He's looking at me conspiratorially. He obviously assumes I want company because I'm on my own. I wish he could see I want to be left alone.

I concentrate on my drink to dissuade him from asking any more questions and, luckily, Helen comes rushing in. She's got her laptop case swinging from around her neck and a stack of newspapers in each hand. 'Sorry, babe,' she says. 'Major story breaking as I left. I think they might call me back in. I better keep my phone out.'

She dumps her BlackBerry on the bar and stares over my shoulder accusingly. 'Who was that who came over? I saw you from the door. Was it Nick? You promised it would be just us.'

'It was nobody. Some random.'

'Are you sure? I wouldn't put it past him to crash. I told you he's a bit keen. I think he needs to back off a bit.'

'You've only met him a couple of times.'

'Trust me, a big sister can tell.' She taps her finger against her nose.

'All right, all-knowing one. Do you know what you want to drink?'

'I'll have what you're having. Let's get a bottle. Make an occasion of it.'

She leans over and helps herself to a glug from my

wine – which she nearly spits straight back into my glass. 'What is this? Paint stripper? Ugh. You can't drink it, Emmy. It's rank.'

'I'll just have water, then. It all tastes the same to me.'

'Don't be daft. We're celebrating.' Helen flags down the same barman. I wish she'd waited for the blonde barmaid at the other end of the bar to serve us. My earlier encounter has rattled me. All men are giving me the creeps right now. 'Right, let's get rid of this shit. We've got to toast properly. Yes. Thank you. Can I have a bottle of your best Malbec? Actually, sod it, I'm on expenses. We'll have a bottle of champagne. You'll drink that, won't you, Em?'

'If you want me to.'

'What have you got?'

'If you want proper bubbles we've got everything through from Laurent-Perrier to Cristal.' Flesh tunnel winks at me again. 'But we've also got a couple of nice Proseccos.'

'I'll take the Laurent Perrier.' Helen sounds affronted at the idea that she can't do better than Prosecco. She nods at me. 'And I'll settle this one's tab, too.'

Flesh tunnel shakes his head. 'That tab's already been settled.' I push the glass away as he gives the table in the corner a significant look. Helen doesn't catch it. I refuse to follow his gaze. I've given that person enough of my life; I will not reward him by being grateful for a poxy drink. I watch the barman pop the cork and pour the champagne. The bubbles look like they're floating in liquid gold.

'I'm proud of you, you know,' Helen says, after he's gone

to the other side of the bar. 'I probably don't say it often enough but I am. You seem different lately. More sorted.'

'Aw shucks.' I duck my head in faux-modesty. 'It's probably the Nick effect.'

'Heaven forbid it could be anything to do with you,' Helen tuts. 'How's it going with the courses you were looking into? Does the first bit of your degree count for something or do you have to start from scratch? How long is a law degree these days?' She takes a drink of the champagne and smacks her lips appreciatively. 'Better. Go on, have some.'

I drink as directed. The bubbles slide down surprisingly easily. It's been a long time since I've drunk champagne. I take another mouthful before answering. 'I was wondering about doing something completely different, as it goes,' I say. 'Nick thinks I'd make a good teacher. He reckons it might be a better fit than law.'

'Oh does he?'

'He thinks I could start volunteering as a teaching assistant and then look at a degree if I liked it. I might even find a school that would lob in something towards the cost.'

'Do you even like children?' Helen raises her eyebrows.

'I couldn't eat a whole one.' I take another drink. 'But it might be a more realistic start, given that I don't have a degree. I thought you'd be pleased for me.'

'I am pleased you're doing something. I just don't think you're at the stage yet where you have to settle in order to be "realistic".' She makes inverted commas with her hands and pulls a face. 'You're brilliant. I still think you should get in touch with college and see if—'

'I've told you, I don't want to do that.' I pick at the

corner of a bar mat then wonder how many other hands have done the same and start picking at my fingernails instead. 'I don't want to go back there.'

'Okay, fine. But promise me you'll look at law. You used to be so passionate about it. If it's a money thing, I'm happy to kick in.'

'I don't want to take more money off you . . .'

But Helen's phone starts flashing. She grabs it and holds it close to her face, her eyes scanning the page. She dumps a notepad and pen from her laptop bag on the bar and starts making notes in shorthand.

'I knew this would happen.' She groans but I can tell from the sparkle in her eyes that she's enjoying it. 'Why these politicians insist on getting caught with their pants down on a Thursday night is beyond me.'

'No rest for the wicked.' I look at the series of dots and squiggles she's written on the page, glad of the disruption. Helen's right. Teaching isn't something I'd naturally gravitate towards but what Nick says makes sense. I don't want to keep treading water as a waitress for ever.

'Look, I'm not saying you shouldn't do it if it's what you want. But don't let Nick push you into it because it suits him better.'

'He's not pushing me into it.' I think of the emphasis he put on travelling during the school holidays. 'He's trying to help.'

'Hmm.' Helen starts tapping a message out on her BlackBerry. I envy her total absorption. The only thing absorbing anything in my job is my clothes. I fuss at the tomato stain.

'All right, I'll look at law again. Teaching's just an option.'

'That's more like it. Now, I'm really sorry, I've got to go. It's all kicking off back at the office.'

'Don't worry about it.'

I must sound dejected because Helen stops packing her things away. 'I can get someone else to cover it if you want me to stay.'

'Go. I'll be fine. I need to get going, anyway.'

'Stay, finish the bottle. Enjoy yourself.'

'What? On my own like a lemon? Yeah, right. I might give Nick a call and see what he's up to.'

'Good plan.' Her brain is already back at the office. She slips her coat on and scans her BlackBerry simultaneously. 'Be good.' She waves from the door. 'I'll call you tomorrow.'

I should slide off the bar stool and go home, ideally via the kebab shop at the end of my road. But the champagne is winking from its flute. The halcyon days of floating from garden party to garden party with Henry at my side, the others bookending us, a bottle tucked under each of our arms, swim before me. I make myself focus on the bar. I'm not going to be driven out by the table in the corner. I could have another glass here and then find out where Nick is. Or jump on the Northern Line to surprise him at his flat in Clapham. Perhaps, since I haven't paid for any of my drinks this evening, I could even splash out and get a cab.

I flick through the newspapers Helen's left behind, sipping the champagne and marvelling at how much my sister has accomplished. Although she's too senior to have a byline, I can see her thoughts and opinions woven through every article and opinion piece. Maybe I should aim higher. I start fantasising about law school, getting my teeth into cases and making a difference. I could get my own flat in London close to Helen. We could travel Europe at the weekends, if I could persuade her to take the time off, that is. If not, I could go with Nick. It might be a bit late but I could finally start living the life I'm supposed to. I only realise I've finished the bottle when the barman comes over with a fresh glass.

'Can I tempt you to one more?' he asks. 'On the house, of course.'

He leans over the bar, a bit closer than I'd like. I jerk back. I know where this goes.

'No, I'm fine. I should get going anyway.' I dig around in my handbag for my mobile. I bring up Nick's contact details and press 'call' but it goes to voicemail. He's probably on the Tube. I'll give him another try when I get to Bank station.

'Wait,' the barman says as I get off the bar stool. I ignore him. I'm sure he's only trying to be nice, but his extra attentions have given me the creeps. I don't like pushy men. I see him starting to make his way around the bar so I stuff my phone back into my bag and hurry to the door. I'm in the glass vestibule between the bar and the street outside when he catches up with me.

'Hey, wait up.' He pulls the bar door open and slips inside, trapping us both in the small space. This close, I can see he's got a small dragon tattoo on his neck. I feel disproportionately panicked by his proximity. I breathe in through my nose, out through my mouth and tell myself to stop acting like such a victim.

'You forgot these.' He hands me Helen's stack of newspapers.

'I actually don't want them. Sorry.' My fingers close around the door handle.

He shrugs and inches closer. 'So . . .'

'I've got to go.' I pull the second door open and throw myself out of the bar before he can finish his sentence. I don't stop walking until I'm past both the bar windows and at the corner of the building. Only then do I look back and check he hasn't followed me. He hasn't. I feel stupid for imagining he would. I hate myself for feeling so rattled but I've had trust issues since college. I know who to thank for that. I take a deep breath and wait for my heart to slow down. I'm about to get my phone out to call Nick again when I smell a waft of cigarette smoke. I gave up a couple of years ago when I noticed the tips of my fingers turning mustard but I miss it when I'm stressed. Like now. I look to my right. There's a thin corridor between the bar and its neighbouring building. A guy with his back to me is smoking about halfway down.

'I'm really sorry to bother you,' I call, being careful not to step too far in. I'm not going to run from one creepy guy into another. 'But is there any chance I can steal a fag off you? I'm happy to buy it.'

When Will Jenkin turns around, it's inconceivable that I didn't recognise him. The back of his head, those broad shoulders; it's all the same.

'Of course you can.'

'I thought you'd gone.' I step backwards, wondering how to get out of this. Our earlier conversation was excruciating enough; he is not somebody I want to be stuck in an alley with.

'Apparently not. Everyone else went on but I had a work call.' The corners of his mouth tug. 'I decided to stay and have a fag. I've been gagging for one all night but I was with a bunch of reformed smokers. This smoking ban will be the death of me. Here, have one. Join me on the dark side.'

He flips open the packet of Marlboro Lights and uses his own cigarette to light a fresh one before I can say 'no'. I hate how confident he is but why should I be the one to scuttle off? I've worked hard to build myself up to a moment like this. The previous five minutes being terrified by a tragi-goth barman aside, I'm so much stronger than I was. This is my chance to prove it.

I rummage through my bag for my wallet and take out a pound coin before I accept the cigarette.

'Don't be mental.' He waves my money away. I notice the cockney rhyming slang's gone in his old age. 'It's only a fag.' He passes me the cigarette and I angle my hand to make sure my fingers don't brush his. 'I'm glad I ran into you.'

'Really? Why's that?' I try to sound as though I haven't been rehearsing versions of this conversation in my head for about five years. And as if I'm not bristling with loathing.

He scuffs his Church's brogues into the wall behind him. 'I've missed you over the years.'

'I find that difficult to believe.' I bet he hasn't thought of me once.

'Aw come on, my folks still ask about you.'

'I doubt that.'

'Do you remember when they came up to visit that morning and we'd all been out the night before? I don't think I'd even been to bed when my mum called. And you said—'

I don't know what I thought I was expecting from this but I can't bear the camaraderie any more. 'Why are you trying to pretend we're friends?'

His face falls. 'That's a bit harsh.'

'It's a bit true.' I take a drag of the cigarette and let the smoke flood my lungs. 'I haven't seen you for about five years and the last time I did see you, things didn't exactly end well.'

I fix my eyes on him, daring him to say something. There's not even a flicker of guilt.

'I've had better nights.'

I throw the cigarette on the ground and stamp on it hard, like I'm driving his head into the bricks. 'I'm glad it was all such a big joke to you.'

'How can you think I think that?' He looks mortified and I remind myself he's always been a good actor.

'Er, I guess maybe from the fact that you never came to see me afterwards.' I look at him incredulously. He must be able to feel the hatred coming off me in waves. 'Or that you left me outside. Or how about what you actually—'

'I'm sorry,' Will interrupts. 'I tried. Do you know how many times I wish I could go back and change things? Tell you how I felt?'

'How *you* felt?' It's like we're talking at cross-purposes. 'What are you talking about? I'm the one who—'

But I don't get to finish my sentence because he bends his head and kisses me. What the fuck? How can he not realise how much I loathe him? I put up both hands to shove him away, hard, but then it occurs to me that it will hurt him more if I go along with it to start with and then shove him away later. I start kissing him back, thinking of the look on his face when I reject him. The ultimate revenge. Even as I'm picturing the humiliation on his face, my body is pressing itself closer to him. His lips find the tender spot where my shoulder meets my neck and I feel a spasm of pleasure. I try to ignore it, telling myself I'm just prolonging the moment to make my final rejection more potent. But I know it's more than that. I don't want to admit it but I'm enjoying this. It takes me back to who I was before. I dig my hands into his hair, wanting him even in spite of myself. Even as I'm unzipping his flies, I tell myself I can still leave at any moment and serve him the humiliation of abandonment I had to endure. Instead, I pull him closer and jam us both up against the wall. I tell myself this is about taking back control as I angle my leg for easy access and grip his buttocks, pulling him deep inside me. But it's more animalistic than that. It's gone beyond a want and become a need. I bury my face in his neck so he can't see my expression and give myself up to the moment.

Afterwards, as he's rearranging his clothes, he gives that trademark grin. 'I have to say, for a second there I didn't know if you were going to shag me or stab me.'

I concentrate on straightening my shirt and belting my coat. Now's the time to recover this. Let him be the one who knows what it's like to be left as if they were nothing. A shame nobody is around to capitalise on his humiliation, the way the pictures he uploaded did on mine.

'Look at you, cool as a cucumber.' He chuckles. 'So, can I call you?'

'I don't think so.' I make my face into a mask. I thought my voice might give me away but I sound suitably removed.

'But I thought – you can't tell me you didn't – what was that . . .' I watch confusion scud across his face. 'Why?'

'I'm seeing someone.' My sensations are returning to normal and a satisfaction, deeper than anything he brought about, spreads through me.

'Who?'

'You don't know him.' For some reason, I want to keep Nick to myself.

'So what? You can't tell me that you didn't feel that . . .' But his words have lost their swagger.

I look him full in the face. I could tell him that he ruined my life, that I could never consider a future with someone who let me down so badly even if they were 'sorry'. But I know the rejection will be more powerful if I don't explain it. I step closer and reach out my hand like I might have changed my mind. Then I drop the pound coin into the pocket of his overcoat. 'Thanks for the fag.'

I walk away, feeling at least a foot taller than I did before I came in here. That three minutes in the alley was worth more than all the therapy Helen's made me have. I'm never going back. I don't even feel guilty about Nick.

That was something I needed to do. Because it's not only Will Jenkin I'm leaving in the alley; it's the self-loathing that I've wrapped around me like a cloak since I left. It might seem like a paltry way of evening the score but I feel freer than I have in years.

Thirty-Six

Now

00.30

I watch the emotions play out across Nick's face. I know him well enough to translate every movement. The way his lips tighten as he tries to dismiss what I've said. His eyes widening as he assesses the situation. His mind is raking the evidence, searching for a loophole. But he only has to look at the twins and their olive skin against the combined pastiness of him and me. Even if he tells himself I'm lying, there will always be a shadow of doubt. His eyes harden.

'How?' He spits the words out.

'I slept with someone before we got engaged.'

'Who was it?'

'Does it matter?'

'You're damn right it matters,' he explodes. 'Who was it? Hawksmoor? I saw the way your tongue was hanging out when you saw him tonight. Frankly it was embarrassing.'

'It doesn't matter who it was.'

His mask's come off. It's telling that wondering who his rival was, not how it affects the twins, is his first concern. I feel a swell of remorse; they deserved to hear the truth before Nick did. But it's too late now.

'If not Hawksmoor then who?' He's still raking over a list of suspects. 'Was it one of the other losers you and Tiff used to hang out with? Some greasy, fat Italian chef.' He's working himself into a rage. 'I mean, who else would possibly have wanted you? An overweight waitress going nowhere. You were hardly a catch.'

The silent contempt he's felt for me over the years is out in the open. I could leave him hanging. Let the not knowing eat away at him. But I want to see his face. I'll deal with the fallout later.

'It was Will Jenkin, if you must know.'

'After what he did?' Nick goggles. 'What is wrong with you?'

'What *he* did? It was you. You who did it all. And I still don't know why. I never did anything to you.'

'You never even looked at me,' Nick shouts. 'I tried to help you that night. If you'd have come with me, you'd have been fine. But you never did know what was good for you.'

'How long have you hated me?'

He doesn't answer. He puts his hands around my throat instead.

We must have stood this close together a thousand times over the course of our marriage. Hugging in the kitchen, dancing at weddings. If it wasn't for his grip and the contortion of his face, we could be locked in a lover's embrace. But his hands are choking the life out of me.

'Nick . . .' I rasp.

But he shuts his eyes. That's how I know there's no coming back. I've smashed his family apart in front of him and here, in his beloved Cambridge too. He's not going to let me get away with it.

They say your life flashes before you before you die. But as darkness reaches out to claim me, it's not the grotty suburban streets covered in cigarette butts and used take-away containers of my childhood that I see. I don't see my parents, or myself on my wedding day, the hint of a bump poking out of my Empire-line wedding dress or the twins when we brought them home from hospital the first time. I see my sister, her face blazing. Her lips move soundlessly, like she's urging me on. And I know I have to fight back.

I start clawing at him but Nick bats me away with one hand, still crushing my windpipe with the other. I splutter. If I can just get him to let me speak. There are things I could tell him, things I should have said, that might make him change his mind. But he doesn't relent.

Just when I feel my consciousness slipping through the cracks, I hear the scratching of the lock. I only have the energy for one last flicker of hope. I don't have many friends left here tonight but perhaps one of them came back. The scratch becomes a scrape and a creak, then there's a whoosh of air. Someone's here. I'm safe. But there's no shout of horror and no sound of footsteps pounding against the floor. Nick's heavy breathing is the only sound filling the room. I feel like I'm underwater. Maybe I hallucinated the creaking. Or my would-be rescuer doesn't want to save me. I think of Will, Henry and Freja; Lyla, Liz; all the people I've fallen out with tonight. Any single one of them might turn and walk in the other direction. I flail my hands one last time. Not waving but drowning.

More by luck than design, my three-carat diamond engagement ring, so heavy I take it off when I'm alone and pottering in the house, hits Nick squarely in the eye. He gives a howl of pain and lets go, putting both hands up to it. I drive my knee into his crotch the way I always thought I would and he doubles over.

Then the door swings wide open and Will rushes in, Chris the porter red-faced and out of breath right behind him.

'What the fuck happened here?' Will looks from where I'm standing, my hands now around my own throat as if I'm trying to keep my head on my neck and Nick bent over with blood gushing from his eye. 'Are you okay?'

It hurts to breathe so I know I need to ration my words. I stagger past Will and Chris towards the door. I don't want to be near any of them. Only when I'm out in the open, gulping in greedy mouthfuls of air, do I speak.

'Call the police.'

The next time I see Will, I'm wrapped in a cloak of silver foil and sitting in the back of an ambulance parked at a ninety-degree angle to two police cars.

'You look like you've run a marathon,' he tells me,

tactfully ignoring the network of bruises running from the bottom of my chin to the base of my clavicle. I must look like I'm wearing a concrete-coloured polo neck.

'Or like a turkey fit for basting,' I croak back. 'Cooked up for the breakfast rush.'

We look out across college together. There's crime-scene tape around the entrance to the Great Hall. Crowds of people in their pyjamas are spilling out of the staircases in the accommodation block like there's been a late-night fire alarm. I can see by the way they're clustering together and frantically jabbing at their phones that the news is spreading. I shrink back into the ambulance and hope they can't make out who I am. What is it with me and this place?

'From the bottom of my heart, I'm sorry.' Will looks devastated. 'I can't help feeling responsible for this.'

I shrug like every word isn't an effort. 'You're not the one who married him.'

'But I knew it was him who took the picture.' Will drives his toe into the gravel in front of him. 'I could have warned you.'

I look down. 'Woulda, coulda, shoulda.'

There are a thousand tiny diversions I could have taken at any point that wouldn't have led me here. Will is just one of them. I don't have the emotional capacity to rake over them for his benefit. All I want to do is get away. I have to put the twins first. I look over at where two policemen are still talking to Chris the porter. I've given my preliminary statement. They didn't exactly say I had to stay around. I could leave. Go back to London, pick the twins up and take them somewhere safe where Nick can't find us.

'Are you going to be okay? Stupid question.'

'I will be.' The police look as though they're almost finished with Chris. The officer who took my statement said they'd contact me in the morning to take an 'evidential statement'. I have no idea what that is or how it's different from what he's already written in his notebook, but if it means I can leave now, it can only be a good thing. 'As soon as I get home.'

'Do you know where they've taken him?'

'There's a police station on the other side of Parker's Piece.' I think of Nick being poured into a squad car with his hands braceleted in front of him, his eye still weeping blood. I can't believe I got him so wrong. Not that I'm exactly blameless after all the lies I've told. The hard nugget of guilt that seems permanently lodged in my solar plexus seems to swell. I need to get away. I stand up.

'Do you want me to take you home and wait with you?' Will asks. 'In case he goes there when they let him out?'

Will's continued presence in my life is exactly what I don't want. After what I accused him of, he has every reason to hate me. I think of my initial plan to raise the twins on my own, the way my mum did Helen and me. I never should have deviated from it.

'It's fine. They told me they'll hold him for at least twenty-four hours and when they release him he won't be able to come back to the family house.'

I don't add that I have no intention of being there, even if he does.

'Let me run you back anyway,' he says solicitously. 'I can have my driver here in two shakes.'

For a nanosecond, I hesitate. After everything that's happened, it would be easy to let Will take charge. Letting a man step in to save the day seems to be my default mode.

'Give us a chance to catch up on the way back,' he carries on. It doesn't seem to occur to him that I'll say no. 'I can offer door-to-door service. All I ask in exchange is a cuppa on the other side. I'm gagging for a brew. And I'd love to meet your kids.'

I stiffen. Was he outside that door longer than I think? And why did it take so long to swing open? I look at his face but his smile is guileless; his eyes are clear. For now. I think of how much he wanted to discuss what happened between us. It won't take him long to put two and two together when he sees Artie's dimples and clocks how old the pair of them are. What will he do then? I can't let that happen until they're ready. Will can wait. I shrug the silvery blanket off and let it fall to the ground near his feet.

'I'm sorry.' My voice is final. However, I've ended up finding it and at whatever cost, this is the independence that Helen was driving me towards. It might not have worked out the way we planned but I think back to everything that happened tonight and hope she'd feel proud. I think of the law school application, the map on my wall at college, the world I haven't had the chance to see. For once the future is going to be on my terms. 'I think I'd rather get there on my own.'

Acknowledgements

My dad died from Covid-19 while I was writing this book and while escaping into writing was a solace, there were times it was hard to keep going and it was the support of my friends and family that pushed me through. *The Reunion* owes something to everyone who raised a glass on 2 April 2020 and also to the wonderful staff at Chelsea and Westminster hospital, who cared for my dad and allowed my stepmother to sit beside him, so he wasn't alone.

While I'm grateful to so many people, special thanks belong to: Celina Teague, Robyn Stromsoe, Shannan West, Hannah Armitage, Sam Armitage, Jo Akram, Lizzie Varley, Ali Davies, Emma Carter, Lisa Kililea, Piero Politeo, Teresa Garin Mendarózqueta, Lisa Kendall, Laura Stockwell, Amelia Haughey, Gaelle Cazavant, Kathy Baillie, Amy Zempilas, Cori Lambert, Holly Shewring, Katherine Saunt, Katherine Patterson, Kate Smith, Helen Cleary, Hannah Talbot, Katie Mounier, Astrid Solomon, Nigel Phillips, Kat Sparks, Topsy Buchanan, Jo Jervis Read, Henry Bourke, Francesca Beighton, Tony Bucknall,

Penny Vallings, Robert Vallings, Jean Dorman, Steve James and Anne James. There are many more so my apologies for missing anybody out.

The book itself focuses on university days – while my time at Cambridge wasn't nearly as exotic or exciting as Emily's, I'm grateful to all the people I met there and the memories we made. I'd also like to thank Richard Partington, Chris Owen and James Bailey for some fact checking as I wrote. All mistakes are of course mine and mine alone and while I went to college with at least a dozen Henrys and Wills, these characters are entirely a work of fiction, as are the set of events that occur in the book, although, embarrassingly, I have to admit I've hurled a couple of drinks in my time.

Thanks as always to my amazing agent, Sarah Hornsley, fantastic editor, Bethan Jones, and the teams at both The Bent Agency and Simon & Schuster for your enthusiasm and insight. Most books are team efforts and this one is no exception.

It's also a huge thrill to be able to thank the readers of *My Best Friend's Murder*. Your support and feedback has definitely informed the writing of *The Reunion*. To my writer friends, Emily Paull, Louise Allan, Natasha Lester, Holly Craig, Pip Drysdale, Victoria Selman, Sophie Flynn and Gytha Lodge: thanks for welcoming me into your world. Finally, to my remaining family: you keep the plates spinning and the world interesting. I thank you for that.

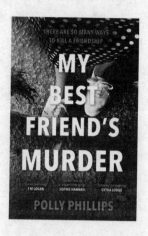

Andaz London Liverpool Street is a 5 star lifestyle luxury hotel in the heart of vibrant East London.

Opened as the Great Eastern Hotel in 1884, the hotel is housed in Liverpool Streets station's beautiful redbrick Victorian building, designed by the architects of the Houses of Parliament, with interiors seamlessly blending modern and heritage designs by Conran + Partners.

Capturing the hotel's location and history, our 267 rooms and suites aim to be creative spaces where the traditionally conservative City meets the vibrant artistic vibe of East London with illustration tattoo art by local artist Sophie Mo and photography of the local area by Hoxton Mini Press' Martin Usborne.

For the foodies, there is something to suit all dining tastes at any of Andaz London Liverpool Street's 5 restaurants and bars, from specialty morning coffee and healthy breakfasts to fresh Japanese, brunches galore, traditional pub fare and perfectly grilled dishes.

Evidence-Based
Clinical Practice in
Nursing and Health Care